THE WILDCARDS

Tricia Trevaskis

To Greg
for his optimism and support

CHAPTER 1

Tim gazed out across the acres of parched, dry grass to where a mob of sheep huddled under the shade of a lone gum tree. The ripe, heavy scent of dung wafted over the paddocks, thickening the warm afternoon breeze. Wrinkling his nose in disgust, he looked at the dust and dead insects coating his mother's car. This time she would have to wash it herself, he thought with some sweet sense of revenge.

Jenny's farewells were lethargic and drawn-out, as if she was reluctant to go on from this moment. Finally, with a last hug and squeeze for both boys, she said in a strained voice, "Please understand. It's not for long. And we can ring every day."

Tim was still too angry about being ditched in the middle of nowhere to do anything more than nod. Jack wasn't giving his mother much either, because he turned away with an offhand wave and said sarcastically, "Yeah. Sure. You know us. We'll be fine."

Jenny let out a deep breath as she got into the car. Winding down the window she said, "This isn't my fault, guys. You know Dad just needs this time to get well. Soon he'll be better, and life will go back to normal. I promise I'll make this up to you." She broke off with a weak attempt at a smile.

Tim knew she wasn't convinced herself of what she was promising, and his look of contempt said it all. "Sure, Mum," he replied as she started the car. Relenting at the last minute as he saw tears well in her eyes, he called out, "Love you," over his shoulder, making a comic, sad face at her as he moved off to join Jack at the gate. Nanna and Pa leaned in towards the car. Nanna gave Jenny a final hug and Pa patted the roof of the car as it rolled slowly past the brothers standing together, their mother blowing lots of air kisses and waving, before heading down the farm's long, dusty drive. The boys watched her as she paused, then, turning left, accelerated off along the highway. As the dust settled, so did the feeling of rejection in Tim's stomach, like a tight knot.

"Well. She actually pissed off and left us after all! I still can't believe she thinks this is a good thing," hissed Jack as he kicked a rock around in the dirt.

"Just unbelievable," Tim agreed. Meanwhile, in a cheery voice that belied his emotions, he called out to Nan who was watching from the verandah, "We might head down to the dam for a bit, Nanna."

"No worries," she replied. "Dinner's not for an hour or so."

The air had a gentle stillness about it, and in the late afternoon summer heat, flies and insects buzzed and crickets chirped. The boys made their way in silence down the track that led to the dam. This was probably their favourite spot on the farm. As little kids there had always been something to discover in its murky, muddy edges. They had collected more than a few tadpoles to bring back to the farmhouse over the years, and in turn had set free several juvenile frogs hatched from their tadpole adventures. These days though, they were happy to skim yonnies across it, rather than go searching for wildlife.

Skipping the first stone across the dam, Jack spoke angrily. "I just can't understand what the hell difference it actually makes if we were still at home? I get it that Dad needs lots of rest and help from Mum, but it's not as if that hasn't been the case for months now. What's changed? We've seen Dad almost on his deathbed. How much worse can things be for us, now he's supposedly over the worst and getting better? If you ask me, it's Dad who has the problem. He's the one who doesn't want us around anymore. He's only interested in himself these days."

These were strong words from Jack who, like Tim, idolised their dad. It had all been said a thousand times, but everyone had tactfully avoided laying any blame on their father. The boys both lapsed into their own thoughts and Jack's bitterness hung over them like a cloud. Tim had no answer. Silently, he contemplated how his father's sudden collapse last September had shaken their world, turning it upside down and throwing everything into chaos. What they thought had been a lingering virus was finally diagnosed as something far more serious. He had leukaemia, and not in a mild form. It had been eating away silently inside him, spreading gradually, like pollution slowly seeping into a river, merging and blending with his cells, poisoning him and leaving him weak and ill. He was immediately prescribed an intense course of chemotherapy, which hit him hard. Just as he was to complete the last of the treatments, he contracted a mild infection. With his immune system defenceless and exposed, it ran over him like a truck. He was placed in intensive care for several weeks, and no-one expected him to survive. Jenny rarely left his side. Jack and Tim kept a vigil at home, waiting for their mother to return or to get the message that it would be okay to see him.

There had been nothing worse than those drawn-out hospital visits, with Dad looking exhausted and ill. They could see the effort it took for him to talk to them. Then there were the visits when they just talked and hoped he was listening, as he lay semi-conscious and unresponsive. Just thinking about it brought back unhappy memories, and even now made Tim feel uneasy. He shivered involuntarily as he thought about the past months. Their father's collapse had shaken their world: everything else was insignificant.

For a long time, they had tried to keep things as normal as possible. An army of friends and family helped out, but nothing was the same. Jenny looked stressed and it showed in the lines that had visibly deepened around her eyes and the firm set of her mouth. She went through all the usual mum routines. She cooked and shopped and tried to focus on the boys' lives as she always had. But her voice was forced and her eyes never smiled. Life had changed dramatically. Her days were arranged around her visits to the hospital and appointments with Mark's specialist team. The family mood was solely dependent on the daily bulletins from the hospital, which governed what emotions they dared feel.

Jack and Tim thought the worst was over when Dad improved enough to leave intensive care. Having seen him most days, they were prepared for the physical changes. They had gotten used to his wasted and weakened body, and his grey, unhealthy pallor; but it soon became obvious that they had expected too much from him mentally. While it was always confronting to see him looking a physical shadow of himself, it was his vacant stare that began to haunt them and brought a new fear. Jack and Tim maintained a convincing charade, telling long stories about school and sport, or reading out footy news from the paper that they knew he would normally enjoy. But there was no spark of interest in his eyes. No sign of the father they knew so well.

When it was time to leave on that first visit to the ward, after he had been in intensive care, they had kissed his cheek and, telling him they loved him and missed him, cheerily waved goodbye. They walked slowly from the room, promising to wait at the McDonald's next door to the hospital for Mum. Once out of sight, united in their anger and frustration, they ignored the waiting elevator, choosing the staircase instead. They covered the eight flights of stairs to the ground floor in record time. Bursting through the doors that opened into the hospital foyer, they dodged a group of people waiting at the elevator doors, missing them by inches. Without stopping to apologise they ran out through the entrance, into the sunshine, into warmth and light and away from the sterility of the hospital and its antiseptic smells. They ran into the sounds of traffic and the city, and as far away as they could from the mute, bedridden figure who was a mere ghost of their father.

After Jenny finally met them back in the car park, they drove home in silence. Jack sulked and said he wasn't going back. Tim called him weak, and a fight was on. As Jenny pulled into the drive at home, they spilled out of the car, wrestling with each other. Jenny tried to separate them, pleading with them to stop as they rolled around the front lawn. In an attempt to halt the violence, Jenny managed a few well-directed hits from the newspaper she had picked up from the verge. Exhausted, and eventually giving in to Jenny's pleas, they rolled apart. That's when the dam burst, and tears began to flow.

Right from the start they had been told that this would be a long, slow recovery. They knew the chemotherapy would take its toll, but they always assumed their father would get better and return to his normally cheerful self. Everything would be the same as before. Now they were no longer so sure. The three of them gave in to their emotions, unchecked, right there in the front yard for all the neighbours to see. Jenny sat on the front steps with her head in her hands while the boys lay sprawled on the grass, facing away from each other.

After a long time, Jenny said, "Come on. Let's go inside. I'll make dinner, you two start your homework, and we'll talk about this later."

Emotionally spent, they each picked themselves up and life went on. They had been too raw to talk about it that night, but there was a new understanding between them all, and they treated each other with more kindness, it seemed.

The family rallied once more and continued to keep up the supportive hospital visits. No-one would ever have guessed— least of all their father—at the subterfuge that was in their hearts. The school year drew to an end, and hospital visits were easier to make without the demands of the school timetable.

Christmas rolled around and there was a new goal to achieve. If his markers were up, the doctors promised that Mark would be able to come home for a few hours on Christmas Day. There was great excitement by the extended family. Both sets of grandparents were able to come, as well as Mark's brothers, the boys' two favourite uncles. This was a milestone in Mark's recovery, and the family was overjoyed to be able to see him finally out of hospital, even if it was only for the day. However, to Tim and Jack, this was no Christmas miracle, and it was still just a watered-down version of their dad who had turned up. There was plenty of food, drink, and Christmas spirit and, initially, Mark tried hard to be part of it all—but in the end it just got too much for him, and he gradually retreated back into his own world. Most of the family kept up the pretence that it was all jolly and carried on as normal, but it was an uncomfortable day.

When it was time for Jenny to take Mark back to hospital, neither Jack nor Tim volunteered to go with her. Jenny could see they couldn't wait for him to be gone. She was quietly shocked to see the relief on their faces as they said goodbye. She was even more surprised to realise that Mark hadn't even registered their reluctance to spend any more time with him. It was suddenly overwhelming, and their lack of understanding and tolerance weighed heavily on her. For the first time, she began to comprehend that spending time with Mark wasn't necessarily a good thing for the boys' future relationship with him, if they saw him as an object of pity. It was hard enough for her to come to terms with her own emotions, to keep loving this man who was so scarred and transformed by his illness. The occasional glimpse of the old Mark allowed her to hang in there for a future that the doctors promised her would be possible. However, she was only beginning to understand the depth of the damage done to their little family by this devastating illness and its side effects.

When Jenny returned home, she deliberately ignored both boys, despite the fact she was sure she could smell alcohol on them. She surmised, correctly, that they had been sneaking a couple of their uncles' beers in her absence. Once all the extended family had left, she ignored the post-Christmas kitchen mess and for once went straight to her room, where she could think long and hard. Cleaning up seemed pointless. She felt utterly defeated.

She said nothing to them to let them off the hook. She knew they were feeling guilty enough about their disloyalty without her having to point it out. It was her own dad's parting words to her that also challenged her to rethink the situation.

"You know you shouldn't be too hard on the boys, Jenny. Mark's sickness has stolen something precious from all of you. You have to be both father and mother at the moment, and you're doing a great job. But don't forget they have suddenly lost their hero. They used to hang on every word he said, and now he doesn't even have the energy to talk. This is going to take more than a few good test results before your lives will return to normal. And you might have to be prepared for Mark to take longer to get over the psychological scars of this illness, even after he has made a physical recovery." Then, giving her a big hug, he whispered, "Stay strong and cut them some slack. They're good boys."

Jenny had convinced herself that Mark's lethargy was just temporary exhaustion while he was fighting his illness. Now she realised that it was much more than that. Whatever dark place he inhabited, he wasn't seeing past himself and his own black world. While she was able to accept this and appreciate the crumbs he gave her to survive on, it wasn't fair to put their two sons through it. She had thought that enduring this illness together was a positive thing, one that would make them even stronger as a family. For the first time since the whole saga started, she recognised that her reliance on the boys may have been a selfish act. Lying on the bed she had shared for so long with Mark, she cried for everything they had lost. She cried even more as she realised that her old life might be lost forever.

A few days later she announced her grand plan for Tim and Jack. They were to go to Winjarra to live with their grandparents until things settled down. Dr Thompson, Mark's oncologist, was also aware of Mark's mental decline. As his immunity had improved, the doctor thought it was more beneficial for Mark to return home and attend hospital for treatment as an outpatient. He would continue to have chemo, but could stay home to recover, with the assumption that the familiarity and routines of home would help with his depression. Jenny knew with certainty that she couldn't cope with the emotional and physical demands of two teenagers, and also give Mark the best chance of recovery. She was convinced, with every maternal instinct she had, that the boys needed a reprieve from this depressed stranger who was nothing like the funny, strong father they knew and loved. While they had been magnificent allies for her over the months of his illness, this last step was a journey she needed to take on her own. She knew they missed the old Mark so much it hurt, but she also knew deep down that she was right. And her gut feeling was that Tim and Jack also knew she was right.

As she drove away from the farm, Jenny was upset but determined. She could see the boys were visibly struggling with so many mixed emotions. Their relief at not having to witness Mark's daily struggle was tempered by enormous guilt at not being there for him. However, the prospect of having to leave home and change schools was indeed a justifiable cause for anger and resentment. But, a resolute Jenny reasoned, if the worst that came out of this was a few weeks' separation from their mates, and maybe a hiccup in their education, it would be worth the short-term pain to preserve whatever was left of the positive image of their father they had in their minds.

At the dam, Tim chose a smooth, flat rock and looked thoughtfully at Jack. Seeing the anger in his brother's face, he made an effort to be positive. Skimming the rock skilfully across the water he said, "With any luck Dad will respond better to the treatment this time, and we'll be home for Easter. And, you know? It might even be fun. We could even be the hot new guys at school!"

Jack, still pessimistic, replied with sarcasm, "Oh yeah? You think so? I think it's going to be the pits."

"Yeah. I think you're probably right," sighed Tim, quickly defeated. Not for the first time since his mother had come up with this crazy idea, Tim felt a swelling of apprehension. "Can you imagine how bad it's going to be for me? I'm starting VCE at a new school! I don't know anyone, and I'm the new kid. Who starts a new school in Year 11? I'm only starting possibly the two most important years of my school life and I don't know one friendly face."

"It's taken me two years to find a good bunch of mates at Deakin High, and now I've got to start all over again. Nobody is going to be rushing over to be my mate either, you know," grumbled Jack.

"I'd be happy if everyone just ignores us. Who knows what bogans go to school here? Let's hope we still have all our teeth at the end of the day."

Tim and Jack had good reason to want to be ignored. At their local high school in Melbourne, new kids more often than not were singled out for "special treatment" by the local bullies. It was much better to be largely anonymous in their over-populated school of upwards of a thousand students. Plus, there were so many different cultures and nationalities, everyone tended to stick with their own tribe of friends. The loners were much more vulnerable for not having a backup bunch of mates.

"Cheer up. They might be rapt to get a new fast bowler just in time for the finals. You never know your luck, Jack-Jack," said Tim, referring to the baby name he had given Jack when he was born.

Jack's shoulders dropped again at the reminder. Leaving home meant they had to quit their respective cricket teams, which were both in the top four on the ladder. Jack had already had a fantastic season and was secretly hoping to win the club batting averages. It was just another in the long list of complaints they had voiced, loud and clear, to their mother over the last couple of weeks.

As they walked back up towards the farmhouse, their grandfather Jim watched them from the verandah. He knew they didn't really want to be there, but he also trusted that Jenny had sent them for all the right reasons. Having two teenagers in the house was going to require some adjusting to his and Moira's lifestyle, but they were only too pleased to help in whatever way they could.

"Come on! Shake a leg, boys," he called. "Dinner's on the table, and if you don't hurry, I'll eat the lot," he threatened.

"What's for dinner, Pa?" asked Jack as he took a running jump on to the veranda.

"What else on Saturday night? Sausages and chips. And there's probably plenty left of the chocolate cake and cream we had for afternoon tea."

The brothers looked at each other and grinned. There were some compensations to make this banishment more bearable, and one of them was Nanna's cooking. Somehow Nanna's culinary skills had managed to avoid any recipe that was vegetarian, vegan or low in fat, which totally suited Jack and Tim. And as they sat down at the kitchen table, Nanna produced the first batch of home-cooked, sizzling-hot chips. For a while, all worries were forgotten.

CHAPTER 2

Tim woke up the next morning to the noisy squawks of a kookaburra showing off its vocal range. When several black crows joined in, their harsh shrieks penetrating the blankets he'd drawn up over his head, he gave up and pulled back the curtains for a look at the day. It was very early. Too early. The sky was still shot with pink and orange hues and the sun wasn't yet visible above the treetops.

He looked jealously over at Jack who was fast asleep, lying on his back, mouth slightly open, his breathing slow and relaxed. Sleeping like a dead man as usual, thought Tim. Jack's bed was always easy to make because he never moved enough to disturb the bedclothes. Tim's own bed, in contrast, always managed to look as if a tornado had struck during the night. He surveyed his tangled sheets and then, readjusting them, sank back down into the soft bed to contemplate the day ahead.

Their bedroom lay off the kitchen, at the rear of the house. Despite the early hour, Tim could hear someone moving around. Pa was probably up, he thought lazily. Farmers like to start the day at all ungodly times, and he knew Pa was no slouch when it came to the farm. Tim kicked his legs free as he began to feel the early heat of the day. The forecast was for an absolute scorcher, and he was already clammy and restless in bed. He had visited the farm enough over the years to know that the weather in northern Victoria was much warmer than in Melbourne. It had its share of cold nights and frosty mornings but generally, even in winter, the days were still and the skies clear and sunny. Not that Tim had any intention of revisiting any fond memories of sunny winter days. He intended to be happily ensconced back home in dreary, grey Melbourne by then.

And then it hit him. That familiar feeling of unease, that all was not right with the world. The nervous punch in the pit of his stomach when he thought of his dad. Life was much simpler when you could tackle a problem head-on and do something to solve it. But this was a problem where Tim knew the solution was out of his control, and he was afraid even to give a name to the dread. The same old questions haunted him in these quiet moments. Was there a way back to their old family life? Would life ever be the same again?

Jack stirred. "What's happening?" he asked sleepily.

"Zilch! And you've been snoring all night!"

"Bullshit I have," said Jack as he stretched and kicked off his covers. "Hey! If I snored, it's because I've had to put up with the smell of your stinky socks all night. It's lucky I haven't suffocated with the stench."

"Stench? Stench, is it?" mimicked Tim, and in one quick movement he had swooped on the offending socks and thrust them under Jack's nose, holding them firmly in place. Jack writhed and gasped, caught totally unaware. But his retaliation was swift as he pushed Tim off and rolled over the edge of the bed. The boys landed together with a resounding thump and proceeded to wrestle as usual, with no consideration as to where they were. Laughing as they grunted with the effort, they banged up against the wall and shoved each other against the beds, overturning a chair in the process. They made enough noise to draw unwanted attention from Pa, who roared from the kitchen, "Knock it off! If you two have got nothing better to do than leap around in your underwear, you can get up and give me a hand with a few jobs."

With a final good-natured shove at each other, Tim and Jack broke off hostilities. Pulling faces and still managing to get the odd well-aimed flick of a tee-shirt away, the boys dressed and straightened up some of the mess they had created in the scuffle. The frequent sibling wrestling was something that regularly drove Jenny mad, and which Mark had often encouraged. It rarely meant anything and there was no malice in it. It was just a bit of one-upmanship to see who was the stronger. For years Tim had always had the upper hand over Jack when they fought, but it was not so clear anymore and Tim had to fight much harder for his victories these days.

As they came into the kitchen, Nan greeted them cheerily. "Good morning, boys. Did you sleep well?"

"Yep. Like a log," said Jack, going straight to the fridge for the milk.

"Yes, all good, Nan. You know I love that bed," said Tim.

Nan was reading the paper as she ate her breakfast. It was a routine the boys knew not to interrupt too much. She loved her morning paper and a cup of tea. The boys had been having holidays with their grandparents for many years, with and without their parents. They knew exactly where everything was in the kitchen, and they could look after themselves. Nanna had always let them have free rein over the kitchen. Also, somehow, miraculously, each time they came she had all their breakfast favourites on hand, and plenty of everything. However, as Tim put seven wheaten breakfast biscuits into a bowl, she did look up and raise an eyebrow. He reluctantly returned one to the packet.

"There's also some homemade apricot jam," she said as she gestured towards the cupboard with a half-eaten slice of toast in her hand. "Delicious, even if I say so myself!" she boasted, winking at them.

After breakfast the boys tidied up their dishes and put away the milk and cereal. Nan had trained them well when they were just little tackers, and she expected them to pick up after themselves. In fact, they showed domestic qualities at Nan's house that they had never revealed to their mother at home. After giving Nan a kiss, the boys headed to the home paddock shed where they knew Pa would be at this time of the morning.

Outside, the sun was already hot. Pa was hauling bags of feed into the ute. "Right, you two. Let's see if you've grown any muscles since the last time you were here. I need a hand with feeding the sheep, so you can both come with me."

The farm was mainly sheep and wheat. The crops had been stripped in December before the boys had arrived. In previous years they had always come up and helped during harvest, but this year it wasn't an option with so much happening at home. Although things were usually quieter on the farm once the crop was in, the long dry spell had affected the feed available for the sheep. Pa had over three hundred sheep and prices were down. Rather than sell them at a low cost, he was hand feeding until the autumn rains came and greened up the paddocks. While Pa drove the ute, the boys stood in the back and hauled the bags of feed over the side, measuring out quantities for each spot he stopped at.

The boys were kept busy with various jobs until after lunch when Pa went off to check out a neighbour's new pump. It was hot. Thirty-five degrees at least in the shade. The air conditioner was going full bore and Nan had the curtains closed against the heat. Inside the house it was cool and dark, while outside the ground cooked and the hot air shimmered, haze-like, in the distance. The tennis was on the television, and Nanna had settled herself in for the afternoon with her ironing. It was too hot to do anything else, so eventually Jack and Tim joined her in the lounge.

The final of the Australian Open was being played between Mats Wilander and the hometown favourite, Pat Cash. It was to be the first time that the Australian Open would be held at Flinders Park, the new tennis centre in Melbourne, and the commentators were predicting a long, hard match. The Open had always been at Kooyong on grass courts, but this time they were playing on the new Rebound Ace. It would be a different match on this surface. Wilander liked to slog it out on the baseline, but he was agile and not afraid of coming to the net to put a volley away. Cash thrived on a serve-and-volley style of play and he was dogged in his ability to fight for every point. Long rallies and exciting play were expected to decide each point. In Melbourne, the weather was windy and rain threatened, and in the uncertain conditions of Centre Court, it was going to be a battle of the fittest. Mildly interested, Tim and Jack stretched out on the rug in front of the TV. The Open was a part of summer in Melbourne. Tennis featured almost every day on TV from mid-December with various state tournaments, culminating with the Australian Open in late January. In the city there were more television channels available, and the boys usually chose cricket over tennis. However, in Winjarra, only the regional channels were available and, in any case, Nanna was obsessive about the tennis, so there was never going to be a choice.

"Do you think Cash can win, Nanna?" asked Jack at the first commercial break.

"Oh, I hope he can! It's about time we had an Aussie win at home. But it won't be an easy win. Wilander has beaten some good players to get to this stage. And look! He's got his own band of supporters to cheer him on." She pointed to the television as the cameras panned across a noisy band of young Swedish supporters, faces proudly painted in yellow and blue, waving Swedish flags. "Whatever the result, it's going to be a great match and I'd love to be there."

"It's Cash's turn to win this year, Nanna. He can't lose! And if he does, Jack will do all the dishes tonight."

"Hey! No dobbing me in! If Cash loses, we'll both do the dishes," replied Jack, good-naturedly punching Tim in the arm. Tim high-fived Jack to seal the deal and they settled in to watch. Both players looked sharp and ready to play. Cash, as always, sported his black-and-white checked headband over his long hair, and around his neck a chunky gold necklace glinted in the sporadic sunlight. Wilander gave little away but looked resolute.

It was an unsettled start for Cash, and although he showed flashes of his best tennis, he lost the first set. Wilander was 4/1 up in the second, and the pro-Cash crowd was getting nervous when rain drew a halt to play for half an hour. As the players walked off court, the trio in the lounge room sank back in their seats. Nan had halted ironing and joined them on the couch after Cash lost the first set.

"It's not looking good, Nan," moaned Jack, picking up some rolled-up socks and bouncing them off the wall.

"It's early days yet, but I wish Cash was the one 4/1 up and not Mats. Now, while there's a break, why don't you two get your school uniforms out and I'll make sure they're pressed and ready to go for tomorrow." Nan ignored the scowls she received from her grandsons. "Go on. Hop to it!"

Reluctantly Tim and Jack moved to their room to collect their school uniforms. They had tried them on once when they had arrived by post last week. They really didn't want to be reminded that D-day was looming in less than twenty-four hours. Resuming her position at the ironing board, Nan shook out their shirts as they handed them to her and then began ironing them.

"It's not going to be the end of the world, you know. You might find you even enjoy it," she said, with a knowing nod of her head.

Further conversation was halted as the commentators continued their discussion on the match so far. There was some concern that Cash had yet to find form. Soon enough the match was restarted, and this time Cash came out fighting. In no time he had broken serve and equalled at four–all, taking the second set 7/6. The crowd was on their feet with excitement, and the stadium rang with their cheers. As the afternoon shadows moved across the court, each point became a test of tactics and strength. It was a four-and-a-half hour, sweat-stained, exhausting battle between two lions of the game. The noise in the lounge room was a steady crescendo of groans and cheers as Cash either won or lost points. Every ball was vital and neither player wanted to concede, playing each point with determination and brilliance.

Another burst of rain delayed play again in the third set, which only added to the tension. The ball boys were kept busy supplying towels to wipe away the rivers of perspiration that ran down the players' foreheads and into their eyes, and to dry their palms so they could grip racquets that were slippery with sweat. Breathing deeply to catch their breath between points, the combatants fought gamely on, hour after hour. Wilander played almost textbook-perfect tennis, while Cash astonished everyone with his speed and high volleys. Jack, Tim, and Nan were swept up in the drama of the battle, the ironing long forgotten in the excitement. "Just like two Greek warrior gods fighting for the golden orb," said Nanna as the final set began, with two sets all.

Cash looked like he was beginning to tire in the final set, but he was spurred on by the crowd. Wilander played stunning tennis, winning rallies he looked certain to lose. Tim loved it. He was totally enthralled by their skills, and their ability to make the ball go anywhere and do anything they wanted. He was in awe as they turned what should have been a point for the opposition into a winning shot for themselves. He was itching to feel a racquet in his own hand and smash a ball around like these two amazing sportsmen could.

Finally, after a five-set marathon, Mats Wilander won. It had taken a tie breaker in the final set, 8/6, to decide it. Nan and the boys were exhausted by the emotional effort of watching the match, and in the end none of them cared who had won. It was a magnificent performance from two superb athletes, and the crowd acknowledged it by cheering and clapping both stars with equal intensity.

Tim felt tingles up his spine as he watched the crowd's adulation. He wasn't envious of the competitors' moment of glory, but he was just as captivated as the crowd by the drama of the game. The players' ability to master a game so completely stirred his imagination. What a blast to be able to be one of the best, if not the best, in the world at something? Leaping up, he served and volleyed an imaginary ball across the room to the TV. "How's my style, Nanna?" he asked as he continued to smash imaginary balls.

"Brilliant, I'm sure, but watch out for my vase with all your leaping around." As Tim volleyed another ball she asked, "Have you two ever played much tennis?"

"No, never," said Jack. "We always play cricket, or footy, and basketball. Sometimes golf with Dad, so Mum says that's enough. Anyway, are you sure you're playing tennis, Tim? You look more like a badminton player to me."

Ignoring Jack's remark, Tim answered, "I wouldn't mind having a go at tennis though when we go home. I reckon it would be great fun, and I'm not playing as much basketball these days."

"You don't have to wait that long, Tim. There's a couple of old racquets in the shed that you could have a hit with if you like. Your grandfather was one of the district's best players in his day. He was the North Central Regional Champion for nine years straight until he did his Achilles. That put him out of action for months, and it took years before he could run again without soreness. A young farmer with two babies can't afford to sit around recuperating, waiting for a tennis injury to heal. He couldn't risk it. So, he went back and played some social doubles matches with his mates, but he didn't play in a serious competition again. He really missed it, but the farm had to come first. He was a great player though, and I'm sure he'd love to give you some hints. He'd think it was wonderful if the two of you got into tennis."

"Why didn't Mum ever tell us Pa had been such a good player?"

"She probably didn't think much of it. It all happened when she was little, and seeing how she didn't show much interest in tennis, Pa didn't push it. It was all netball in winter and softball in summer for Jenny. Anyway, come down to the shed with me and I'll see if we can find these old racquets."

Jack and Tim, full of enthusiasm, followed Nan down to the shed. It was past six in the evening, but outside the late afternoon air was warm and the concrete footpath, still hot from the day's heat, burned their bare feet. The house was a sprawling old weatherboard, with a gracious Australian verandah that wound around all four sides. The garden was carefully laid out with bushfires in mind, and any tall gums were set well away. Creepers and ivy grew around the water tanks, softening their appearance, but otherwise mainly low flowerbeds and shrubs grew close to the house. There were some lovely old fruit trees scattered over the lawn, providing some shade and screening from the paddocks. It was an attractive oasis of green in what was, in summer, a flat, dry dustbowl.

It took them a few seconds before their eyes adjusted to the gloom of the dark shed after the harsh brightness of the outside. Light came through the cracks and gaps in the roof and walls, casting golden patches across the dirt floor. Dust slowly spiralled downwards, caught in the pockets of daylight. Squinting, Tim could just make out Nan searching through an old wardrobe at the rear of the shed.

"I'm pretty sure this is where I put them. There should be three because Jim had two and I had one as well. Don't look so surprised," she said, looking sideways at them and smiling. "I used to play as well. How do you think I met your pa? I used to play all the time before I had kids and even after I had them. We had a midweek ladies' comp back then. That was about the only time I got out for the week. Mind you, I wish I had done a bit more gallivanting around when I could. Now I've got all the time in the world to play tennis but not the energy, or the young back!

"Okay, boys, lift off this crate for me. I think they're behind it."

Sure enough, there were the three racquets. They were old all right, thought Tim. Ancient wooden racquets with small heads and leather grips. Tim thought enviously of the deadly-looking silver racquet Cash had wielded with such expertise. But racquets they were, and the boys grabbed them, eager to feel their weight.

"You might be better off with mine, Jack, because its grip will be slightly smaller, although it still might be a bit heavy for you. Tim, you can have your Pa's, even though it will be heavy as well. We both liked a bit of weight in our racquets and frankly, there wasn't much choice anyway. And I've just remembered I've got a new tin of balls! I won them in a raffle at the club last year. I knew they'd come in handy one day."

As Nan went back into the house to fetch the balls, the boys swung the racquets around to shake off the dust and get the feel of them. They looked at each other dubiously.

"What else are we going to do?" said Jack. Tim shrugged in response, and they went to collect the balls.

CHAPTER 3

New balls in hand, Jack and Tim looked around for a spot to hit. Nan had suggested just hitting up against the wall of the shed because there wasn't space to hit across the yard to each other. The shed was in shadow at this hour, so it was also much cooler. One wall was clear of any obstruction and the ground in front was flat, bare dirt, baked hard by the sun. An odd weed had sprung to the surface here and there, so there were some uneven patches, but it was mostly smooth, and it gave a good bounce.

Conditions may have been challenging, but the boys, restless for some action after an afternoon of being housebound, approached it with enthusiasm. The shed was made of horizontal timber slats, which made the ball return a tad unpredictable. If the ball hit a crack or a protruding nail—and there were plenty of them—it could shoot off in any direction. Rather than detracting from the game, all this heightened the fun of it.

Jack's racquet had all its strings intact, but both of the other racquets had a string missing. It didn't seem to make any difference to Tim, so he didn't let it worry him. For the next hour or so they attempted to smash balls against the shed wall, considering it a major achievement if they fluked it to hit two or three in a row. Most of the time they spent chasing wayward balls, becoming increasingly hot and sweaty by the minute.

By the time Pa's ute came roaring up the drive an hour later, they were worn out. As he got out of the car, he called out to them, "Hello, hello. What have we here? Two budding tennis stars? What brought this on? I thought you two only played cricket?"

"We watched the tennis final with Nanna. Wilander only just won after a marathon game. It was such a fantastic match, we've been inspired to have a go," said Jack, wiping his forehead and leaving a grubby streak of dirt.

"Sorry about all the marks on the shed," said Tim, noticing for the first time that the shed was now covered in dusty spots, like a spreading rash.

"Don't mind that. It's only the shed and I'm happy to see you both having a hit. I loved my tennis days, and it's about time you boys got started. Most of the young ones around here play. Between tennis and cricket, they keep themselves busy enough in summer. If you're keen to play, it would be a good way to make a few friends."

Tim grimaced. "But we're absolute beginners. No-one's going to want to play with us."

Tim liked to think of himself as being a handy sportsman. Everyone who knew him considered him good at sport, and he took pride in that tag. Teachers, friends, and coaches all wanted him on their team, and he was always chosen in the top teams. So was Jack, for that matter. Tim couldn't quite share his grandfather's enthusiasm for looking like a complete beginner at anything. His ego was already too finely balanced at the moment at the thought of facing a new school and a bunch of strangers. Jack also looked threatened at the thought of suddenly being thrust into playing a game he knew nothing about.

"I wouldn't worry too much, fellas," said Jim. "Paul Maclaren takes PE at the high school. He was a ranked tennis player in his day, and he gave up professional playing and coaching only a few years ago to teach PE. His passion is tennis though, and I'm sure it makes its way into most of the PE lessons at the high school. He's a fantastic coach and a great guy. If you're prepared to have a go, I think you'd find him more than helpful."

Tim and Jack looked at each other doubtfully.

"Why don't you give it a rest for now, and then after dinner we'll come out and I'll see if I can give you any pointers. You won't have to line up at school with a racquet tomorrow, so I'm sure we'll have a bit of time to find some form. It's not rocket science. If you can manage to return a hit from the dodgy shed wall, you're halfway there," Pa offered reassuringly.

Still talking tennis, they left their racquets on the verandah steps and went inside to wash off some of the dust that had found its way onto almost every part of their bodies. Dinner was a substantial affair yet again. Nanna had a theory about the heat, believing it was best to counter the heat with heat. Consequently, she dished up a spicy spaghetti and meatballs, her own special recipe that all her grandchildren loved. It was just delicious and guaranteed to send rivers of cooling sweat down every face. Replenished and fortified with some choc-chip ice-cream, at the end of the meal the boys helped clear away and do the dishes as promised. In the meantime, Jim had gone to shower and change out of his working clothes into the oldest pair of white tennis shorts the boys had ever seen.

"What have you got on, Jim?" shrieked Moira, laughing. "Where on earth did you find those shorts? I'm sure I tossed them years ago."

"Indeed, you did, my love. But …" Jim paused to adjust the waist of the shorts and replied with an injured look on his face and a wink to the boys, "I rescued them. I can't believe you even considered tossing out my lucky shorts. I won the A Grade singles in these shorts four times."

Jack let out a whoop of approval. "Fantastic, Pa! You are rocking it, especially with those lily-white, hairy legs. Let's do this!"

There was plenty of daylight left and Jim started the boys hitting practise balls up against the wall. Despite the tennis outfit, Jim sat on a chair placed strategically out of the line of fire and watched his grandsons' efforts, shouting encouragement from the sidelines. Occasionally he would take a racquet and demonstrate the correct grip or foot movement, but mostly he called out directions as they played. Tim had initially doubted there was much point to all this; however, as the hour wore on, he found himself caught up in the moment. Even in the short space of time they had been hitting he could feel himself improving as he took note of his grandfather's advice. He was surprised to feel disappointed when the light faded and Jim called a halt to play.

"You boys are doing amazingly well for kids who haven't really held a racquet in their hands before. I have to say I'm impressed by the way you keep your eye on the ball. That's the hardest thing for most beginners to learn, watching the ball on to the racquet."

Putting his arms around them both he nodded his approval, saying with feeling, "Good job, fellas."

"Now, showers and bed," interrupted Moira from the porch where she'd been watching as well. "The school bus pulls up out front at 8 am, and it won't wait for slow coaches."

The next morning, with ten minutes to spare by the kitchen clock, Jack and Tim set off down the farm drive to the main road. The bus arrived on time as Moira had predicted, slowing down to stop just where they stood.

"You must be Jenny's boys," said the driver as they climbed on board. "You've both got your mum's good looks," he added, winking at them. "I went to school with Jenny. Max Reynold's the name. Say hi to your mum for me."

"Will do, Max," replied Tim, hoping his mum would remember this friendly man. He wasn't used to bus drivers doing more than collecting the fare and sighing as though the world was coming to an end if they had to give you change. Finishing their chat with the driver, the boys turned to look for a seat and noticed everyone's eyes were on them. Rapidly scanning the bus for a space, Jack quickly spotted that the nearest spare double seat was immediately behind the driver. Kicking their bags under the seat, they both slumped down low, striving to retain some degree of anonymity. The noisy chatter that had greeted them as they entered the bus had dropped to a low murmur, punctuated by a few giggles. Jack and Tim stared at the road straight ahead, trying to ignore the fact that they were very much the elephants in the room: or on the bus, as it turned out.

"What year are youse guys in?" called out a voice from the back. Breathing in, Tim turned around to face the mob. He was immediately distracted by a pair of soft brown eyes and a magnificent mass of curly red hair on the girl sitting two seats back. Dragging his eyes away and towards the sound of the voice, he pointed to himself and said, "Year 11 and he's in Year 9."

Embarrassed by the scrutiny, Tim tried to turn back towards the security of the front window, but no-one was going to let the conversation finish there. Several kids called out they would be in their classes, and soon both Jack and Tim were fully turned towards the rest of the bus answering questions from all sides.

"Do you blokes play cricket? Chuckers or hitters? Not that it matters, we'll take you anyway," said a guy that looked too old to be sitting in the back of a school bus.

"Spinner," mumbled Tim.

"I don't mind either. I bowl and bat a bit," offered Jack, with an air of modest bravado.

"Great. Training is after school tomorrow on the footy oval," the man-child informed them, without bothering to even ask if they could make it. More questions followed, and by the time the bus lurched to a stop, it seemed to Tim and Jack that their entire life's stories had been extracted in twenty minutes. Their stress levels were already in the red zone and they hadn't even reached the school gates.

Winjarra High had been built in the typical Victorian Education Department style of the sixties. Three grey-brick rectangles stood in formation next to each other, with paved areas and garden beds in between. Corridors down the centre of each building divided the classrooms off to either side, and each building was connected by a central passageway. The grounds weren't large, but there were several significant shady gums spread across the lawns, and well-maintained garden beds bloomed with bright yellow marigolds, roses, and native bushes. Pigface grew wild in patches outside the school's fences, and the rear of the school, situated on the edge of the township, gave way to the bush. The school occupied what could be described as the only hill in town, so from most areas of the school you could see the town stretching out in all directions.

Spilling out of the bus with the others close behind them, Jack and Tim found themselves caught up in the throng of students greeting each other effusively after the long summer break. Trying to absorb their new surrounds, they navigated their way around the hyped crowd of teenagers, all heading through the school gates. For the moment they were thankful that no-one seemed interested in them. Jack spotted the "Administration" sign and nudged Tim. Their instructions were to go to the office and report in when they arrived. Inside the admin building the venetian blinds were already lowered against the sun, and the air conditioner hummed quietly. Tim hadn't realised how hot it was outside until the cool air greeted him, a soothing balm to his frazzled thoughts. A smiling registrar directed them to sit on some green vinyl lounge chairs in the foyer while they waited for the vice principal, Mr Aitken, to see them.

"They all seem friendly enough," whispered Jack once they were alone.

"Almost too friendly," complained Tim. "But it's certainly better than having the Toad's gang of tossers to deal with," he added, referring to the notorious gang of bullies everyone was in fear of at Deakin High.

"Do you think they were serious about playing cricket? I mean, they didn't even ask how old I was. And hey! Did you see the tennis courts up the side of the school?"

"Shush! No, I didn't see the tennis courts, and yes, I do think they meant it about cricket. After all, look around! They don't exactly have a cast of thousands to choose from, so this could be our chance to really star."

They were still grinning when Mr Aitken came bursting through the double swing doors that divided the reception area from the school offices. Dressed in shorts, a rugby shirt, and track shoes, he looked more like he was ready for a Sunday barbeque than work. With friendly efficiency he completed the last details of their enrolment forms, and within minutes Tim and Jack were officially Winjarra students and heading off to find form teachers. By the time the bell had rung for assembly, the boys had finalised subjects and timetables, and been issued with textbooks.

Assembly was held in the quadrangle outside the admin building, at the front of the school. With the Australian flag raised and the morning sun beating down on them, they sang the national anthem. Tim stood through the long speeches that followed, trying to gather some understanding of what was happening and, more importantly, attempting to exude an air of confidence he was definitely not feeling. Spotting Jack standing in the Year 9 lines, he hoped he was okay. He did have a sense of being the big brother in all of this and feeling responsible for Jack was just another of his worries. He realised with a start that he hadn't even given either of his parents a thought all morning.

Jack was similarly taking in his surrounds. His eyes darted around like laser beams. In a way he was quite enjoying himself and he was beginning to think this might not be such a negative experience. Mrs Holloway, the principal, was telling the students about some events that were already planned for the year and detailing some new school rules. She welcomed the Year 7 class to the school and then, to Jack's horror, singled out Tim and himself as new students, and invited everyone to make them feel welcome. A round of applause, the universal symbol of welcome, made Jack want to disappear into the ground. He caught sight of Tim, whom he thought looked as mortified as he felt himself.

They were both relieved when assembly finished, and they were able to move off to their first classes. School in Winjarra was definitely going to be different. For a start, there was the novelty of having the luxury of an air-conditioned classroom. Air conditioners in Melbourne were a rarity at school—especially government schools. The day continued with one new experience after another, so that both boys were soon well and truly overwhelmed. It was a bonus that the school was small and the physical layout followed a simple plan, with classrooms off a central hallway. Deakin High had over a thousand students, and the schoolyard was littered with portable classrooms brought in to cope with the growing population. You could go there for six years and still not know half the teachers' names or even all the students in your year. Tim could see that with only three hundred students, things would be much easier. However, he was beginning to realise, as was Jack, that being anonymous in a big school had some advantages.

Here at Winjarra, everyone already knew them on sight, while they knew no-one's name and every face was new. It was also becoming uncomfortably apparent that soon they would be expected to be able to put a name to a face. The task of learning names was doubly impossible because most kids had their formal name that teachers used in class, and then also a nickname. It seemed that lots of these names had been used more than once so there were several Puds and Jackos, and Trackers and Chucks. One name, however, that Tim did zone in on, and not forget, was the red-haired Karen Jennings from the bus. Karen, he discovered, was not only in his year but in most of his classes as well. Tim was not disappointed at all about the prospect of seeing her every day. He thought she was a knockout.

Towards the end of the last period, Mr Maclaren, the sports teacher, came in with a list of sport options for the term. Tim was mindful about what Pa had said about Mr Maclaren being a hot shot tennis coach, but it wasn't until he saw Karen put her name down for tennis that he made up his mind and signed on for tennis too. By the time the dismissal bell had rung, both of the boys were more than ready to get back to the quiet refuge of the farm. Moira had arranged to meet them after school as she had shopping to do in town that afternoon, so they were saved another interrogation on the bus home. However, they soon realised Nan possibly had an ulterior motive for picking them up when she conned them both into helping her shop at the IGA.

The "quick trip" to the shop took almost an hour as Moira managed to run into every person she knew in town. Jack grumbled halfway through that he thought she must have known they would all be there. Moira, on the other hand, ignored the boys' complaints and relished every minute of letting the town know these were her grandsons and they were staying on the farm with them for a while. To their credit, the boys smiled politely despite their frustration, and did their best to charm all Nan's friends and cronies. They knew what Winjarra was like from their mum's stories about growing up there, so they didn't disappoint Nan, whom they loved. Permanently red from embarrassment, they sweated their way through the ordeal, both making a mental note to go home on the bus next time.

Back in the car Jack exclaimed ruefully, "Gee, Nan. Did we miss anyone you know?"

"Well, Jack, you know how it is. I've lived here all my life. Of course, I know everyone. And besides, I knew they were all dying to meet you two. It doesn't take long to spot a newcomer to town."

"Tell me about it," said Tim. "All day I felt like I had a sign on that said, 'I'm Tim Anderson, say hello'."

Ignoring his sarcasm Moira replied cheerfully, "Well, that's good to hear. I'm glad everyone made you feel welcome. How was your day, Jack?"

"Pretty good, Nan. I met a few mates, one called Chuck, and Steve and Ted. I'm not too good on all the names yet, but I'd have to say all the kids were friendly enough. And even the girls talked to me. At Deakin, no-one bothers to talk to anyone who isn't in your home group, especially new kids you don't know anything about. So, it wasn't too bad."

"True," agreed Tim. "But I wouldn't mind if someone ignored me just a little. It's hard being the star attraction."

Moira laughed. "You'll get used to it, Tim. I'm surprised you haven't been approached by the cricket and footy teams already and asked to play. They usually like to check out the newcomers to see if they have any talent."

"Don't worry. They're not slipping. They did that already on the bus this morning."

Chuckling to herself Moira changed the subject, asking about the courses and subjects they had chosen. When she followed up about what sport option they had taken, she was pleased to hear that each of them had opted for tennis. "Your Pa will be pleased," she said, smiling at them both.

CHAPTER 4

A couple of apples, a chocolate milkshake, and several of Nan's homemade peanut biscuits, and the boys were ready to start hitting tennis balls again. This time they drew a chalk line across the shed wall. A racquet-length-and-a-racquet-head high, the height of a net, just as Pa had instructed them. Using a stick to mark the ground, they drew several more lines in the dirt at equal intervals away from the wall. The aim was to make five consecutive hits with safe returns at each line before moving on to the next. Racing the clock as well as each other made it more interesting than just hitting.

While it looked simple, the concentration and effort required was intense and went a long way to shaking off the day's tension. The uneven surface of the wall and the unpredictability of the ball's bounce off the ground combined to make this no easy task. The variables and uncertainty of each shot had both of them totally engrossed. Tim had to work hard to keep ahead of Jack. He was used to having the older brother advantage, but Jack was fast catching up and this new skill of tennis was pretty much a level playing field. Tim wasn't about to let Jack get ahead and have to concede superior status in anything just yet.

Secretly, Tim gave himself credit for much of Jack's sporting ability, because he'd always used him as a practise partner in cricket or footy, and he felt he'd taught him well. Jack definitely had great hand-eye coordination though, which was a potential threat to Tim's dominance. However, when Jack hit a wayward ball off the edge of his frame, costing him precious time while he chased it down, Tim was relieved to finish the clear winner after two hours of slogging it out.

Slumping on the steps of the verandah, the boys soaked up the late afternoon breeze as they recovered from their efforts. Jack broke their companionable silence first. "Well? What did you think of school?"

Tim took a while to answer as he weighed up the events of the day. "It seems okay so far. It wasn't what I expected. I mean, everyone was so friendly, and even the teachers made an effort to chat. Can you imagine what it would have been like at Deakin? We'd probably be looking for icepacks now, instead of playing tennis."

Jack nodded. "You said it, mate. It's small though. The library is really only a couple of classrooms joined together, and there's not much tech stuff either."

"It's small, all right. And how was it when the principal mentions us by name, in front of the whole school! And literally everyone seemed to know who we were before we even arrived!" complained Tim.

"Embarrassing stuff, no doubt," said Pa, overhearing the end of their conversation as he wandered outside and sat down on the steps with them. "But if being recognised is the worst thing that happened today, then I don't think you've got too much to worry about. Right now, your grandmother is ready to dish up, so hurry and wash off some of that dirt, and we can talk about things over dinner."

As promised, they discussed the day over another of Nan's excellent dishes: an egg and bacon pie, and a tossed salad. Jack and Tim discovered that not only did their grandparents know most of the teachers, but they seemed to have a connection with almost every person they mentioned. No wonder everyone had known about them well before they arrived!

"Well, that's the way it is in a small town like Winjarra," explained Pa. "We play bowls and golf with different ones in town, and we hear the news about their kids or grandkids. Whatever happens at the school or the footy club, we'll hear about it eventually."

"Don't forget there's only about eight hundred people who live in town, and we'd probably be lucky to have three and a half thousand in the shire. So even though we're spread out a bit, given time, it's hard not to know most people. Plus, we've been passing on news about you two since you were babies, so plenty of our friends already know lots about you. Besides," said Pa with a chuckle, "last week there was little item in the Winjarra Gazette, in the social news, about how you were coming to stay for a while."

Tim was horrified and thought he must have been joking, until Pa reached over to last week's paper and began to flick through the pages. Jack grabbed it and read aloud, "Tim and Jack Anderson, of Seaford in Melbourne, will be staying with their grandparents Moira and Jim Jones on their property at Snake Gully. While they are here the boys will be attending Winjarra High School. Tim will be in Year 11, and his younger brother, Jack, will be in Year 9.

"No wonder everyone knew us," said Jack, appalled.

"Don't let it bother you," said Nan. "All you have to do to fit in is to be yourself and meet people halfway. Naturally we get a little curious about newcomers, but that's all it is. Just a bit of curiosity, and it will die down. Be open-minded and join a few clubs or teams. Once they see you're prepared to have a go, people will bend over backwards to make you feel welcome."

Tim couldn't help but feel a little overwhelmed and threatened by all this talk of fitting in. If it weren't for the fact that they couldn't miss so much school, he would have been perfectly happy to just stay on the farm and help out his pa. The phone rang before he could think of a reply.

"I'll get it," said Tim instead as he jumped up from the table. "I bet it's Mum ringing up to find out about school."

Just as he thought, it was Jenny ringing to find out about their day. Tim brushed off her questions about school with a quick reassurance that all went well. He was more interested in his father's prognosis and how long he and Jack might have to stay at the farm. Jenny was bright and cheerful, and reported that the first outpatient chemo treatment had gone well and that their dad was resting at home and had, so far, seemed to handle it fairly well.

"Did the outpatient doctor say anything? Is it normal for Dad to be still feeling sick after all this time?" Tim demanded, hoping for some positive scrap of information.

"Oh, Tim," replied Jenny ruefully, "I can't give you any answers yet. He didn't say anything new, just to expect tiredness and nausea. That's why you're staying at Nan and Pa's, remember? To give Dad a chance to recover at home."

"Yeah. I remember. Just don't you forget that this is only a short-term arrangement!"

Tim's mood darkened even more and, in a bad-tempered moment, he shoved the phone at Jack, who stood listening at his side, and went back to the table to finish his dinner. Nan and Pa wisely said nothing, but the scowl on Tim's face and his flushed cheeks reflected his emotions. Tim had shocked himself with his sudden anger towards his mother. He felt he had no control over his life anymore and, although deep down he knew it wasn't her fault, she was the only one he could lash out at.

Jack's conversation with Jenny was much calmer and he filled in the details that Tim hadn't mentioned, even making her laugh when he described the assembly when they had their names read out. Coming back to the table he said, "Mum says hi to you guys," he nodded at his grandparents, "and that she will call later. And she reckons she might be up Friday week, and if she does, she'll stay for the weekend."

"That will be nice," said Nan. "Did she say how your dad was going?"

"Nothing new. He seems to be okay so far. It's still a waiting game," sighed Jack, more resigned to hearing the same old news than his brother.

For a while no-one spoke, each of them processing Jenny's call in their own way. Tim finally broke the spell by collecting plates and taking them over to the sink.

"Are we all having ice-cream and stewed apricots?" asked Nan, serving out dessert. "And then it's probably time you did some homework. I heard you both complaining in the car you had homework, so you better get on to it."

After dinner, while Nan and Pa went in to watch the evening news, the boys finished up the last of the dishes and then, spreading their books out on the kitchen table, began the homework tasks set that day. The rest of the week followed in a similar vein and by Friday both Jack and Tim found themselves feeling comfortable with the familiar routine. Each morning by eight o'clock they would be waiting at the end of the drive for the bus. Like clockwork, at about a minute past the hour, Max would come rolling around the bend in the highway and pull up with a rattle and a jerk in front of them. Initially they were greeted with the usual curious stares and polite greetings, but with each new day they could feel themselves becoming less of a novelty. By Friday they felt almost part of the scenery. There was always a bit of rivalry and teasing on the bus between different groups. Max, their driver, was generally very laid back about the commentary, turning a blind eye, or ear, to the antics that went on. Tim could concede that the daily trip to and from school was lots of fun, and certainly beat the drudge of the public transport they took to school in Melbourne.

Once they arrived at school, they generally had about fifteen minutes to get ready for class. It was just enough time to catch up with the town kids, or to play a round of handball. Tim had already attached himself to a couple of mates. Tony Dean, one of his friends, was also relatively new to town, having moved there only six months ago when his father took up a position as the bank manager. Tony only lived a few doors from the school in town.

Right from the start he had been keen to connect with Tim because he could remember vividly the feeling of being the new kid at school. Tim liked Tony immediately and he could readily understand, as they got to know each other, that Tony was also missing his former friends and school. Tony had at least lived in a small town before, but it was on the coast and a long way from Winjarra. He and Tim found another connection as they both missed being near the beach.

Tony had teamed up with a local guy, Nick Chandler, whose family was born and bred in Winjarra. His dad was a farmer, so he lived on a farm out of town too, but his mum was the local kinder teacher. He didn't usually catch the bus, because his mum drove him to school and back. This meant he spent a fair bit of time after school in town while his mother did class preparation, which was how Tony and he had become mates. They also loved their sport, and Tim found them easy to be around. By Friday, when school finished, he was confident enough to call out to them, "See you Monday," as he boarded the bus.

Lunchtimes and recess were spent playing handball and cricket in the nets. There was no footy oval in the school grounds, but the town footy ground and hockey field were part of a huge recreation centre that was just across the road, and they doubled up for school use. The rec centre, as it was known locally, also bizarrely contained a trotting track that was used officially once a year on Winjarra Race Day. Adjacent to this were the netball courts, and further along towards the main street lay the bowling club and lawn tennis courts. The tennis and bowls club shared facilities and a clubhouse. In the far corner of the rec centre property was the swimming pool, a fifty-metre Olympic pool that was the envy of many surrounding towns. Once the school day was over, it would be invaded by all the town kids, and any other out-of-town kids lucky enough not to have to catch a bus home.

Such a wealth of facilities at the school's disposal during the school week meant that the actual school grounds were reasonably small, but beautifully maintained. The grounds were well thought out. There was plenty of sports equipment, courts marked out for basketball, netball or handball, as well as undercover areas. There were no restrictions about moving between areas and year levels mixed freely. This meant that age and year group were no barrier, and you found yourself making up the numbers for cricket, basketball or handball, or whatever was happening, with anyone who was interested. This was very different to Deakin High, where students were segregated into certain areas according to year level, and where the availability of sport equipment was almost non-existent outside of structured PE lessons.

Jack had made several new friends. He had been adopted by a large group of boys in his form. Their current favourite pastime was a game called brandy, and Jack spent his recess and lunch times chasing or being chased around the school by his mates, trying to tag each other with a tennis ball, the focus being to get the other guy "out". Jack loved this game as it involved very little chat but gave him great acceptance among his peers for his deadly aim and his nifty speed. Within a day or two he had become highly sought after when teams were picked.

Tim had been worried that starting Year 11 at a new school would damage his chance of doing well next year in his final VCE exams. However, by the end of the week he realised he quite liked all of his teachers and in his favourite subjects of English, maths, and PE, he thought he might have actually struck gold. The classes were small, and the teachers relaxed and friendly. They seemed to know everyone well and weren't afraid to share a joke with the students, even at their own expense. Tim found the implications of the small-town structure reinforced on a daily basis. It meant that everyone literally knew everyone else, including their parents and siblings, cousins, aunties, uncles, and grandparents. There was no chance of staying under the radar, so if you didn't put in an effort at school, your parents would soon find out, one way or another.

He particularly liked Mr Maclaren, the PE teacher. In his first lesson he had worked the class until they dropped, which was his intent, as he commenced a series of fitness tests on each student. This was the kind of stuff Tim thrived on, and he pushed himself to the limit as they completed timed runs around the trotting track, and various strength and agility tests in the gym. The second PE lesson involved skill and development in a particular sport, and Tim was pleased when he learned that tennis was the first sport the class would try. He could have shown off much better if Mr Mac, as they were allowed to call him, had chosen cricket, because he was proud of his cricketing skills. However, as he and Jack had continued to fool around with hitting tennis balls up against the shed each evening after school, he was keen to get some tips on how to play.

As Pa had promised, Mr Mac knew lots about coaching tennis, and he did so in a way that made it easy to interpret and grasp the skills, even for a complete beginner. He was matter-of-fact and very patient as he taught the correct grips and stroke play. On Friday after school, he added an extra session for any interested students. Tim and Jack signed up for this as well, along with several other beginners who took up the offer—mostly younger than Tim and Jack. Both brothers found hitting the ball wasn't too difficult: but keeping it in the lines of the tennis court was a different matter. Also, they loved the school tennis racquets, which made their strokes look so much better than their grandparents' old wooden ones did. Completely absorbed in what he was doing, Tim initially failed to notice Karen Jennings, on a court further down, hitting buckets of balls by herself as she practised serve after serve. As they finished that afternoon, he asked one of the other kids why she was there.

"Karen's a really good player. She plays A Grade on the weekend in Bendigo, and Mr Mac coaches her. He wants her to play in the state interschool competition this year, so they often train down here after school. And even if she doesn't win at the state champs, she should win the North Central Regional Championships. Why are you so interested anyway? Have you got the hots for her?"

Then, without waiting for a reply and with a very knowing look, he added confidentially, "I wouldn't waste your time on her. She goes out with Perko in Year 12, and he's got his licence. I don't think she'll be interested in a loser like you." And he swiftly put Tim in his place, softening the blow by a wink and a friendly flick of his jumper. "Gotcha!"

Tim was saved from any further potentially embarrassing conversation with the cocky Year 8 by the honking sound of Max's bus horn. He always did a double bus run on Fridays, so that any kids who chose a sports practise could make training and still get the bus home. Settling back into his seat, Tim looked out the window to where Karen was talking to Mr Mac as she walked towards the school gate. He had to admit to himself he was more than a bit interested in Karen.

She was different to the usual girls he liked, and because she was in some of his classes he'd had plenty of time to check her out. She had long, curly red hair, which she usually wore tied back severely in a long ponytail down her back. However, it was hair with a mind of its own. By the end of the day, much of it would have managed to escape its elastic band and she would blow the wispy red tendrils of hair out of her eyes as she sat in class. Her eyes were a light hazel, framed by deep auburn lashes, and when she spoke, they would widen a little, as if she was surprised by what she had to say. She had the pale skin of a redhead, but only a dusting of freckles, and Tim wondered how she never managed to tan in this hot, sunny climate. When she smiled, her face lit up, and Tim felt drawn to her easy going nature.

When Tim realised she was the school tennis champ, she appealed to him even more. He had a strong feeling that they would get on, especially since they both loved sport. Tim had never understood the girls at school who did everything to avoid PE lessons and huddled together in groups at lunchtime talking or walking aimlessly around in pairs. So far, they hadn't said much to each other, but Tim was hoping that given they were on the bus together each day, at some point he'd have a chance to get to know her.

Max gave a final hoot of his horn and started the engine when Karen started running towards the bus. As she sat down next to her bus pal Annie, Tim reflected on his chances now he knew she had a boyfriend. He wasn't conceited but he knew he wasn't bad looking, and the fact that lots of girls smiled at him gave him a bit of confidence. He was lucky enough to have never gone through a pimple stage, and he had good skin. His hair was naturally light brown, but at this stage of summer it was always streaked with some blond after spending time at the beach, swimming and surfing. He had a nose that could politely be termed strong, but that had so far thankfully shown no signs of developing into the family conk, which his uncles on his dad's side seemed to have.

His mate Aaron, and several other guys he knew in Melbourne, had been shaving for months, and they proudly showed off hairy chests, arms, and legs. Tim's facial hair could be described as wispy at best; however, he was tall for his age, and he was glad because this gave him an edge over most of his mates. Tim knew he was physically strong and he had great natural core strength, so there were not many who would take him on in a tackle and bring him down. Jack was quickly following in the same physical pattern as Tim. It was easy to guess they were brothers, with Jack being just a few centimetres shorter and having grey eyes instead of Tim's green. Although Tim knew they didn't look exactly alike he could see that Jack was a good-looking kid, and he hoped the same went for him. However, this boyfriend was an unknown quantity, so he felt he would be wise not to get his hopes up.

As the bus chugged its way back to the farm, Tim's thoughts eventually moved on to the past week at school. All in all, it hadn't been too bad, and he'd even found himself enjoying the change. Despite the promising start to school, Tim still often felt dragged down by thoughts of his father and what was happening back home. He found himself looking forward to his mother's visit—if not to see her, then for the information she would bring.

The next week passed quickly with Jack and Tim slipping into a daily routine of school, tennis, jobs at the farm, and homework. As promised, Jenny rang every night, but for the most part she had remained very noncommittal. Tim still didn't believe he was being told the full story. He hadn't given up on looking his mother in the eye and asking her the tricky questions she was so evasive of on the phone. The following Friday afternoon, it was Jenny who was waiting for them at school after tennis training. She had left Mark in the hospital for respite over the weekend so she could visit Jack and Tim.

After initial hugs and greetings, they headed back to the farm. Both boys were keen to ask her just how things were going. Jenny seemed very bright and positive, but Tim found her answers still mostly evasive. Jenny noticed his exasperated look as she finished explaining what she'd hoped would be enough to satisfy them. When she got to the farm turn-off, she stopped the car in the driveway and turned to face them. "Your dad is physically getting better. I can honestly say that the doctors are happy with his progress and the chemo. While it makes him really nauseous, it's hopefully doing its job, and he doesn't seem to be reacting quite as badly to it as he was. He's tired and exhausted but he did send his love and kisses to you both, and he wants me to tell him about everything you've been up to. So that's a good sign. But," she paused to reach out and grab their hands, "he still has a long way to go, and he's still not himself yet."

For a moment they sat in silence as Jack and Tim took in what their mother had said. The words "he's still not himself yet" sat with them in the quiet car. Eventually, after a final squeeze of their hands, Jenny started the engine again and they drove slowly down towards the farmhouse.

Despite the news that Dad was still obviously suffering from depression, the boys managed to make the most of their mother's visit. They quickly slipped into familiar territory as she picked up on their lack of manners or personal hygiene. It was almost fun to be admonished once more for talking with their mouths full or wearing the same socks three days running.

Jim and Moira clearly appreciated having Jenny around, too. They spent one evening going through the old slide photos Jim had taken on various family holidays, and there were lots of laughs as it brought back memories for them all. Jim was in fine form, full of yarns and plenty of family stories that he completely exaggerated for effect, keeping them all laughing, especially Jenny. For the first time in months Tim and Jack had a glimpse of their old mum, as she used to be, without the harried expression she now constantly wore.

As she was preparing to leave late Sunday afternoon, Tim managed to catch Jenny on her own. For a brief moment there was no-one else around and Tim made the most of his chance.

"Mum. If this therapy doesn't work, do the doctors have any more treatments planned?"

The question took Jenny by surprise, and she took a moment to answer. Looking straight at Tim, she held his gaze like a magnet as she debated with herself how much to give away. Tim held his breath, willing her to answer honestly. Finally, she put her arms around him and drawing him close to her, she said very quietly, "I don't know."

His next question though was the one that really hit home. "If Dad does recover, do you think he'll ever be the same again?"

Once more Jenny whispered, "I don't know. But," she added, as the spectre of Mark's mental struggles hung over them, "we have to keep treating him as if he is the same old Dad, and be as normal as we can. Because I think that's the only thing that might bring him back to us. That, and time. Just give him time and hopefully, eventually, these days will be all forgotten."

They stood there holding each other close as unspoken thoughts circled around them. Jack's voice from the verandah, calling to Jenny, brought them back to the moment. They broke apart, Jenny assuming the cheerful mask she had worn for so long as she readied herself to face Jack. Arm in arm, they walked together down the hall and outside to the car. Jenny hid her mixed emotions well as she took her leave, thanking Jim and Moira for the fantastic job they were doing with Tim and Jack. As she started the car and waved goodbye, Tim, knowing his mother was upset, but unable to stop himself, opened the door to the car, saying emphatically, "We're only staying here long enough to give Dad the best chance to have this shitty treatment, and then we're coming home. Don't forget he needs us, too."

Jenny gave a long sigh but nodded. "I love you, Tim, and I miss you both so much. It's a deal. You can come home at the end of term." As she drove away, Jenny wished for the umpteenth time that she did have a crystal ball and could see a happy future on the horizon.

CHAPTER 5

The days and weeks continued in a pleasant routine of school, sport, and the farm, and Tim realised that the end of the first term was fast approaching. The weather had continued dry and hot—a long, extended summer, dominated by clear blue skies. Although it was autumn, there had still been no rain and the sun continued to beat down on the red dirt, slowly sucking away any remaining moisture. Tim watched his grandfather search the skies daily for a change in the weather. Jim spoke often of the need for early autumn rains so he could begin seeding the paddocks for the year's wheat crops.

His anxious gaze was contagious and had them all scanning the skies. Each evening and on weekends, Tim and Jack found themselves carting water and feed to the sheep, and helping herd them, when necessary, into other paddocks. Jim weighed up the prospect that he might have to sell off some sheep in the coming months unless the rain arrived soon. He worried how long he could hold out before seeding. Did he take a chance and go early? Or wait for the first rain and hope it was wet enough to plant, but also not too late to germinate before the cold weather set in?

Finally, the weather changed. It was a Sunday morning when red clouds of dust blew down from the Mallee, and the wind raged, rattling windows and doors, threatening to tear any loose sheets of iron off the sheds. Moira had all the windows shut tight but, despite her best efforts, dust still managed to coat every surface of the house. Finally, in the late afternoon, menacing black clouds rolled across the sky, and the day grew prematurely dark. Bolts of lightning pierced the dim skies, and thunder rang, first distant, then closer, like cannons approaching. When the storm broke it was a pent-up fury of nature that lashed the district with blinding sheets of rain and strikes of lightning that sent everyone racing indoors, while the sheep huddled together in bleating masses in corners of the paddocks.

Trees, dried out by the long summer months, became damp and heavy and, as the rain continued to pelt down, some branches cracked and fell crashing to the ground, blocking roads and at times pulling down power lines. The power to the farmhouse was cut and Moira, Jim, and the boys waited out the storm in the kitchen, playing cards. For three hours the storm raged, and it was very late in the day before they ventured outside to survey the damage. Rivers of water ran across the house yard, and the dirt was now thick mud. An eerie orange glow from the setting sun bathed everything in a soft light that muted and blurred all the usual harsh edges. Everything looked quite beautiful, framed in the post-storm dusk.

There were a few branches down around the house, and Moira's veggie patch and garden had taken a battering. Broken shrubs and bruised flowers lay strewn across the lawn, and the roses had been stripped of petals and leaves. However, the air was moist and filled with the promise of new life and they could picture the dams beginning to fill again with water. They surveyed the debris and destruction from the verandah, and could hear water trickling off the roof, into downpipes, and flowing along to the water tanks at the side of the house. Out in the paddocks the sheets of water were gradually seeping into the soil, leaving it wet and heavy, ready to plump up the wheat seeds when they were planted.

It was a magnificent sight and Tim could see the relief on Pa's face. He felt a new respect for his grandfather, who had carried the brunt of the worry about the drought, and he began to also appreciate, with much more understanding, the precariousness of farming life. Jim was almost euphoric as he headed off to repair some of the damage and check on the sheep, and it seemed to Tim that the lines on Pa's face were visibly relaxing by the minute. As Jim strode away Tim could almost hear him already busy mentally calculating just how quickly he could get the machinery out to start the planting.

The rain continued on and off for the next few days, but even the dull grey skies couldn't dampen the feeling of excitement and anticipation the rain had brought. The Easter break was in sight, and the beginning of the footy season almost due. A holiday mood permeated the school. With the district's farming fortunes so closely linked to the wellbeing of the entire community, no-one could remain indifferent to the early promise of good crops after such plentiful autumn rains. In a good season everyone benefited, as the farmers spent money in town on goods and services, employing the local tradies, and cash flowed through the town. On the other hand, a bad season or a drought had everyone tightening their belts. No money spent in town with the local businesses often led to very hard times all round.

Tim had to concede, as the end of term loomed, that it hadn't been too bad after all. He and Jack had each made several good friends and the feeling of being the odd ones out at school had long faded. Mum had visited often as promised, but the news was much the same, and Dad's sickness lingered on, leaving both Tim and Jack still worried and uncertain about the future.

With the end of term came the Year 11 school camp, and Tim was looking forward to it. He had slipped into an easy friendship with Tony and Nick, and all three of them were keen to try the outdoor adventure activities available at the Grampians-based camp. Canoeing, rock climbing and abseiling, orienteering, and bush hikes were all on offer. Nights promised to be even more fun as the teachers laid out the long list of rules that were begging to be broken.

It was Karen's idea to let off crackers outside the teachers' tents at 3 am. While the instigators fled to the safety and seclusion of their own tents, the sudden popping of crackers sent the teachers leaping from their sleeping bags and out into the night. The hilarious sight of their teachers arrayed in their pyjamas was worth the five-kilometre punishment run before breakfast the next day.

The evening campfires were also fun, and the teachers gave the students some space and free time, as they congregated around the tables in the rec room planning for the next day. Karen and Tim often ended up sitting together in the same group, and he began to hope she enjoyed his company as much as he did hers. On the last night at camp a ranger from the park took everyone on a bush hike with torches, to spot the nocturnal native animals. It was a dark, cloudy night, and they had plenty of success spotting possums and even a wombat. As they were returning to camp a light drizzle turned quickly to heavy rain.

The orderly groups they had been in broke up as everyone ran for the lights of the camp and shelter. Tim saw Karen stop as she dropped her torch in the confusion and he slowed down to help her look for it. As Karen scrambled about on the ground Tim shone his torch around and within moments, he found it. Triumphantly, he cried, "Bingo!"

"Great work, Tim, but it doesn't look like it was worth saving, does it?" she laughed as its half-dead glow barely cut through the darkness.

"Maybe not, but I still think it's worth a reward, don't you?" replied Tim cheekily as he stretched out a hand for her to grab, and pulled her to her feet.

"I agree totally," said Karen demurely. Then in an unexpected quick move, she grabbed Tim's face and drew him towards her, planting a big, smacking kiss on his lips. Before Tim could recover, she gave him a friendly push and ran, laughing, down the path back towards the campground and the lights.

"What are you doing, standing in the rain like a twit?" called out the last remaining teacher as he hurried past with his group of stragglers. "Get a move on, Anderson, so we don't have to send out a search party for you."

Later, as Tim lay in his sleeping bag, he thought over what had happened. Once he had gotten back Karen totally ignored him as they headed for showers and to change out of their wet clothes. What on earth was he supposed to make of that? And then the terrifying thought came to him that he should have kissed her back, but that it all happened so fast he wasn't ready. Confused thoughts circulated around his head all night, and they continued the next day as Karen made no further reference to the kiss—in fact, behaving as if nothing had even happened.

To add further to Tim's unsettled emotions, by the end of the camp he was feeling as though he had really cemented strong bonds with his new friends, and yet he felt almost a sense of betrayal towards his old friends. He was ridiculously bothered that he had so quickly moved on from his mates in Melbourne. It was also the first time in many years he could remember when he'd had to actually work at making new friends. He realised with a shock that this was probably not only good for him, but it had been fun as well. The effort to be interesting and to learn about other people's lives demanded social skills of a higher order, and he'd had to dig a bit deeper and be more open than he was used to, after years of hanging with the same old crowd. While he missed that familiarity, he understood that he also liked the new challenges and the rewards that came with making and developing new friendships.

Sport had always been Tim's happy place. He thrived on its physical demands, and he loved pushing his body to the limit. With the new school came opportunities to shine, and with his height and coordination, he had been highly sought after for local teams. He had joined the cricket team as a reserve halfway through the season, but through injury and circumstance, he ended up playing enough games to be eligible to play for the grand final–winning team. The footy club was also anxious to secure him for the Under 18s but he reluctantly declined, knowing it would be too difficult for Nan to get him in and out to town for training, especially since they would most likely be heading back to the city just as the season started.

Instead, he and Jack had found themselves most afternoons after school with a tennis racquet in their hands, smashing balls against the shed wall. Once school was over and farm jobs were done, there was little else to do, and the brothers were well and truly hooked. Jack needed no other incentive than to be able to beat Tim at the various challenge stations they had set up. Spurred on by some extra after school tennis coaching from Mr Mac, they always had a new skill to practise.

Eventually, with Pa's help, they had measured out a half court from the shed wall. This meant they could train at more than just hitting and keeping the ball in play. Daily the strokes became more familiar and their skills steadily improved. They switched from backhands, forehands, volleys, and serves with dexterity, gradually gaining consistency. Their eyes were glued to the path of the ball as it flew unpredictably off the wall or bounced with erratic speed off the uneven grass.

Tennis practise after school had become the highlight of their week. Within weeks, despite their newness to the sport, Jack and Tim found themselves quickly outstripping the others in the class, with the exception of Karen, who was in a league of her own. Tim and Jack had made enormous progress. The advantage of a decent surface, good racquets and a net, and some timely coaching was pure bliss. Mastering the depth of the court was impossible playing against the shed wall, and Mr Mac's coaching was thorough and specific. He insisted on sound grips and correct stroke technique, and he reinforced his messages, constantly checking and observing, not allowing them to develop bad habits.

Mr Mac set the squad up across the three hardcourts at the rear of the school. There was little time for any mucking around because Mr Mac let them know emphatically that he expected dedication and concentration if he was going to give up his personal time. Slowly their appreciation of the game lifted into a deeper understanding. Tim loved serving most of all. The full swing of racquet and arm, the arching of his body and transference of weight to achieve greater power resonated with him. Every muscle was needed to master this skill with accuracy, and Tim thrived on the challenge. He knew his initial attempts were not as stylish as he optimistically visualised, and his ability to land the ball in the service court was erratic: but the lovely feeling of power the movement created was there right from the start.

One afternoon, as they took a breather after an intense workout on the net, Mr Mac walked over. "Well done today, boys. You are really starting to impress me."

"Thanks, Mr Mac," gasped Jack, catching his breath in between much-needed gulps of water.

"It strikes me that it's a shame you've not had a chance to play before. How does it stack up against other sports for you now?"

"We love it. Don't we, Tim?" said Jack, looking to his brother for confirmation.

While Tim nodded enthusiastically, Mr Mac continued.

"You know, you've both surprised and impressed me. Not only are you each good athletes, but in all my years of coaching I've never come across such a rare combination of raw talent, athleticism, and mindfulness. You both have the ability to process information and instructions and put them into practice. And I can see you both have the mental strength that's needed to be a winner. That's even harder to achieve. But to have all of that is remarkable."

By this time Tim and Jack were hanging off every word.

"I know you're only here for a short time, and there are many other demands on you with cricket and school. It's also an almost impossible gap to make up, to compare you with kids who've held a racquet since they could walk, and who have had the benefit of years of playing and good coaching … But," and he paused as he looked them both in the eye, "I think that with hard, dedicated work, you two could play at the highest levels."

"Really?" managed Tim after a few seconds.

"Yes. Really." Mr Mac nodded. "I think you are both capable of anything. But with that said, it may not be what you want, and," shrugging his shoulders to emphasise his point, he continued seriously, "it would mean a total commitment to tennis. Just keep it in mind. Think about it." With that he walked off, gathering up balls and school racquets as he headed back towards the PE shed.

"What the hell! What was that all about?" said Jack. "Like, where did that come from? What does he mean?"

"Beats me," answered Tim. "I mean, he's never said anything much at all to us and now he thinks we could play at the 'highest level'. Not that I wouldn't love to be a great tennis player, but surely there's a bit more to it."

As they picked up their school bags and headed for the gate, both Tim and Jack basked in the unexpected praise of their coach, which fed their egos with a much-needed boost.

Keen to continue to earn Mr Mac's admiration, they began to practise with even more purpose, spending as much time as possible either hitting up on the courts at school, or going through the makeshift challenges back at the farm. Their infatuation with tennis even began to concern their mother on her occasional weekend visits. She was worried, as always, that they were sacrificing their studies for time spent playing tennis, when they already had so many sporting commitments.

Tim knew he was clever enough, but he had always been a lazy student. His report cards were always dotted with comments such as, "Could do better," or, "Not working to potential." Tim had decided long ago, with the impeccable logic of a teenager, that if he worked hard and got good marks, then he would raise expectations unnecessarily and he would be expected to continue as an "A" student. It was a flawed argument, he knew in his heart, but he figured he could turn it around when he wanted to in Years 11 and 12. The trouble was he was now in Year 11, and it was time to get cracking. Jack, on the other hand, enjoyed study. He was clever and he liked showing off with good marks, and with just a little bit of revision it all came very easy to him. So far, especially with Nan on their backs to get schoolwork done, they'd made a good start to the year, and Jenny really had no reason to be concerned. It also helped that there were far less distractions in the country than the city, which certainly allowed more time to study. Once she realised they were both keeping up with the school workload, she was unexpectedly in favour of them taking up tennis.

Both boys looked forward to their mother's visits, because she was their only connection to their life in Melbourne. She brought news of their mates, and Tim and Jack found themselves wavering between the fear that they were missing out and smug complacency, deciding that nothing much at home had changed in their absence. Living with Nan and Pa was becoming Tim and Jack's reality, and their life in Melbourne seemed less and less relevant to them.

His initial awe at the way everyone knew everyone else had never left Tim. Instead of being irritated by it, he had come to respect the close-knit community where there was genuine friendship and concern for each other. He was very appreciative of the way everyone had so readily accepted him into their friendship groups and lives, and their generosity of spirit had touched him. In fact, when he considered it, Tim decided he had met more people in the first few weeks in Winjarra than he had after living in the same area in Melbourne for sixteen years. Most of his friends he'd known from primary school days, and most of their parents were also friends with his parents, and so it was a fairly small, familiar circle he moved in. With some embarrassment he recalled how reluctant his gang were to accept anyone new, and that it took ages before you gained acceptance unless, perhaps, you were a sporting legend.

Here he spoke happily to everyone, from the old farmer down the road to the guy at the servo and, in the end, he said hello to anyone he passed just in case he had met them and forgotten! The other thing he liked was the lack of pretence. It didn't matter what clothes you wore, no-one judged. Even the best cricket players didn't necessarily have the most expensive gear. In fact, more often than not, everyone shared the club gear. Everyone was accepted and they didn't need to be decked out in the right brands. They just had to be a decent person.

So it was with some regret one Saturday morning towards the end of term that Tim lay in bed and thought about returning to Melbourne. He knew he would miss the endless sunny days, as well as Nan and Pa, with whom who he had become very close. He contemplated reluctantly what awaited him when he returned home, and he kicked restlessly at his sheets. Tim knew his thoughts were disloyal to his dad, and he felt bad.

Wasn't going home to be a family again what he'd wanted and railed against his mother for? And yet, the thought of Mark sick and lethargic left him with a feeling of dread. Cocooned here at the farm, it was a reality he hadn't had to confront for quite a while. Confused and impatient with his thoughts he rose early, careful not to wake Jack, snoring gently in the single bed next to his. He tiptoed down the passage to the kitchen.

"Morning, Tim. You're up early for a Saturday," Pa greeted him, looking up from the Saturday paper. "Pity you're heading home this week just as you're starting to keep farm hours. Maybe I'll make a farmer of you yet," he joked.

Looking a bit closer at Tim, and taking in his subdued demeanour, Jim asked, "Is there something bothering you, mate? You look a bit out of sorts."

"I don't know. Just thinking about going home. I've gotten used to it here and it's been fun, even though," he confessed with a grin, "Jack and I didn't really want to come, you know."

"I might be old but I'm not stupid, Tim. Your grandmother and I both knew you boys didn't want to be here. But, I have to say, we're proud of the way you both knuckled down and got on with it. And we've loved having you, and we'll miss you both very much when you've gone."

"Thanks, Pa."

"But it's more than that, isn't it? You're worried that when you get home things still won't be back to normal?"

"Well, Dad hasn't really spoken to us since we got here, and even before. He's just different now. And it's hard. I don't know how to be with him anymore."

"You just have to be yourself, Tim. Just think about this. Your dad goes from being a successful architect, respected by his colleagues and his friends, to someone whose life is suddenly dominated by hospital, doctors' visits, tests, medication, and treatments. Without warning, life as he knew it was snatched away, and he's reliant on the whim of medical experts for his every move. Depression is very understandable in these circumstances. No doubt he's also worried and even guilty about the effect all this is having on all of you. I know your dad. He's a good, strong man and I know he will be doing his best to get well."

Tim nodded in agreement.

"And think of your mum. Jenny's been his carer and sole companion through all of this. It's time you boys take over some of the workload and give her a break as well." Pausing for effect, Jim continued, "My advice is to go back and treat your dad just the same as always. No kid gloves. Annoy the daylights out of him and just watch how quickly he'll get back to normal."

As Tim laughed, Jim reached over and gave him a big hug. "Now, go and get your brother up, because we've got some lambs to feed and I'm going to get as much work out of the two of you as I can while I've still got you here."

CHAPTER 6

Tim trudged home, his dark mood matching the heavy, grey Melbourne sky. Above him loomed a great expanse of pondering clouds, waiting to swell and burst with yet more rain. He'd dodged out of school quickly, as soon as the bell sounded, avoiding his mates, seeking some solitude and the chance to think. More often than not these days he found himself craving some space.

Life was really pretty good. He was getting good marks at school and the time spent at Winjarra High had set him up well for the year ahead. He had a permanent spot at last in the First 18 school footy team, and they had won their first couple of matches so far, which gave him great satisfaction. He had slipped back into his group of old mates as if he'd never left. However, the issue of Dad's illness was constantly there preoccupying his thoughts.

Tim and Jack had been shocked when they first got home and saw him. He looked thin, clearly ravaged by the chemo treatments, and there remained an unhealthy tone to his complexion. He had lost weight, his skin stretched and taut over his cheeks, his clothes loose on his frame. But when he looked at them and smiled, a light switched on in his eyes and

Tim was almost reassured, for the first time in many months, that there might be a way ahead in all of this. Dad's pleasure in seeing both of them home was as unexpected as it was obvious. There was so much to catch up on and Mark was hungry for every detail the boys had for him. Despite his frail and tired state, they talked for hours that first night, and Mark was happy to listen to all their stories.

It was the beginning of a long but visible haul back to health. As the chemo slowly left his system, and his blood count rose, Mark's strength began to return. Gradually, his skin lost its grey tinge, and his wasted muscles started to recondition. He began to walk, first around the garden, then soon around the block, going further each day. He hadn't lost all his hair but what he did lose was now coming back, curly and thick. Having the boys home was the spark Mark had needed, and for the first time in a long while he could feel an energy creep back into his days.

Jack had never considered that there would be a problem returning home, and it was probably he, more so than Tim, who broke down any barriers or reserve that there might have been. While Tim was wary of his fragile dad, Jack just accepted that Mark had at last emerged from his self-absorbed cocoon of illness, treating him as if nothing had happened. Mark welcomed the distraction their presence brought, never once complaining, even when their antics tired and drained him. Although the final prognosis on his illness remained uncertain, there was no doubt the black cloud of depression had lifted, and they had a glimpse of their old dad back: even if he was still just a translucent version of himself.

As Mark's strength and temperament had improved, Jenny had gone back to teaching, so when the boys got home from school, Mark was ready and waiting. After a day on his own he was keen to catch up on everything that had happened. With time on his hands, and out of sheer boredom, he had learned to cook pancakes, muffins, and scones, and there was often something freshly baked when they walked in the door. By the time they had demolished that, and given up every detail of their day, Jack and Tim would be ready to escape just as Jenny arrived home. Before she could think up any jobs that needed doing, Tim and Jack would grab the second-hand school racquets they'd been given by Mr Mac as a farewell present, and head to St Aiden's Anglican Church down the road where, behind an ancient and unkempt hedge, they had discovered a disused tennis court.

The abandoned court had seen better days, and cracks littered its asphalt surface where weeds once enjoyed uninterrupted growth. However, it did have one redeeming feature, and that was a practically new net that stretched proudly across the court, reminiscent of a time when it was used every day for church tennis teams. At least Tim and Jack were able to judge the height of their shots—and the surface, despite a few weeds, was a decided improvement on the dirt patch behind Pa's shed. Gradually they pulled out all the weeds, discouraging any new growth. Matches could be played at last, rather than just practising drills, and they were fiercely contested. Neither Jack nor Tim were willing to concede a shot and they gave each other no quarter. Tim acknowledged that he had a slight height and strength advantage, but Jack more than made up for that by his ability to run everything down. While Tim might be strong, Jack was wily and quick.

They had been using the court for several weeks most afternoons, and hadn't sighted anyone, when one afternoon, in the middle of a game, a man had approached, wearing the garb of an Anglican priest. Unsure of whether to run or stand their ground, the boys stopped play. Seeing as he hadn't asked them to leave yet, Tim had taken a stab and said politely, "Hello, sir. I hope you don't mind us using the court. There was no-one here and we hoped that it would be okay."

Ignoring Tim, the priest had continued to look from one to the other carefully, before answering a question with a question. "Are you brothers?"

"Yes, I'm Tim Anderson and this is my brother, Jack. We just live down the street a bit, and we don't belong to a tennis club, and we———"

"We didn't think anyone ever used this court, so we hope you don't mind," interrupted Jack in support.

"Of course you can use it. I don't mind at all. Not one person in the parish has shown the slightest interest in this tennis court for years, which I've always thought a shame. Go ahead. Enjoy yourselves as often as you like," he had said, before disappearing off behind the hedge with a backward wave.

Jack and Tim had high-fived each other across the net. Imagine that! Permission to use their own private tennis court! They had looked into joining a club, but they didn't really know anyone, and it all seemed a bit too complicated. Their one and only attempt to join was thwarted when they realised that the availability to use the courts as they wanted was limited. There was not an afternoon when the club courts were not being used for junior practise or lessons. They liked the freedom this old court offered them: especially being able to use it whenever and for as long as they liked. They couldn't believe their luck.

Tim had fist pumped the air. "Yes!" he declared. "This is unreal! I can't believe we were so lucky to find this spot."

"And no more sneaking in and out either. WE HAVE PERMISSION!" said Jack, laughing as he did a celebratory jig of his own.

As Tim rounded the corner of the street that led to his home that grey afternoon and reflected on all of this, he smiled again at the memory of Jack's victory dance that day. Tennis had given them both an outlet, especially when Dad's regime of tests and doctors' appointments continued to dominate their home life. His pensive mood was shattered though as Jack came racing by on his bike, swerving to a sudden skid-stop in front of him.

"Hey, guess what? You know that loser Jimmy Perkins? Well, he was bragging today about the new graphite Prince racquet he got for his birthday. $110 his olds paid for it, but he reckons it's worth almost $150. And I think he'd be crap at tennis! You should see him try to hit a cricket ball. Useless! So, I'm thinking, maybe we could get a couple of new racquets? What do you think? Do you think Mum and Dad would buy us new racquets?" rattled off Jack, barely taking a breath in between sentences.

"I would love a new racquet!" enthused Tim. "I mean the school ones are okay, but they're still old. Not that I'm complaining. It was great of Mr Mac to give them to us, and they are a major step-up on Pa's old wooden things. But to get a graphite racquet! That would be awesome. I'm not sure if Mum will be up for it though. Maybe try Dad?"

Jack was not patient at the best of times, so almost the second they went inside, with just a quick look to gauge whether his dad had had a good day or not, he jumped in. Starting with the story of Jimmy Perkins getting a new bargain racquet, it was a quick leap to why he and Tim should also get new racquets. And then he took the ultimate plunge, saying, "You know, if we buy these racquets now while they're on sale, we'll be practically saving money. It's such a good idea. What do you reckon? Can we get new racquets or not?"

He held up the old racquets for Dad's inspection. Although they really weren't too bad to play with, they had been well used already by countless students and they did have some decent scratches. The grips had definitely seen better days. Jack had always been the far better nagger out of the two of them, and Tim was happy to leave it in his more than capable hands.

"We could play much better if we had decent racquets. I mean, these are small heads and if we had bigger heads, we'd have a much better sweet spot for a start," Jack continued, "and then who knows how much better we could be?"

"Well, I suppose the question is how serious are you about this? I thought this tennis was just something to keep fit and fill the time?" Mark asked, a little surprised at the animation Jack was showing. He knew that the boys took off to play every afternoon, but he hadn't given it much thought, figuring it was just a fad. They had always been footy and cricket obsessed and they still were. He was genuinely taken aback.

Jack took a moment to consider before he said aloud the words he hadn't yet admitted to himself. "I reckon we're more serious about this than we've been about any sport. We love it and Mr Mac thinks we could be really good at it. He said we had 'great potential' even though we have just started." Looking at Tim, Jack threw out a challenge. "In fact, I'd rather play tennis than any other sport at the moment, even footy!"

Tim nodded in agreement. Their dad raised his eyebrows at this. But once Jack had finally verbalised it, they both knew it was true. They would rather play tennis than anything else.

"Come and watch us, Dad," Tim said. "See what you think. Maybe we are just kidding ourselves. Come now. Come and watch."

"I'd love to. It's probably too far for me to walk but when Mum comes home, we'll drive down together."

It was decided that Tim and Jack would go on ahead and warm-up, while Mark waited for Jenny to get home. While Jenny was surprised, she was happy to go along with things because it was the first time in ages that Mark had looked keen to get out of the house for anything other than a gentle walk. By the time they arrived at the court and found the almost hidden entrance in the hedge, Tim and Jack's game was well underway.

With a critical audience for the first time, the brothers were keen to show off their skills. Neither of them was prepared to concede, and they scrambled for every point. Jack slowly gained the lead, and at 6/5 was serving for the match. With a crushing first serve he sent Tim wide off the court. While it was a superb effort to reach the ball, Tim could only manage a weak floating forehand in return, which Jack immediately ran to the net to volley hard away to the opposite back line and claim the set at 7/5.

"Game, set, and match!" called out Jack jubilantly, as Tim stood flat-footed on the baseline.

"Great set, guys! Fantastic!" cheered Jenny, blown away by the level of skill she had just seen.

"We had no idea your little hits were as serious as this," said Mark, also impressed. "You have absolutely stunned me. I used to play a bit, but you two are pretty good. It's incredible how quickly you've managed to improve in such a short time. You look like you've been doing this for years!

"We need to get you two some lessons. You should be playing in competitions … This is great!" Mark enthused, with more animation than he'd shown about anything in such a long time. Quickly Tim pulled out of his backpack the folder Mr Mac had given them before they left, along with the two school racquets. In it were several training workouts for them, with detailed instructions and graphics covering each step, and in what order to go about it. There were also photocopied coaching points and diagrams, detailing how to break down each stroke into separate skills. It was their manual for how to go about each practise session. It had not only given their training sessions purpose, but it also gave them an incentive because they knew what standards they were working towards achieving.

"This is what we use already when we practise," said Tim. "Mr Mac gave it to us, and it's got everything in it."

"So yesterday we did serves and forehands, and today we would have done forehand volleys from midcourt," surmised Jack. And they both quickly assumed positions on court for what was now a well-rehearsed drill.

"Hold on. This is early days yet," Jenny admonished with the voice of reason. "Don't get me wrong, boys, but you already play footy, basketball, and cricket. Where is tennis going to fit in all of this? And let's not forget schoolwork! I hate to dampen this enthusiasm but how can you seriously consider adding another sport to all of this?"

As both boys began to protest, Mark stepped in. "Okay. Point taken. But let's not discuss this here. We'll talk about it at home. And it's getting late, so you two should finish up soon. And have a think about what your mother has said."

Later, riding home slowly on their bikes, the boys were quiet. It was a bit of a turning point for them both. Just how serious were they about all of this? Were they serious enough to give up other sports?

"I don't know yet if I do just want to play only tennis, Jack," Tim admitted as they put their bikes in the shed. "I love my footy too, and I like being part of a team. It's hard to imagine not being involved with the footy club. But I don't really want to stop playing tennis, either."

"Hmm. I know. I don't really want to either, but Mum's right," replied Jack glumly. "We're late starters. If we're going to make a go of this then we don't have much time, and we might just have to give it everything if we want to be any good. We know there's a heap of guys out there our age who are already way better than us. We're kidding ourselves that we can catch up to them. It's a joke we even think we can."

"Yes. But we need to try, or we'll never know, and that would piss me off more. The not knowing if we could have," challenged Tim.

"Okay. Let's do this," said Jack. And, squaring their shoulders, they went inside to convince their parents.

CHAPTER 7

In the end, after an animated discussion, things weren't decided one way or the other. While Jenny conceded she was quite happy for them to get new racquets, she wasn't as convinced that this wasn't just a passing fad. Mark was more perceptive that this was important to the boys and, being also acutely aware of his absence in their lives over the last year, he was keen to be proactive. He took things into his own hands, and the next day he not only picked them up from school, but drove them straight to a huge sports store, where there were literally dozens of racquets to choose from.

This is where their enthusiasm ran into a brick wall. Not one of the three had any real idea of what racquet would suit them or how much they should pay. Tim and Jack felt a lighter frame and a bigger racquet head would help, and they were dazzled by the new graphite range of racquets. They also wanted something that would give them more power to their shots. As they stood aimlessly looking at the racquets displayed gloriously before them, the very informative Don approached them, and no doubt rescued them from any potential bad choice.

Don was a fountain of knowledge and an expert on every brand of racquet and what each style offered. He was a man who knew everything there was to know about the subject of tennis racquets, and he enjoyed his work.

After about forty-five minutes of hearing the virtues of almost every brand of racquet ever made, and getting totally confused, Mark interrupted. "Okay. Basically, they need a racquet that will stay with them as they improve. They're well past the beginner stage and, in fact, they are A Grade players. These boys could go all the way," he confided with a knowing wink at Don.

While Tim looked away embarrassed, Don looked them over much more closely, as Jack boldly nodded in agreement, going along blissfully with his father's undisguised boasting. In the end Don gave them a great deal on two Prince graphite racquets with new gut strings, which he offered to restring to give more power than just the standard factory strings, and two tins of balls. Tim and Jack drove home with Mark on a high. They couldn't wait to try them out and they raced straight off on their bikes to the court. Mark reluctantly gave in to his exhaustion and collapsed thankfully on the couch, the prospect of a couple of quiet hours all his body could cope with.

Their first hit with the new racquets was an absolute blast. Without the constraints of broken or dulled strings the balls pinged off their racquets almost without effort. Back and forth they hit to each other, trying backhand and forehand with a new enthusiasm and exhilaration. With each stroke they felt themselves soaring high on a learning curve that was rising sharply. Caught up in the excitement of discovery they hit balls until they could hardly see in the encroaching dusk. For the first time, they began to have an understanding of the power they could generate and appreciate the exquisite feeling of playing with a light touch, which brought its own special magic to their game.

Mark was drained by the excursion, but he waited impatiently until they returned home and burst into the kitchen with all the news of their first hit. Their visible excitement gave him enormous satisfaction, and their obvious delight with the racquets gave him a rush of adrenaline: a strength that he'd almost forgotten feeling. He vowed to himself he would not miss another practise session if he could help it.

From then on, every possible day after school, Mark met the boys at the tennis court. He would bring muffins and fruit and water bottles, and a plan. From a basic knowledge of the game, Mark had transformed himself into a tennis guru. He had poured over Mr Mac's coaching plans in detail, and his study was now strewn with tennis magazines and books on the finer points of tennis. He had researched several players and studied their fitness and skill regimes. Taking note of many sources of advice, he devised a training program covering the skills and strength required to be a top player. Jenny thought it all totally extreme, but she wisely held back her opinion because, for the first time in so many months, she could see glimpses of the old Mark returning. If he was a tad over the top about coaching the boys, it was a small price to pay for his general good health and mental wellbeing.

Tim and Jack were also cognisant of the fact that these tennis practises meant more to them as a family than just an improvement in their tennis. Starved for so long of the dad they remembered, they were only too happy to be caught up in his enthusiasm for the game. Mark had even developed long-term goals for them. His vision was a style of play that was well rounded, consistent, and flexible enough to cope with anything an opponent could deliver. Between his own research and Mr Mac's practise session guides, Mark had worked out a range of skills and drills that were specifically targeted to Jack and Tim.

He had even contacted Mr Mac several times, to keep him updated and get some more ideas. Normally a busy and productive man—bordering, in fact, on being a workaholic—he threw himself into this new project as he once did when his firm was in the planning stages of a new development.

Part of the frustration of his illness had been the sudden loss for him of all that had filled his life before. No longer able to be fully involved in the daily routine and ongoing ventures of his architectural business, he had lost interest in everything as his life was reduced to hospital treatments and medication. The constant weakness and total exhaustion had made him very introverted. Mark knew he was being slightly obsessed by coaching the boys with such intensity, but he also acknowledged that this distraction was what he needed. So he pushed on, even on days when he felt bone tired, because he knew that despite some setbacks, he was definitely regaining his strength.

No longer did he fill his days watching daytime television from the couch. Now he watched tapes of old tennis matches and compared playing styles of the greats with his own home videos of the boys' skill sessions. With alacrity, he took notes on technique, strategies, and skills, and analysed them methodically. His mind, once drained and battered by drugs, was now an encyclopaedia of tennis facts and information. Having once been a footy player and cricketer, he had spent many hours at training himself. He remembered from those days that coaches who could vary training sessions made the experience so much better.

Jack and Tim were more than happy to get caught up in Mark's passion. He took pride in making their practises fun and his enthusiasm fuelled their own. Each session was a constant cycle of skills and technique: practise, analyse, and evaluate, and practise again. Their sessions at the court were a tight routine and they were hooked.

It could have been tedious playing the same person each day, but their game was being constantly refined, which kept them interested. Often the improvement was slight, but the process was absorbing for each of them. Their true strength lay in the constant sharing and pooling of knowledge, and their willingness to test out new ideas. They had no outside competition to consider, so they were free to be in their own experimental bubble because there were no consequences. Jack and Tim could work on their own individual styles, exploring what worked best for each of them. And so they relentlessly ploughed through a labyrinth of techniques for serving, forehands, backhands, lobs, topspin, smashes, drop shots, and more.

Jenny happily tolerated the constant discussions about tennis. Mealtimes were adapted to allow for the often late arrival home from practise sessions. As winter wore on to spring and the evenings allowed more time for tennis, she maintained her easy going attitude. Her patience was slowly being rewarded. Just as gradually as he had absented himself from the day-to-day running of his business, Mark slowly returned to the office, meeting clients once again, and bringing plans home to work on. Jenny offered silent thanks to the tennis gods that Mark, her best friend and husband, was back.

The only thing Jenny had insisted on through all this was that Tim and Jack continued to play at least one other sport. She believed that if they grew tired of tennis, they would regret giving up their other sports. She also understood that the friendships gained through playing in a team were important in their lives, and that they needed the company of other friends.

Tim continued to play footy, while Jack continued with his basketball. Football and basketball did give each of them more balance. Tim especially thrived on the mateship football offered, and the rough nature of the game appealed to him after the discipline required to chase a small ball all over the court. And if that meant that he was expected to push and tackle and put his body on the line to help out the team, Tim was as physical as the best of them. However, as much as he loved his footy, it was tennis he thought about as he drifted off to sleep at night.

As planned, his two friends from Winjarra, Nick and Tony, were coming to Melbourne for the first week of the September school holidays. They had kept in touch over the last few months by regular phone calls, and they were looking forward to it. Although Tim was also keen for the visit, as the day of their arrival approached, he began to get a little nervous about having them stay with him for a week. He wasn't sure how they would fit in with his footy and school mates and he wondered if they still had much in common. Waiting on Platform 7 at Southern Cross station for the Bendigo train to arrive, Tim, with martyr-like conviction, talked himself into giving up a week of his holidays to do the right thing by these country mates. His halo was almost visible as the train pulled in. With a smile plastered on his face he searched in vain among the disembarking passengers for his friends. As the crowds filtered out, he began to get concerned. Country bumpkins, he thought. They probably got off at the wrong stop! How was he going to find them now?

Peering hopefully into empty carriages for signs of them, Tim was concerned and distracted. Eventually he noticed that the platform was nearly empty. Most people had already met, embraced, collected luggage, and were on their way out of the station. Abruptly, he sensed the menacing presence of a couple of blokes unusually close to him. Only too aware of the rough types and thugs that hung around the station at night, Tim cursed his own carelessness. He began belatedly to move towards the other end of the platform, where the few remaining passengers were heading towards the exit. His heart began to beat a little quicker as the footsteps of the two potential thugs followed him closely, barely a step behind him. Even in broad daylight it wasn't unknown to be attacked and robbed. He thought of the $40 he had in his wallet. Should he just give it to them now and then he'd be left alone? Suddenly a hand shot out and grabbed him by the back of his jumper.

"What's a little prick like you hanging around here for?" sneered an ugly voice in his ear.

Tim froze. Feeling the strong grip on his jumper, Tim knew he wouldn't be a match for both of them. He looked around frantically for help. Shrugging off his attacker's grip he turned to face them. The penny dropped.

"You bastards! I was shitting myself!"

"Yeah. We thought you might be. We've been trailing you for a good five minutes, wondering when you'd have the nous to look around."

Nick and Tony cracked up as they mimicked Tim peering into the deserted carriages.

Tim's anger evaporated quickly in the good-natured teasing that followed, and so did any concerns he had. There was no tension as they picked up the threads of their friendship without a hitch.

It was a magic week to be in Melbourne. The footy finals were on and every day there was something new for them to do. They went to movies, had a couple of trips into the city, and went to see a couple of bands. There was so much news to catch up on and Tim was genuinely interested to find out what everyone was up to. It wasn't until a couple of days into the visit that he managed to casually enquire about Karen.

"I was beginning to think I'd lost my bet!" teased Tony, grinning like a Cheshire cat. "Come on, you owe me five bucks," he said, putting out his hand to Nick, who reluctantly fished the money from his wallet. "We had a bet you'd ask about her and I won!" Pocketing the money with a flourish, he threw out his arms dramatically and pronounced in a deadpan voice, "Okay. She sounds a bit like you. All she does is play tennis. She won the regionals in June, and now she's training for the state championships in December. Mr Mac still coaches her, and she goes all over the state for competitions, so she's off most weekends at tournaments, and I think she's even in Melbourne next week for one."

"And," interrupted Nick, "I can also say that she said to say hello, when she heard we were coming here this week. And …" he paused dramatically, "you'll be interested to know that she broke up with Perko, and he's gone to Adelaide to take up an apprenticeship in the steelworks there."

"Well, how is her tennis going?" asked Tim, trying to look cool and ignoring the sly wink Nick gave him with the last bit of information.

"Actually, she is deadly serious about it. She works really hard, and she is easily the best female player in the district. She demolished the club championships, winning the open section by a mile. She's also playing in some big-deal lead-up tournament to the inter-regionals, and the write-up in the local paper gave her a good chance at winning this year. It's at Kooyong, and there will be heaps of really good players there. You should go along and watch."

"I might," said Tim, giving nothing away even though his mind was racing, and he asked about someone else to change the subject. He had rung Karen a couple of times, but although she said she was training with Mr Mac, she hadn't boasted about her tournament wins. She also hadn't said she was going to Melbourne in the holidays, and she definitely didn't mention breaking up with her boyfriend. Their chats had been friendly with no hint of anything more than that, although Tim had gone over them in his mind several times, searching for some hint of her feelings. Now he concluded that she certainly hadn't wanted to see him, otherwise she would have told him she was in Melbourne.

The week flew by, and by the time Tony and Nick were due to leave, he knew he would miss them. They were a different tribe to his Melbourne friends, but they were very easy company and he often felt more in tune with them. Arriving home after farewelling them at the train station, he was contemplating a lazy afternoon in front of the television, and then maybe getting back into some tennis with Jack, which he'd mostly missed while he'd had Nick and Tony around. His mother, though, had other plans.

"Up off that couch, you've got jobs to do," said Jenny, her hands on her hips. "You may not have noticed but your brother has been busy helping Dad sand down the window frames this week while you've been the tourist guide, showing off the city sights."

"But I'm tired. I need a rest! It's hard work making sure people have a good time!"

"Tell me about it. I've been cooking all week trying to keep up to the appetites of four teenage boys and two adults. Not that I minded," Jenny said, smiling. "They were lovely boys, even if they tell enough dirty jokes to make your father's hair fall out again. And I thought they were innocent county kids!"

"Hey! Don't bring my hair into this!" interrupted Mark. "I'm quite pleased with my new curls," he said, running his fingers through the curly fuzz.

"Here's the sandpaper, bro. I'm off to the movies. I'll be back in time for tennis though, Dad," said Jack as he sauntered down the passage and out the front door.

"This sucks," Tim grumbled, reluctantly taking over sanding the window frame where Jack had just been.

CHAPTER 8

The next few days passed quietly, with Tim and Jack sanding and sometimes painting the outside windows with their dad. By Thursday most of the job was done and the boys were ready for a break. The tennis results at Kooyong had been published in the paper each day, and they knew that Karen was still in the draw for the quarterfinals, so they had decided to go and watch. Mark had intended to go as well, but the lure of finally finishing the painting was too tempting, and so he stayed home.

Jack and Tim were rapt to be finished with the drudgery of the windows, although they both had to admit there was some satisfaction in looking at the freshly painted Federation-styled sash windows of their home. It was also the absolute normality of it all that made them smile. Twelve months ago, they would not have believed they would be sharing this mundane job with their father and appreciating the moment.

It was a lovely spring day when they arrived at Kooyong Tennis Centre, and the sun shone down on the hallowed courts. It was the first time either of them had been there, and they were stunned by the amount of activity that was going on. There were players of all ages, many of them hanging together in groups, talking loudly and excitedly. Across the top of the babble, there were several announcements for players to register and proceed to their respective courts. Further announcements for umpires followed, and as they looked around at the melee of players, parents, coaches, and spectators, Tim and Jack felt more than a little overwhelmed.

Kooyong. The traditional home of tennis in Melbourne! Tim felt an absolute buzz just being there, and he wanted to absorb everything. He could tell that Jack was feeling much the same as they steered themselves almost by instinct towards the main stadium. In awe and anticipation, they climbed the covered steps and emerged from the cool, dark tunnel to the sunlit stadium, where they gazed in reverence at the famed Centre Court. A few others like themselves stood quietly. They also had made this pilgrimage to see at firsthand what they had only ever seen on television. Not in use for this minor tournament, the court looked still and calm, its closely cropped grass glistening under a thousand fine sprays of water. A solitary curator attended to a particular spot near the far baseline, checking maybe for weeds or any imperfection.

Tim took a seat on the worn, slatted wooden benches and let his imagination run. Having hungrily devoured the old video tapes his father had collected of the last of the Australian Opens to be played at Kooyong, he could almost hear the roar of the crowd as a sweat-stained John Newcombe, moustache drooping in the January heat, battled against a younger, tenacious Jimmy Connors.

He imagined it was him there. Serving, volleying, dropping clever little shots across the net, stretching to return the impossible. It was just a fantasy, but he felt the excitement, and his heart beat a little faster at the thought of being out there, watched by crowds all cheering for him.

"Oh man," sighed Jack. "Wouldn't you just love to have a game on that? Can you imagine how perfectly the ball would land on that grass?"

"Would I ever!"

"I'd love to play on lawn courts again. Remember how it was in Winjarra when we got a chance to play on grass? We should go back up soon and have a go. Dad would be up for it, I'm sure. I know the courts wouldn't be a patch on this, but it would be fun giving it a go again, especially now we are so much better."

Tin nodded. "Yep. Why not? And Pa hasn't seen us play for a while. I'm sure he's got a few more hints, and we could see Mr Mac. C'mon though. Let's watch some games, and we should find Karen if we can."

Making their way back through the crowd they spotted a huge white scoreboard where several people were gathered, studying it closely. The draw for the day and the results so far were written up in large black lettering. They scanned the board.

"There's a K. Jennings in the Under 18s and one in the Under 19s," reported Jack.

"Show me," demanded Tim. "Hmm. She must be playing in the Under 19s for experience, I suppose. Beats me. Looks like Court Fourteen is for the 18s and Court Five for the Under 19s. Let's check it out. It looks like she's on Court Five now."

"She must be doing okay if she's still in the Under 19s," said Jack, impressed. Approaching the court, Tim nudged Jack and pointed towards a familiar figure. The peaked cap and sunglasses couldn't disguise the long scrawny neck and wide shoulders of their old teacher.

"It's Mr Mac," hissed Tim. "He must be here coaching."

Waiting patiently behind some other spectators, Tim and Jack—not wanting to distract Karen and maybe put her off—unobtrusively took their seats only after a break in serve. Karen's hair was pulled tightly back into a ponytail, and her visor was pulled firmly down across her forehead. She was clearly a bit puffed, and she looked flushed from the effort of playing. Athletic and strong as she was, she was still in sharp contrast to her opponent. While Karen was dressed simply in a blue, collared tee-shirt and white skirt, the other girl was resplendent in a green silk dress with matching headband. She looked confident and moved with a calm, lithe professionalism. For the first time, Tim took notice of the score. Karen was love–forty down. Mr Mac and Karen's mum, who Tim could see now next to Mr Mac, looked anxious.

"What's the game score?" he whispered to Jack.

"I think it's a set each and she's 5/6 down in this set. If she loses this, it's all over."

Tim could see Karen pause and take a deep breath as she steadied herself to serve. Tossing the ball high in her usual way, Karen arched back and met the ball in a solid, crisp movement, sending it speeding down the centre-line. Her opponent was caught out wide and was slow to react to the pace. She lunged late towards the centre-line, but only managed to tip at the ball and send it spinning ineffectively into the net.

"Fifteen–forty," called the umpire as both players moved to the forehand court.

Karen again took another steadying breath before she served. This time her opponent was ready, moving quickly, and returned service deep into Karen's court. The rally continued for another two shots, each girl pressing for a weakness in the other. Finally, Karen sent a high, lobbing ball deep into the girl's backhand. A risky shot. Tim held his breath as it landed safely inside the baseline. Using a two-handed grip, Karen's opponent steadied and lobbed it back to Karen, but it lacked enough depth, landing midcourt, and Karen pounced on it to smash it away for a winner.

Still down set point, Karen faulted on her first ball, missing the line by a whisker. With the pressure now intense, Karen's second serve was more cautious, landing well inside the line. In her eagerness to put it away and finish the set, her opponent misjudged the spin Karen had put on it. At the last second, she had to reach further for it than she had anticipated, and she overshot the sideline she had been aiming for. Out.

With the game now at deuce, neither girl was willing to concede. As Karen headed back to the baseline to serve, Tim could see a visible lift of her shoulders. Two more points. It took several rallies with each girl pressing hard to take advantage of the other's weakness but, in the end, Karen was in luck as a slightly wayward ball hit the tape of the net and dropped safely to the other side, impossible to return.

Tim and Jack resisted the impulse to cheer loudly.

"Six games all. We now play a two-game advantage," called the umpire as everyone let out a collective breath.

Karen's lucky shot had clearly unnerved her opponent, especially after being up love–forty. Karen, however, was looking fresh and keen, and she stepped lightly from one foot to the other, eager to attack the ball. Although the match continued to be close, with several hard-fought rallies from both girls, Karen closed out the next two games and the match was hers. Running to the net, Karen, visibly excited, shook the umpire's hand and hugged her opponent across the net. Not bothering to collect her things beside the court, she ran to her where her mother, Clare, and Mr Mac were now standing, both still clapping. Meanwhile, Tim and Jack watched the losing girl, with a face set in fury, fall into the arms of a woman they guessed must be her mother. They were close enough to hear the exchange between them.

"I know, darling. You were so unlucky," soothed the woman, putting her arm around her and carrying her bag as she led her away from the court. As they walked away Jack asked the man next to him, whom he had noticed writing down the score, who she was.

"Ali Baulch, from Melton."

"Is she any good?"

"She's supposed to be one of the top juniors, but the lass from North Central has certainly given her something to think about. That was a solid performance," he replied, looking across at Karen talking excitedly to Mr Mac and her mum.

"But then, I see she's got Macca as a coach, and he knows when he's got something to work with." And catching Mr Mac's eye he gave a wave and a thumbs up, clapping his hands at Karen. As the three turned in his direction acknowledging his congratulations, Tim and Jack caught their attention, waving at them as well. They made their way over to the group.

"Great game, Karen. You were awesome," said Tim, giving her a hug.

"You were fantastic," said Jack, following suit and hugging her enthusiastically.

They both shook Clare's hand and then high-fived Mr Mac.

"Jack and Tim! Great to see you both! I didn't notice you. Were you there for the whole match?" said their old teacher, clearly happy to see them.

"No, we only saw the last few games. What a fightback, Karen!" said Tim.

"Yes," said Clare. "She gave us quite a fright. My heart was pounding. But she won and that's the main thing."

"I gave myself a fright," laughed Karen. "I lost the first set 1/6, and then I thought, just go for it, and I scrambled in the second and won 6/4. And she's the fourth seed! Now I'm in the Under 19 quarterfinals! I really didn't think I could win but I'm so happy," Karen gushed, brushing her hair away from her face with both hands. "And it's so great to see you guys."

"Gee, that's not a bad effort," said Jack with genuine admiration. "What about your Under 18 matches? Are you still in that?"

"Yep, this afternoon. I've got another match. It's a quarterfinal, but I think I've got a good chance. Can you stay and watch?"

"We were hoping to, if it won't put you off or anything?" replied Tim.

"Karen won't even notice once she starts to play. She's a very focused girl," replied Mr Mac, looking proudly at her. "But, as your coach, I advise you to settle down for now, eat an early lunch, and rest as much as you can. You've had a big four days to get to this point, and your hardest matches are yet to come."

Clare handed Karen her jacket. "I'm off to get a coffee and I'll ring Dad to tell him the news. Have some fun catching up with Tim and Jack and meet me at our spot at two o'clock. That will give you plenty of time to start your pre-match routine."

"Okay, Mum," Karen promised. Giving her mum another hug, she said again, "Can you believe I won?"

Laughing, Clare returned the hug before they began packing up Karen's kitbag.

Mr Mac turned to the boys. "I was hoping to catch your dad while I'm here," he said. "It would be nice to meet him in person after all our phone calls. And I'm keen to see how your tennis is going, guys. Your dad has been telling me good things as well as picking my brains."

"He'd love that, Mr Mac," said Tim. "I'll let him know you're in town."

Karen interrupted by grabbing both their arms and leading them off, leaving her mum to roll her eyes and gather up the racquet bag she had carelessly left behind. "And don't sit in one spot too long. You don't want to get stiff!" she called after her.

"I'm so glad you're here! I didn't mention it because I thought you'd be too busy doing fun things in the holidays. But it's so good to see you both," said Karen, linking arms with them. "I've got so much to tell you and as much as I love Mum and Mr Mac, I am ready for a break. Now, you won't believe what happened this term!"

Walking companionably together, Karen launched into all the snippets of high school gossip that she thought might interest them, entertaining them with her anecdotes. In no time she had them both laughing, embellishing her stories with her own witty observations. As they talked, they walked past court after court of young tennis hopefuls, all slugging it out in either singles or doubles. Most matches were fairly subdued with the occasional burst of applause, but angry voices drew their attention to a court where a surly, long-haired teenager was remonstrating angrily with his umpire. Quite a few bystanders had also been drawn towards the unsportsmanlike spectacle.

In a low voice, Karen filled them in. "That's Paul Todd. He's from Mildura, and a really good player, but he can be such a bad sport. He thinks he can carry on like this because every now and then he plays amazing tennis. He's just so arrogant. See the lady in the green sun visor and the man next to her in the white jumper? They're his parents. They never even try to stop him. In fact, I've heard that his mum is just as bad and has had a go at the umpire if she doesn't like the calls. I can't believe the referees haven't ever reported him, but I think they all believe he's good enough to play nationals, so they just ignore it."

Curious, Jack and Tim moved closer to get a better view. As play restarted, the three of them quickly squeezed onto spare courtside seats. Both players were about Tim's age, he surmised. While Paul continued to mutter to himself and occasionally bad-temperedly hit balls into the net after a point didn't go his way, the other boy was the complete opposite. While Paul scowled, his opponent maintained a steady demeanour, his face giving nothing away whether he won or lost a point. It was quite early in the game and as they warmed to the task, both boys appeared evenly matched. While Paul could certainly produce some brilliant shots, he was also capable of some shocking mistakes. His opponent, who they discovered was from Geelong, was impressive in his consistency, and he had slowly gained the lead at 4/3 in the third set when they had to leave. Karen needed to eat, and she had to start thinking about warming up for her own match.

"How's your dad?" Karen asked as they settled themselves at a table near the food stalls. Jack had gone in search of hamburgers and Tim had stayed with Karen while she ate the healthy lunch her mother had packed.

"He's getting better," Tim said with genuine relief. It felt good just to say it. "He pushes himself a bit, and I don't think he always tells us if he's having an off day. But the treatments are finished for now, so it's just a waiting game till his next blood tests and we see if there's any leukaemia cells left." He paused. "You know what's crazy? He spends most of his time being Jack and my tennis coach. And he's actually pretty good at it, too."

"Yeah. Mr Mac told me you guys were still playing. And he said your dad had asked for ideas to use in your practise sessions. That's so cool! We should have a game soon!"

"I think the plan is to go up to the farm over Christmas, so we can catch up then. That is, if you're not going to be away?" Tim asked hopefully.

"Hell no! Dad would never leave the farm at that time of year. He's way too worried about bushfires and getting the crop in. I'm playing a few tournaments in January, but I'll be around most of the time."

"Good, that'll be fun," smiled Tim.

"Anyway, what club did you join here? Are you playing pennants yet? It's a pretty high standard here in Melbourne. The competition would be really good for your game, and you and Jack could play doubles together as well."

"Doubles!" repeated Jack returning with hamburgers. "We're not even members of a club yet."

Tim went on to explain. "We looked at joining a club, but it all seemed a bit complicated. Just by luck we found this old court near our house that no-one uses. It's owned by a church. The minister there is a nice guy, and he lets us play there as often as we like for free. Sometimes we see him watching us practise and Dad has chatted to him a few times, but mostly he just lets us be. There just didn't seem a need to join up anywhere, seeing as we can use the court any time we want. But," Tim took a breath and looked around, "I can see it would be fun to play in something like this eventually. Even if we got thrashed, I think I'd love it."

Jack nodded. "I agree. These courts are fantastic. I'd love to play on them."

"You should! You know you're not going to really get better just playing each other. After all, what's the point of that?"

stated Karen, bemused. "Anyway, I've got to run or Mr Mac will kill me. Are you coming to watch my match?"

"Absolutely! Good luck and break a leg," said Jack, giving Karen a high-five.

"Same. Good luck. You'll blitz her for sure," said Tim, high-fiving her as well before she raced off. As Karen disappeared into the crowd, Jack eagerly turned to Tim.

"Well? What did you think of the match we saw? What do you reckon? How far off the pace are we?"

Taking a big slurp of his drink, Tim answered thoughtfully. "Those guys were good, but yeah! I wouldn't mind hitting up against them. I don't think we are that far off at all. They hit lots of deep balls, and they're really consistent," he mused. "And their serves look like they have a real kick to them. I bet they've been playing much longer than us … but we can hit some pretty decent balls ourselves."

"I know. I wish Dad could see this. I'm almost itching to have a go. Let's check out some more matches before we go to see Karen play. Maybe there are better players around."

They finished their lunch and continued to wander between courts, attracted to any games that looked to be their own age-grouping. Watching as objectively as he could, Tim couldn't help but be optimistic. He wasn't alone in his excitement. Jack was feeling much the same. There were certainly some strong hitters out there, but Jack didn't see anyone play that he thought he couldn't return a shot to. He admired their consistency though, and the way they could press the net to put away a shot. Jack could see that some of the older boys knew how to out-think their opponents, and he realised that this level of gamesmanship was something he and Tim knew nothing about. But, when it came to most shots, and both boys decided this together, they would definitely almost hold their own. It was certainly something to think about.

Eventually they settled down to watch Karen play her match. Karen's opponent looked young, and they guessed she was also playing up a grade. While they watched Karen easily demolish her younger opponent their minds were busy, racing with anticipation and excitement. How could they move from their isolated tennis practise to this level of play? Was it even possible?

"She looks really young to be playing in this age group," remarked Jack as they stood together after the match.

"She is," answered Mrs Jennings. "I think she would be lucky to be thirteen. She's clearly after the experience and, in all honesty, she's done pretty well to get this far. If she keeps it up, she should be a very good player."

"Why wouldn't she keep it up? I mean if she's this good at thirteen why would she even think about stopping?" asked Tim incredulously.

"Peaking early doesn't mean you'll end up a superstar, or even that you'll continue to get better," answered Mr Mac. He gestured around. "These courts are full of promising juniors, but not all of them will have the dedication or mental toughness it takes to get to the top. Dedicating all your life to the one sport can come at a high cost and, sadly, many burn out with the hard work and effort, and just the plain boredom of it all. It's tough and it takes sacrifices to get to this level, and not everyone can keep it up. They'll always be great tennis players, but only a handful will play at a national level, and even fewer will make tennis a career."

"And these are mostly country kids, remember," said Karen. "The state comp takes in the metro kids as well, and that's when the standard really jumps up. I wouldn't even attempt to play up a grade at the state champs."

Tim and Jack went home on the train that afternoon, each thoughtful about how the day unfolded. Karen's indication that the state championships were an entirely tougher level of tennis was sobering for Tim, while Jack couldn't even imagine becoming bored with tennis as Mr Mac had warned. He was longing for the chance to have a go at a tournament like that. He couldn't wait now to play someone other than Tim, whose shots he could almost predict before he drew his racquet back.

Tim also couldn't help feeling some excitement. He knew he had no experience, but he, like Jack, was busting to play and test himself at that level. Because they had been training in a virtual bubble, they had no yardstick to measure their progress against their peers. Tim's only comparison were the tennis greats he'd watched on TV. Maybe, just maybe, he could play as well as the guys he'd seen today. Even at his most self-critical he believed he could. It was time to move on from just playing each other.

Tim turned to Jack as they neared their station. "We need to join a club or something. We'll have to talk to Dad. We can still train, but we have to have a go at playing other guys or we'll never get any better."

"I totally agree, bro," said Jack, nodding. "We are more than ready to start playing seriously."

CHAPTER 9

Tim and Jack returned to Kooyong a couple of days later to watch Karen play in her Under 18s final. This time Mark accompanied them, keen to see everything for himself. Karen had apparently played well but had been beaten in her Under 19s semi the day before. This was no disgrace, because the older age group competition really did rev up to a higher standard.

Mark was intrigued by everything going on around him, just as Tim and Jack had been. He enjoyed Karen's struggle and triumph in her match, noting in particular how cleverly she varied her shots to wear down her opponent. Just as curious as his sons, he was keen to watch some of the boys' matches: in particular, the age groups similar to Tim and Jack.

There wasn't much difference between the standard of the boys and the girls, but Mark did note that while the boys he watched had power, they inevitably had a weakness in their game, and were often undone by a well-placed shot to their weaker side, or deep into the court. The girls, on the other hand, appeared more strategic and consistent, their games showing maturity and patience. They were more likely to rally, waiting for the right moment to play a winning shot, whereas their male counterparts wanted to put away their opponents quickly with a flashy shot. And as he watched all these teenagers put their hearts onto every shot, spurred on by coaches and parents, his admiration grew for what his own boys had achieved largely on their own.

"What do you think, Dad?" whispered Jack as they watched two boys who looked about his age battle it out. "How do you think we'd go?"

"I think you'd give them a run for their money, mate. You certainly wouldn't be out of your league here. We just need to get used to all of this," replied Mark with a wink, gesturing to the organised chaos around them. "It's a far cry from our little court at the back of St Aiden's. I mean, where are the all the hedges dropping leaves on the court for a start?" he joked.

Mr Mac called in to see them on his way home to Winjarra, as promised. Apart from meeting at Kooyong, and despite their numerous phone calls, this was the first time Mark had had a chance to talk at length to Mr Mac in person.

"Call me Paul," he said as he shook hands with Mark and Jenny. "Hi, Tim. Hi, Jack."

"Hi, Mr Mac," Tim and Jack echoed as they greeted their old teacher.

"It's good to see you again, fellas. And I'm keen to find out, what did you think of Kooyong? Did you enjoy it?"

The conversation quickly took a turn to tennis as Jenny offered afternoon tea. Paul was keen to get an update on what the boys had been doing in training, asking several relevant questions. It was obvious that he had been following their progress via his long-distance phone conversations with Mark. Finally, he said, "I'd like to be on my way home by five, so I avoid the kangaroos. But I'd love to watch you two have a hit-up. Can you show me what you've been up to?"

It took Tim and Jack only seconds to swallow the last of the cake, rush up and grab shoes and racquets, and be back downstairs ready to go.

"I take it that's a yes then," laughed Mark. "Okay, get in the car, boys. I'll drive you and Paul can follow us."

"Thanks, Jenny, for the delicious afternoon tea. I'll say hi to your mum and dad when I see them next," said Paul as he wished Jenny goodbye. "But I hear you might be able to do that soon yourself," he added quietly as he followed Mark to the car. Jenny nodded and smiled and shrugged her shoulders, a gesture the boys didn't see.

At the courts the boys warmed up, hitting back and forth, while Paul said to Mark, "I gather the boys don't know what you've been thinking about for next year?"

"No. We're going to talk with them about it tonight. They'll need to be on board or it won't work. I'm well aware of everything they've had to give up over the last twelve months, so we're only going to do it if they're one hundred percent behind it. They've been such good sports through all this, I'm not going to force it. So, we'll see …" Mark trailed off.

Paul nodded. "Fair enough." Turning to the boys he called out, "Okay. Show me some nice, deep, forehand rallies." As he took the boys through their paces, he grew more and more focused, stopping to confer occasionally with Mark. Finally, he became aware of the time and, checking his watch, called the boys over.

"Congratulations, guys. That was amazing! I can't believe how much you've both improved in a few months. Lovely shots, and such good technique! I'm so impressed! Certainly, there are some areas to work on, but I can really see how hard you've been working. And great job, Mark! Whatever you're doing with them is perfect. Just keep it up."

"So, Mr Mac. Do you think we could be good enough to play in a tournament like at Kooyong one day?" asked Tim. "I mean, are we practising for nothing, or do you think we could match those guys?"

"You know, there's nothing wrong with just practising something to get good at it, especially if you love it, Tim. Tennis is a great sport, and you can play it for life and just enjoy it for what it is. But," he added emphasising his words, "of course I think you should keep it up. We do seriously need to get both of you off this court and out into the tennis world. No more hiding away in here." He gestured his arms around their hedged court. "We need a plan so you can play lots of other people. That's the only way you'll really improve from now on. But I'll let your dad talk to you about that. Now, give me a high five, because I'm really very proud of you both. Great work, boys."

As they high-fived and shook hands, he said, "You never know, I might see you both sooner than you think. Keep up the good work." And with a final hand on Mark's shoulder, he bent his head, saying quietly, "Good luck. They are fantastic. I'd love to continue this, and I really do think they have what it takes. I hope you can convince them."

Mark smiled wryly, looking over to where the boys were packing up. "I hope so, too."

Later that evening, as they sat down to dinner together, Jenny interrupted their endless chatter about Mr Mac's comments with a question of her own. "Well, how would you like him to be your full-time coach?"

"What?" said Tim incredulously. "Is he coming to live in Melbourne?"

"No. He'd never do that. Would he?" asked Jack. "I thought he loved it up there."

"No, he wouldn't be the one moving," said Jenny, leaving her comment to float in the air.

"What?" exploded Tim, the first to catch on.

"Wait a sec. You want Tim and I to go back to Winjarra? On our own? I thought you promised we'd never have to do that again?" fired off Jack angrily as Jenny's comment fully dawned on him.

"Calm down, Jack. You wouldn't be going on your own. We'd all go together this time," replied Mark, looking earnestly at them each in turn. "But, it depends on how you both feel about it. It's got to be something that suits all of us or we stay put."

"But what brought this on?" asked Tim, still taking in the bombshell his parents had just dropped. "Why would we suddenly up and move? What about your jobs?"

"It might sound sudden but it's actually something we've been discussing for a while. Long before I got sick your Mum and I had talked about the possibility of a tree change. We always imagined it would be later, when you were off doing your own thing down the track, when you were at uni, maybe. But, as you know, lots of things have changed for us since I've been sick, and now we think that just twelve months away from the city might be good for us as a family. It would be a chance for all of us to slow down and spend a special year together, before the two of you are off to uni and starting careers."

"But what would you do for work? You can't just do nothing, can you? And what about all your friends?" queried Jack.

"Well," said Mark, looking at Jenny and taking a deep breath, "Brian and I recently put in a tender for the new Winjarra Shire Offices, and we've just heard we got the job. You know they've been in temporary premises in the town hall since they had the fire two years ago. Well, we started drawing plans soon after the fire happened and once it was advertised, we were ready. It's lucky we were proactive because when the money came through from the insurance company, we had drawings ready for Council to approve. We can start finalising the plans and costing it out." Jack and Tim were speechless. This was clearly a well thought out plan.

Mark continued, "This is a huge contract for our little firm, and I can be there on the job while Brian takes care of what's happening down here in the city. Last month, we put on a graduate architect to help with the general work, and she's proving to be a real find. She's most competent, with terrific design ideas, and we think we can employ another grad as well now. So Brian doesn't need me as much here in the office, and anyway, it's a short trip back to Melbourne when I need to."

Jack found his tongue and interrupted. "What! How long have you been planning this?"

Mark put his finger up to stall Jack and continued to enthuse, "And Winjarra Shire, thanks also to Brian and I, put in an application for an additional Commonwealth grant for regional sports facilities, and for a new shared sports facility to be built between the footy, tennis, and netball clubs. The Department of Sport and Recreation have contributed as well, with a regional sports facilities grant. It's going to be a fantastic bonus for everyone in the shire and the surrounding towns." He beamed excitedly at Jack and Tim. His smile faded though as he took in the complete shock on both their faces.

"And," said Jenny a little more tentatively, realising this was all a bit overwhelming, "I've arranged for a twelve-month teacher exchange with a young teacher at Winjarra Primary, who's keen to move back to Melbourne for the year, so my job won't be affected. But," she paused and looked at them both, "no matter how keen we are on this, we won't contemplate it unless you boys are totally on board with it. We promise."

"Whoa," was all Tim could muster before falling back into silence, his brain working overtime. This had not been on his radar at all. He was about to say, "But what about school?" but he answered his own question. Despite it being his Year 12, he already knew the teachers he would most likely have at Winjarra, and he not only liked them, he respected them. He'd already been impressed by the extra lengths they went to before to help him settle at the beginning of the year, and he knew the smaller class sizes would be a bonus. He also knew he had good mates in Nick and Tony and the gang. He could see more of Karen, which was a definite positive, even though he was still no wiser about where he stood with her. And then he recalled the start of the conversation. They would also have the added bonus of a proper tennis coach in Mr Mac.

Jack was similarly astonished, his face reflecting everything he was feeling. It was really way too much to process, and he wasn't sure how he felt about it. His mind raced as he weighed up the thought of going back to Winjarra, just as he was getting back into the swing of things back here in Melbourne. He really couldn't understand the timing of it all, with Mark only barely recovered. Was it good for his dad to be so far away from the hospital and specialised medical help?

"Just think about it, guys. We don't need an answer yet. Let's sleep on it and we can talk more tomorrow," said Jenny, motioning them to continue eating.

"Okay. Just one question though," said Jack. "What does Dad do if he gets sick? Doesn't he need to be near his specialist? What if he has to go back to hospital? And, Dad, you're still not very strong. I see how tired you get, and you still have a lie down in the day. You can't do that and be at work," he challenged.

"You're absolutely right and it's a good point. I'm hoping that my next round of blood tests confirm that I am in remission and, as you know, Dr Thompson is very hopeful. Obviously if I need more chemo, it's all off the table. But, fingers crossed, we can be positive, and I like to be positive," he said, giving a wry grin. "I'll be able to work from home and can rest if I need to. No more commuting to the office for clients, they'll be literally just down the street. It will actually allow me an easy transition back to work, I hope. And there's all that fresh air and a change of pace, a chance to just slow down a bit, I guess. But," he emphasised, "this is going to be a family decision, and I'll respect that."

They ate the rest of the meal with little conversation, as everyone sifted through their own thoughts. Mark caught Jenny's eye, hoping to gauge if she thought it went well. She raised her eyebrows in a gesture that meant, "I don't know." Despite his promise that he would respect their decision, Mark was really counting on them to agree. He had his heart set on it.

Later that evening, Tim slipped into Jack's room. Jack was flat out on his bed, eyes closed, listening to Jimmy Barnes sing about flame trees on his Walkman. Tim stepped lightly in and gathered up Jack's discarded sports socks before twisting them into a ball and throwing them at Jack's head.

"Jeez you give me the shits when you do idiotic things like that," said Jack, throwing them back at Tim and removing his headphones.

"I couldn't resist it, mate," taunted Tim.

"You'll keep," muttered Jack, sitting up and putting his Walkman aside. "Well, what do you think? Is this a crazy idea or what?"

Tim shrugged. "Dad seems pretty keen on it."

"And Mum." Jack shook his head. "I can't understand it. I mean, eighteen months ago you couldn't drag him away from the office. Then he's too sick to go near the office, and now he wants to leave it in Brian's hands, yet again, and live blissfully in the country?"

"Yeah, I know. It's crazy. But I think there's more to it. They want this to be a special year, a year where we all hang together. Who knows? It might be fun …"

Tim had his back to the door as he spoke. Jenny had slipped soundlessly into the room, and he didn't realise she had overheard him until he heard the soft click of the door shutting.

"You're right, Tim, there is more to it, and there is something I want you to consider before you make your decisions." Sitting down on Jack's bed, she continued, "Your dad wouldn't want me to say this, but we three need to be as honest as we can to each other. I promised you, Tim, a while ago that I would tell you the truth if I could, so I'll tell you as much as I know. While your dad looks better now than he has for a long time, Dr Thompson still can't give us a guarantee that he will fully recover any time soon. He's at a crossroad. The prognosis looks good at the moment—really good, in fact—but he needs to get through the next twelve months before we can begin to relax. If he can stay in remission for the next twelve months, then he has much better odds of full recovery. He's already defied the early predictions, but if … if he does deteriorate, then we're told he could go downhill very quickly."

Brushing away a tear, she continued. "So, if we stay here in the city, next year will be just like any other year, with nothing to make it special. But if we go and it does end up being our last year all together, then we will have done something very unique and memorable for us. It would be a year away from all the daily distractions and interruptions: all that outside stuff that drags each of us in so many directions. We can focus on just being a family."

Tim nodded. He felt he was beginning to understand the possibilities. Jack, however, wasn't completely sure, and his face showed it.

"I'm not explaining this very well, am I, Jack?" Jenny sighed and took another tack. "Take Dad's interest in your tennis lately. You'd have to agree he's never followed your sport, even your footy, with as much interest as this? Not that it would have mattered particularly what you chose to do. He just wants to be involved in your lives. I think he's trying to make up for all those times he was too busy to kick a ball with you in the backyard or take you to the beach. He needs to feel that, if the worst happens, you'll remember that he shared something with you … not that it makes up for what he missed, but I know that you guys are his priority now, not work. However, this contract in Winjarra means he can have both. He can have a rewarding professional life, and you know he loves his work. And he can still be involved in the family."

Grabbing one of each of her sons' hands, Jenny squeezed them before continuing. "Now, I know we can go on quite happily here. Your dad could make a weekly visit to Winjarra and stay overnight with Nan and Pa, and still manage the project. Some people faced with Dad's prognosis might choose to travel or stay in some exotic paradise. Other people might crave normality and continue life as usual. Dad wants to spend his time with us. Not that he expects us to sit around all the time with him," she added quickly. "He just wants us to have a change of pace and scenery so that it becomes a year that stands out. A year we can look back on as different. Besides the work angle, he genuinely loves it up there, and I think he figured it would be less disruption for you both, because of the time you spent there last year. But you each know only too well the things you'll miss out on—your friends and the beach, decent TV, and everything we take for granted in Melbourne. Like shopping ..." Making a droll face, she then smiled reassuringly and stood, saying, "C'mon. Give me a hug. There will be sacrifices all round if we do this."

After they shared a group hug, she stepped back.

"So, you need to consider this, but," she paused, adding softly, "this can't be a half-hearted commitment. You have to be totally sure you are up for it because I couldn't bear dealing with recalcitrant, sulky teenagers who would rather be somewhere else. No mooching around and complaining that it's too boring or that you wish you'd never come. Now, give me a kiss and think on it. I won't be cross if you say you aren't up for it. Just be honest with yourselves because we all know it's a big ask."

When Jenny left the room Tim sagged back down to the floor. Jack lay face down on his bed. Neither boy spoke for quite a while. Finally, after a long time, Tim stood and stretched his muscles. "Looks like we're off to Winjarra, Jack."

"Apparently we are," was the muffled reply as Jack contemplated his own situation from underneath his pillow.

That may have been the end of the discussion, but Jack was still very much undecided. He wasn't quite as philosophical as Tim about going back to Winjarra. The experience had been great but, despite making lots of friends, he hadn't quite bonded with other kids as much as Tim had. He thought he could work on connecting with mates though. Then there was Mr Mac. It was self-centred and shallow, perhaps, but he really did like the idea of being coached again by Mr Mac. He was such a good coach. And there were Nanna and Pa to consider. It would be good to see more of them. And so, very pragmatically, he gradually talked himself around to the idea.

The relief on his dad's face when he declared he was keen to go was more than enough to take away any lingering doubts that he had made the right decision. And, as Mark's enthusiasm for the idea grew, Jack couldn't help but be carried along with it and even find himself looking quite positively towards the year ahead.

Several weeks later, towards the end of term, the family drove to Winjarra to spend the weekend sorting out many of the logistics of the move. They stopped first at the high school to gather booklists and information packs for the next school year. The welcome was quite overwhelming from the principal, teachers, and the few students that were still at school on a Friday afternoon in the second-last week of term. Jack and Tim were quite flattered that everyone was so happy to welcome them back. Tim caught up with each of his Year 12 teachers, who gave him holiday reading lists, and even some assignments.

His maths teacher explained that he needed to keep his mind working mathematically. "We don't want to have to revise everything before I start, so if every week you could work through one of these chapters and the problems at the end, we should be ready to roll on day one."

Once again, Tim reflected that he certainly would get an advantage at Winjarra High in a small class, compared to his huge secondary college in Melbourne, where there were multiple Year 12 maths classes instead of only the one.

While Tim completed his appointments with his teachers, Jack found some classmates who were well into a game of mixed cricket. The number of students around was low as many of the local kids had summer jobs hay bailing or working on the wheat bins. He was soon conscripted into a side, and by the time his parents arrived back to collect them both, he was hot and sweaty, while Tim was burdened with photocopied booklets and textbooks for five subjects.

"Nothing's changed," gasped Jack, sinking back into the car and gulping from his water bottle. "This place is still hot as hell, and I seriously don't think anyone notices. Turn up the air con please, Dad. I'm dying here."

"What on earth have you been doing?" asked Jenny, laughing.

"Playing cricket. And can I fill in tomorrow afternoon for the Under 16s? They're short because everyone's off doing summer jobs."

"And I've got a party on tomorrow night," said Tim, hoping to slip his request in while the going looked good.

"I wouldn't let him go, Mum. You can't trust him," piped up Jack, dodging the punch in the arm Tim tried to give him.

"Cut it out, you two," admonished Mark as they drove away. "Don't forget your grandparents will want to see you both. But I don't mind either cricket or the party. What about cricket gear though?"

"Ben's lending me some old cricket whites. And I can use the club bats and gloves."

"And who's having the party?" asked Jenny.

"It's at Nick's place and his parents will be there." Figuring the truth would come out anyway, Tim confessed the rest before the inevitable questions from Jenny. "It's his eighteenth, so there will be alcohol."

"Mmm," was the noncommittal reply as they pulled up to their grandparents' place and got caught up in welcome hugs and kisses.

Staying once more in the back bedroom off the kitchen at Nan and Pa's brought back many memories. So much had happened since those first few days in Winjarra. Jack and Tim were both much more confident and chilled about the year ahead than they had been almost a year ago. This time everything felt so familiar, and the couple of hours they had just spent at school reinforced the feeling that they had made the right decision. Their dad's state of health was still uncertain, but at the moment it all felt like nothing bad could stalk them here.

Tim was feeling very positive about the move, even though theoretically he should have been the one person who stood to lose the most. After all, he was missing out on doing Year 12 with the mates he'd known all his life. However, he only needed to look at the change in his dad to confirm the decision. Mark was certainly a great deal more relaxed, and happier than Tim ever remembered him. Not quite a workaholic, maybe, but Tim always had the feeling that his dad put work above the family. Jenny was the one he went to first, because Mark had always been busy. He worked long hours designing and working on projects, trying to build up the business. That's just the way it had always been. It was great when his dad was around: it just didn't happen that often.

But coaching them at tennis had revealed another side of their dad. Not only was he genuinely interested, but he was patient and encouraging. He offered criticism, but its edges were smoothed with positivity, and he was a wonderful motivator. Jack was continually surprised by his dad's grasp of the finer points of tennis. He'd never really seen him as a sportsman. Mark seemed to be always sketching away at a drafting board and Jack assumed he wasn't interested in sport, other than as an armchair observer. Jack now realised, after spending so much more time together, that he had played lots of sport in his day: cricket, tennis, and footy. He'd just let sport slide while he worked on his architecture career, a sacrifice that Jack was only now able to appreciate.

Mark had been in his element over the last few weeks, masterfully coordinating all aspects of the move. Seeing his excitement grow, it was difficult to imagine that they had ever even contemplated saying no. He was fun to be with, and his enthusiasm was certainly infectious. It was two very contented boys that sat down to dinner that evening with their parents and grandparents. Nanna, of course, had cooked up a storm. Despite the warm weather there was roast lamb and Nanna's famous chocolate cake with cream. There was so much to catch up on, between the family news and the plans for next year, that it took some time before the subject of tennis came up.

"So, school looks sorted. And I think you'll like the house your nan and I picked out when you see it tomorrow. Now, tell me about your tennis plans. I talked to Paul Maclaren when he came back from seeing you in Melbourne and he was very impressed with your game. What's been happening?" asked Pa.

"I think you'll be impressed as well, Jim," said Mark. "They've really worked hard, and I have to give them full credit for their efforts. I've been able to help them a bit lately, and Paul Mac has been sending me lots of ideas, but these two have shown a dedication and work ethic that has really been outstanding."

Tim and Jack felt themselves glowing in the warmth of Mark's high praise. He'd praised them often when they were on their own, but it gained in significance when he said it to someone else in front of them. Pa looked at them both proudly and said, "I'm not surprised. You should have seen them hitting balls up against the shed wall all last summer. I thought I was going to have to replace the wall if they had stayed any longer," he joked. "Well, when can I see you play? You'll obviously be joining the tennis club, but I have to warn you, there aren't many tournaments around here until later in January."

"Well, that's the thing," said Mark. "So far they have just been playing each other and practising. They need competition and to play someone else. It's ridiculously too predictable for them at the moment. They know each other's game inside and out. One day Tim wins and then the next, Jack will. There really isn't much between them. They definitely need to join a club and get out there and compete."

Jack and Tim listened intently. They had been reluctant to mention joining clubs and tournaments while so much was going on planning the move. They knew that Mr Mac would take over coaching them, and that was something they both looked forward to. An earnest discussion ensued between Jim and Mark, talking about some of the old greats and their game styles. Once again Jack understood he had very much mistaken his father's lack of interest in sport. Mark continued to speak enthusiastically about his plans for training; however, Tim could see his energy levels diminish as the night wore on. It had been a very full day.

Finally, Mark admitted exhaustion. "I might have to leave you all, and head to bed. I think I've hit the wall. I don't quite have the energy I need to keep up with these two, so you might have to take over occasionally, Jim. And I may get busy working some days, so it would be good to know you can help out sometimes." Mark smiled ruefully as he rose from the table.

"Well, of course I would be happy to give a hand if I can. I'm keen to see these boys play, and if an old codger like me can pass on a few tricks, I will."

The next morning, they all had a look at the house Pa and Nan had picked out for them to rent. It was a lovely old weatherboard, complete with a bull-nosed verandah that ran around all four sides of the house. Built to cope with the warmer weather, it had high ceilings and wide passageways. Best of all there were two recently renovated bathrooms, and Jack and Tim each had their own bedroom, just like their home in Melbourne.

The house was within walking distance of most places. The high school was nearby, and they were also close to the sporting fields and recreation area. They had a slightly elevated view of the town, and they could see the town swimming pool from their verandah. Mark would also be able to keep an eye on the construction site for the new municipal offices from the side verandah that faced the town.

Tim thought it was going to be heaven being so close to everything for a change. They would literally be able to roll out of bed and be at school in five minutes. He was definitely not a morning person.

He stood on the front verandah looking out over the town and took in the view. He could see the high school on his left, and down to his right was the main street. The occasional truck was visible as it lumbered through town on its way north. On one side of the town were the spires of the Anglican church, an imposing bluestone building that had served the needs of the town for many years. Opposite it on the other side of town was the less imposing spire of St Peter's, the Catholic church. Of weatherboard construction, it possibly gave a good indication of where the spiritual loyalties of the town lay.

Mark stood with him on the verandah and called to Jack to join them. Jenny was busy examining the kitchen with Nan, and Pa had already bailed up someone passing by to talk to.

"Come for a walk," Mark said. "I want to show you both something."

Leading the way, he headed towards the recreation fields, or the rec ground, as it was known locally. They walked through the rec ground, which was adjacent to the high school. This proximity was a great advantage to the high school because it was a quick short cut through to the town's hockey and soccer fields, the lawn tennis courts, netball courts, and the footy oval. The swimming pool was on the far side of the rec ground, but it was all accessible by foot, which meant the school was able to share facilities with the community and vice versa.

As they neared the southern end of the rec ground, Mark pointed to a shiny new fence that extended along from the last of the lawn tennis courts that were, at that time of day, full of Saturday morning juniors playing competition pennant tennis. "Take a look, boys," he said. From where they were Tim and Jack couldn't see much at all. The new fence was still a couple of hundred metres in the distance, and it wasn't until they got quite a bit closer that they understood their father's excitement.

"Jeez!" exclaimed Jack. "When did that happen?" Both boys quickened their pace towards the gate in the fence. In front of them were three beautiful new hardcourts: but not just the usual bitumen courts typical of a local tennis club. These looked just like the new Rebound Ace surface, laid at Flinders Park for the Australian Open. They hadn't yet actually seen a Rebound Ace court anywhere, except when they had watched the matches at Flinders Park on television. This was the first time they had seen one in real life.

"Are you kidding us, Dad? Is this the real thing?" Tim called out to Mark, who was following at a slower pace.

"It sure is. The council and the high school put in a joint application earlier this year as part of their shared community facilities program. Mr Mac's tennis program was obviously a big advantage and featured heavily in the grant application. Once the application was successful, he used a couple of his old tennis contacts to fast-track the construction. They've only just been finished. He's kept it all fairly quiet, but he thought it might be a nice surprise for you. Now the town and school can boast having some of the best regional tennis facilities outside of Melbourne. What do you think?"

"This is unreal. Can we get on it, though? Is it open to everyone?" asked Tim as he walked out onto the courts. He knelt down almost reverently to feel the surface. "They say it gives a really true bounce and that it's better for your body. Less injuries and stress on your joints so you don't get as tired."

"Absolutely. It will be a much truer bounce than the lawn. And yes, not so hard on your legs as normal hardcourts, I'm told. As far as I know, Mr Mac will be able to coach using these courts, but obviously they will have to be available for the tennis club outside of school times. I think you'll get plenty of chances to practise here. Not a bad unexpected bonus, is it? Almost worth the move, I would think," Mark said with a wink.

After a last look they walked back together to the new house. Tim was even more convinced he had made the right decision. The year ahead was looking better by the minute. He hoped Jack was feeling the same. Moments later, as he watched Jack rush up the steps of the new house to Jenny, telling her what they had just seen, he realised that perhaps Jack was totally cool with the idea of moving after all. Still looking euphoric, Jack took off soon after lunch to fill in for the cricket team, while Tim helped Pa on the farm. The afternoon passed quickly as they bailed hay—a hot and dusty task—and Tim was tired when Pa signalled the job was done for the day. It was already after six when he raced in to shower and change for the party.

While he was in the bathroom showering off the afternoon's dust, Jenny talked quietly to Mark. "What do you think about this party? Tim's not eighteen till June, and I don't want him to think he can drink yet. And I know how much these country kids can drink! I was one of them, once," she said, rolling her eyes and making a guilty face.

"I agree, but he's going to have to work this out for himself one day. Probably far better he has a couple of drinks in a safe environment—like at Nick's, with parents around—than down in Melbourne somewhere with no supervision and trying to sneak into a pub underage."

"Nick's parents are very sensible, I know. And he's their third son so they must have some experience with all this. I don't want to look over-protective, but I don't want to encourage underage drinking, either. I don't know that I'm ready for all of this," sighed Jenny.

"Hey. I think we've been extremely lucky so far. Not that we've had tabs on him all the time, but he doesn't ask to go out much, ever. I think we need to trust him and give him the chance to work it out for himself," replied Mark, putting his arms around her. "We have to let them grow up sometime."

Tim came out of the bathroom smelling strongly of deodorant and aftershave and looking suddenly grown up. Jenny felt a pang in her heart at the same time as a surge of pride. With his strong, broad shoulders and tall, fit physique, she could see the man he was to become emerging. He smiled at them both standing there, a smile that lit up his handsome face and showed off his lovely green eyes.

"Can we pick up Karen?" asked Tim. "I told her we'd give her a lift there and back, if that's okay? Her mum is away this weekend, and her dad's minding her two little sisters."

"Absolutely no problem," said Mark, picking up the car keys. "It will be nice to see her again. I'll have to ask what tournaments she's signed up for this summer. And, of course, you will probably be seeing lots of her once Mr Mac starts coaching the three of you together."

Tim nodded. He certainly hoped to see lots of Karen himself next year, and he was glad Jack wasn't around to say anything embarrassing like he usually did. Jack knew exactly when and how to give him a hard time. To Tim's relief, Mark took over the conversation on the drive to Nick's. Tim was still surprised by this new version of him. Mark had often been so absent-minded, preoccupied with designs and drawings, that he was lucky to know the names of Tim's friends. Yet here he was, talking away to Karen about tennis as though they were old mates. He shook his head in wonder in the backseat.

When they arrived, the party was still quiet, which was good. Tim had thoughtfully brought a present from Melbourne, and he was glad to see Nick have the chance to open it. It was a cassette of their favourite band, and he was rapt that Nick's reaction was so positive.

"Thanks, mate. I love this! I'll put it on now," he exclaimed, putting the cassette in the stereo and turning it up.

Karen and Tim moved to the open fire pit, in the yard at the rear of the house, where a group of their friends were already ensconced on hay bales. School was almost over for the year, and the holiday mood was infectious. It wasn't long before Tim was caught up in the conversation as though he had never left. Summer stretched ahead, and a few talked about heading off on camping holidays to the beach, but others would be busy working on family farms or on the wheat bins while the crop was harvested. For those staying at home, the talk centred around the summer basketball comp, and meeting at Old Tom's waterhole, a natural spring that offered the only swimming possibility other than the town pool.

Nick's mother kept up a steady supply of food as the night wore on. There were plenty of cans of beer available, but all were low alcohol so there wasn't as much danger of kids getting too intoxicated. Eventually, several girls started to dance on the makeshift timber floor Nick and his dad had laid out on the flattest spot of grass. Losing their inhibitions, the boys finally joined in, and soon most of the party goers were on the dance floor. Occasionally Nick's dad would wander out and turn down the volume, but just as soon as he went back inside the dial was turned back up again.

Around midnight most kids had reached their curfew and were starting to leave. Mark had said he would be back at half past twelve to collect them, so Tim and Karen said their goodbyes to Nick. As they walked around to the front of the house to wait, Karen linked arms companionably with Tim. One by one their friends were collected, until finally they were the last two left. Tim extracted his arm, putting it around Karen, drawing her in close. With his heart pounding in his chest at the move he was about to make, Tim bent his head towards Karen, hoping she would be feeling the same. Their lips touched and the gentle kiss that followed seemed very natural. It was without all the usual awkwardness that his previous attempts with other girls had entailed. But just as he was emboldened to kiss her again, car headlights rounded the corner and they both jumped back abruptly in response.

Tim let his arm drop from around Karen's shoulders as the car rolled to a stop in front of them. He got into the front while

Karen sat in the back. Mark, oblivious to their heightened emotions, was again full of chitchat.

Later, as Tim walked Karen to her front door she asked, "When will you be back?"

"In the next few weeks. Soon after Christmas, I hope."

"I've got a tournament in Geelong the week after Christmas, and we might be able to plan something for New Year if you're around. I'll ring."

Nodding in agreement, Tim kissed her once more, lightly on the cheek, knowing his dad was probably looking, and headed back to the car feeling quite proud of himself. Next year was looking better all the time.

CHAPTER 10

Tim sat hunched forward on the hard, slatted bench seat, intently watching a bull ant struggle with its prized burden of a breadcrumb. Slowly it traversed its way through tufts of grass and insurmountable mounds of gravel, resolutely forging a path to its destination. Absorbed in the solitary journey taking place before him, Tim missed hearing his name being called over the loudspeaker.

Jabbing him gently in the ribs, his father snapped him out of his reverie in time to hear the repeat announcement.

"Under 18s boys singles. T. Anderson and B. Stavros to Court Twenty. Thank you."

Standing quickly, Tim stretched himself to his full six feet and one inch and looked down on Mark and Jack. "Well, I guess this is it."

"Good luck, Tim. You can do this," encouraged Jack, standing up to give him a hug and a slap on the back. Despite the two-year gap in age, there was very little difference in height, and their eyes met in a mutual recognition of the significance of the moment, at almost the same level.

"Go out and enjoy it, Tim. Have some fun and just play your own game and you'll be fine," said Dad, handing him his racquet, handtowel, and drink bottle. "You've done the hard work, now get some reward for it all."

Outwardly Tim looked calm, but inside he was almost sick with apprehension. Nodding, he asked, "Are you coming to watch?"

"Of course. You go ahead and check in and we'll be there for the start. We'll stay until Jack gets called up for his match," said Mark, patting him on the back.

As he walked away, Tim turned back and called to Jack, "Hey! Good luck to you too, bro, if we end up playing at the same time."

Tim did a little jig from side to side to warm-up as he walked towards Court Twenty of the Mornington Lawn Tennis Club. He tried to remain calm despite the adrenaline surging inside him. His heart was thumping in his chest: he could almost feel it under the strap of his racquet cover. He wanted to make a good first impression, but his mind was still whirling with this sudden turn of events.

Two days ago, it was Christmas, and any idea of him stepping out to play in a tournament was still just a vague plan. He and Jack had woken up Christmas morning, not quite as early as they would have several years ago, but nevertheless a little earlier than usual. After all, it was Christmas! According to their Christmas morning ritual, he woke Jack and together they went to discover if Santa, alias Mum and Dad, had left something in their Christmas stockings. The stockings had been handmade by Jenny when they were babies. Brightly coloured in a reindeer pattern, they featured the letters T and J on them, so there was never any mistake about the recipient. Tim wasn't sure about who enjoyed the Christmas pretence more—he and Jack, or their parents. Jenny and Mark would appear on cue, generally still half asleep but not willing to miss this special part of the day. There would be great exclamations about what Santa had brought, just as if it were the first time either of them had ever seen the Santa gifts. This year was no exception.

"That's some fancy tennis gear," commented Mark in feigned surprise, in reference to the matching new shorts and tennis shirt on the top of their stockings.

"Nice one, Dad," said Jack as he put them aside and delved deeper into the stocking to find more surprises.

Mark gave them a few minutes before he pointed to the tree, saying, "Check the tree. There's something else on there if you look carefully."

"Sweet!" said Tim, spying an envelope with his name on it tucked in the branch of the Christmas tree.

"Oh man! I hope it's cash! Thank you, guys," said Jack, grabbing his and ripping open the envelope. It wasn't cash. Quickly scanning the content of the printed page, Jack sat down with a thump on the couch, squashing all the presents he'd just ripped out from the stocking. "What? You can't be serious? I'm not ready!"

"Come on, Dad! You're shitting me? I can't play in this! And what? It's for this week! No way!" remonstrated Tim, angrily throwing his Under 18s singles entry form down on the carpet.

"Oh no. I'm not kidding," said Mark. And reaching higher into the tree he brought out another envelope. Opening it, he read out, "Under 18s boys doubles team, T. Anderson and J. Anderson."

"I'll get breakfast started. Merry Christmas, boys." Giving both Jack and Tim a kiss, Jenny made a well-timed exit, leaving Mark to deal with the fallout of his own Christmas surprise. He had hoped it would be something the boys would be pumped about, but it had backfired on him, and it took most of

Christmas morning to calm the boys down and get them to see it in a positive light. As usual there was an extended family gathering for lunch of cousins, aunties, and uncles.

In the end it was Sally, one of their cousins, who, after listening to their complaints over lunch, managed to put their fears into some perspective. "It's no big deal, surely? You both told me you play all the time, and it must be so boring just playing each other. It's just another game. I don't know why you're carrying on so much about it. Just have a go and see what happens."

Uncle Bill had then declared emphatically, in his booming voice, "Sally! You have nailed it exactly! What is the point of forever playing each other? You do know how crazy this sounds? What are you worried about? If you don't have a go, you'll never know. Now, forget about it. Enjoy Christmas Day because this year is a great one, and we have so much to be thankful for." He had raised his glass in Mark's direction, and the family had clinked glasses to acknowledge Mark's good health. Tim had felt slightly ashamed at his carry on. From that moment, he and Jack did their best to put any qualms they had aside and enjoy their day. However, Christmas was over, and this was now crunch time. The moment to play had arrived.

Just another game, thought Tim to himself, quickening his footsteps towards Court Twenty. He knew he was ready but, despite the adrenaline rushing through him, he felt a sudden loss of strength as he neared the court. Backing out was not an option. It was time to find out one way or the other if he could play. Walking onto the court he saw his opponent was already waiting for him. He looked poised and completely at home as he casually bounced a ball on his racquet.

Taking a deep breath, Tim walked towards him with a confidence he didn't feel. "Hi. I'm Tim."

"Bernie. Do you want to toss now?"

Tim had watched several other players begin their sets, so he had a good idea of the court etiquette required.

Taking a coin from his pocket, Bernie asked, "Your call. Heads or tails?"

"Heads." Tim followed the coin's progress as it flipped high into the air, falling softly to the grass, head side up. Whew! Tim was relieved that he didn't have to decide which end he preferred. He hoped by serving first he could get rid of the nerves that threatened to overwhelm him.

Formalities over, both boys went to their ends and began the five-minute hit-up they were allowed. Mark had gone through this with him the day before, so he knew the expected routine. First both boys hit to each other from the baseline, each trying to find a rhythm and some depth. Then, in turn, each of them moved to the net to try a few volleys, and finally they returned to the baseline to serve several balls into either court.

As they were finishing their last serves the umpire called out, "Two minutes."

Tim heeded the umpire's warning and returned to the side of the court where his things were. Suddenly parched, he had a swig of water, and dried his already-sweating palms on his towel. Stretching his neck from side to side, he walked towards the service line, collecting two new balls from the umpire as he went. He took several deep breaths, trying to control his scattered thoughts and get some air into his lungs. The sight of Jack and Dad arriving to sit courtside helped to steady him. He held up the two balls to Bernie and the umpire called out for play to start.

He began with a double fault. At this end, the sun was in his eyes, and he could understand why Bernie had wisely chosen the other end, giving himself an advantage for the first game. His next serve was more cautious as he tried to compensate, making sure he got a serve in. Bernie pounced on the weak serve and drove it straight down the sideline, out of Tim's reach.

Another two shaky serves, and two devastating returns from Bernie, left Tim flat-footed and out of position. He lost his first serve and first game without scoring a point. This played heavily on his mind as he changed ends, and he still hadn't composed himself when Bernie began to serve with devastating accuracy. The sun factor didn't seem to be bothering Bernie, while Tim struggled nervously with every shot. The racquet felt foreign in his hand, and he was second-guessing every stroke he made. Very quickly he lost the second game, and he was two–love down.

It's all happening too fast, thought Tim, his brain in a whirl as he collected the balls for his next serve, this time from the non-sunny end. It was a knockout tournament, one set only, played as the first to eight, with a two-game advantage. He couldn't afford to let this guy get too far ahead. Steadying, he threw off his cautious play, telling himself to have a go. In his panic he went for every shot. Too often he attempted the impossible, and in trying to close down a rally too quickly, he overplayed his shots. In no time at all he was four games down and yet to score. This was not going at all according to plan. Tim's anxiety level hit the red zone and he felt he had lost all control.

As he gathered balls from Bernie for his next serve, he couldn't help but notice the relaxed swagger of his opponent. Not only that, but when he set himself up to receive Tim's first serve, Bernie stood well inside the baseline, indicating that returning Tim's serve would not stretch him too much. It was absolutely a silent insult from his opponent. Tim looked over to where Dad sat, expecting a glum face. Instead, he got an encouraging smile and nod in return. Jack also responded with a thumbs up and a wink. It was just enough to settle him. Halting in his serve preparation, Tim took a moment. His dad and brother didn't look concerned. They must think he still had a chance here. He took a determined breath this time. "No more cheap points," he said to himself as he stared down the court at his opponent. Time to play. His father's words echoed in his head: play your own game. "Play your own game," he repeated to himself and, wiping his hands on his shorts, he braced himself to serve.

Tossing the ball out in front, he pivoted and hit down with a full wrist action, finishing perfectly balanced. His right leg moved through, and he planted his foot firmly down onto the court. For the first time in the match, he served with power and purpose, and he was rewarded. Bernie was caught out too far forward to make a decent return and Tim was able to move quickly to the net to put away a smartly angled volley. Prior to serving again, Tim took the time to visualise his serve before he began his toss. He did this for the remainder of the game and, as he slowed his thoughts and his pace of play, his serving improved markedly. No longer did Bernie edge forward to return serve. Sensing a change in Tim's tactics he had quickly adjusted his own game. Tim had to be patient, and he worked for every point. However, shot by shot, Tim rallied back and forth with Bernie, gradually playing himself back into form, until he won his first game.

It wasn't an earth-shattering performance, but Tim finally felt his brain switch on and his nerves calm. He began to ease back into his comfort zone. Bernie looked unruffled as they changed ends at 4/1. This time, though, Tim faced Bernie's serve with a steely determination. He'd stupidly given four games away, but he believed that he still had a chance. Tim knew that longer rallies would be to his advantage. Shrewdly discerning that Bernie had already won this set in his head, he hoped it might make him careless. When he won the next game, taking Bernie's serve at thirty–forty, Tim knew he could beat him. He just had to keep the ball in play and let Bernie make the errors. Simple. If only he hadn't given away four games so cheaply!

As play continued, Tim put all those hours of practise to good use. Patiently he rallied back and forth to Bernie, who was certainly a worthy opponent—but, Tim realised, not as quick or accurate as Jack. Watching every return for an opportunity, Tim attempted to place the ball just a little out of Bernie's reach, making him really work hard to produce his shots. It was basic gamesmanship, and it didn't always work but, courageously, Tim clawed his way back into the match.

Bernie knew he had blown a significant lead and it began to bother him. At 5/4, he was only one game ahead, and starting to tighten up in his shots. The next two games were vital for the match. Both boys won their serves, but Tim had won his easily while Bernie had only just held on, conceding several advantage points to Tim. The score was 6/5 to Bernie when Tim stepped up to serve. He and Jack had been practising a spin serve over the last few weeks—in fact, ever since they had seen Karen use it in her final to devastating effect. Bernie was becoming wise to his shots and Tim thought it was time to surprise him.

Keeping his mind totally focused, Tim tossed the ball to serve, arched well back and, bringing his racquet across the side of the ball, sent down a spin serve that bounced truly but curved suddenly away, catching Bernie totally unprepared. Ace.

Tim repeated the inwardly curving spin on his next serve. Totally surprised by the first ball, Bernie was not expecting another, especially when it looked like it was going to fall short on the centre-line. As Bernie moved to take advantage of the slower-paced ball with a forehand winner, the ball curved suddenly into his body and, even with a quick adjustment, his return crashed uselessly into the net.

Well aware that he had played two risky shots, Tim now steadied, retreating to his patient game. However, his change of tactic created doubts in Bernie's mind, and this time it was Bernie who was second-guessing shots; more unforced errors began to creep in. Tim continued to play deep, forcing Bernie into a defensive position as much as he could. It wasn't exactly a lightning-bolt moment but, finally, after all those theoretical discussions about tennis strategy, Tim observed firsthand just how they could play out in reality.

The final game was an anticlimax. Although it could not be said that Bernie gave up at any point, Tim simply discovered that his own killer instinct was alive and well. Once he sensed victory, his shots became even more precise and ruthless, and the last game was almost technical perfection. As Bernie sent the last ball wide and the umpire called out the final score, Tim was overcome with the pure joy of winning. It was an emotional soup of pride, glee, astonishment, and satisfaction, and he tried his best to hide it as he shook hands over the net with his opponent.

With exceptional good sportsmanship Bernie said, "I could have done without that comeback. You were just too good in the end. Thanks, mate, and good luck in your other matches."

"Thanks. I think I was just lucky," replied Tim, feeling very generous himself now the game was his.

Tim gathered his bag and water bottles and, after thanking the umpire, looked over to where Dad and Jack had been sitting. He had been so absorbed in his game, it was the first time he realised they were gone, which could only mean one thing: Jack was on court playing his first match. Tim was very keen to get to watch Jack, but as the winner he had to hand in the results of his match to the tournament office.

As he handed in the score to the officials, he was met with a quizzical look. "That's not a bad effort, mate. You've just knocked off the fourth seed in the first round. Don't go too far. Your next match will be at around one o'clock."

Tim wasn't quite sure what to make of the official's comment, but he smiled politely and said thanks. A quick look at the tournament whiteboard helped Tim to locate Jack's court.

He slid quietly into the seat beside his father. "I won. 8/6."

"That's great." Mark grinned at Tim, putting his arm around him and squeezing his shoulders. "I knew you could do it! But you gave us quite a fright in the first four games. What the hell happened out there?"

"I don't know. I just went into zombie mode, and I forgot what to do. Sounds crazy but I just wasn't switched on. And, hey! I've never even played anyone other than Jack, and it just felt weird," protested Tim, still looking a bit shell-shocked.

"I know. Maybe this wasn't really fair on you guys, entering you in a tournament like this. I just couldn't help myself! But you can see why now, can't you? It's time we got you out there. Here," he gestured to the courts around them. "And, c'mon, tell me. You looked like you were starting to enjoy yourself by the time we had to leave."

"It was fun," admitted Tim, "but only once it was over. Or maybe the last game was a blast. Okay. Maybe even the last few games," Tim grinned. Gesturing towards the court he asked, "What's the score?"

"He's made a few very silly shots as well, but nothing like how you started. The kid he's playing isn't as sharp as that Bernie kid you played, and Jack's been able to settle into his game much quicker. He's up 7/2, so fingers crossed."

Jack was tested in his final game but eventually won 8/2 and came off the court elated and grinning widely. They ate lunch, talking furiously about their respective games and reliving key moments. They had learned so much in one set of tennis, and they were keen to share their experiences. On cue, Tim was called to his next match at one o'clock. This time Jack and Mark were able to watch the whole match before Jack was called up for his.

A much wiser Tim began his set with greater confidence and some sort of plan. He was even composed enough to take notice of a possible weakness in his opponent's forehand during the warm-up. The games went on serve for each of their first three serves, before Tim gradually found his rhythm and was able to dominate his opponent. He won his second match comfortably at 8/4.

Jack stormed through his match with even greater ease at 8/1, as Tim and Mark watched on. However, despite feeling euphoric, Jack was also plagued with guilt, spending the drive home wondering if he looked like a show-off.

"Jack," said Tim, totally exasperated with Jack's thinking, "if you're playing a social game of tennis with mates, then it might be an option to lose a couple. But seriously, this is a tournament! It might not be sheep stations, but you're entitled to be the best you can be—and if that means winning by a mile, then that's okay. What if you go out there tomorrow and face someone who takes you to a tie breaker, and then you're too tired to compete because you played extra games the day before, so you end up losing? And don't forget we're going to have extra sets because we play doubles as well from tomorrow on, so you'll need to conserve your energy for that."

Jack nodded, seeing the common sense in this. "I forgot about the doubles. Can we get out of those, Dad? I honestly have no idea what to do in doubles."

"You'll be fine, Jack," replied Mark with reassuring confidence. "The doubles will be fun. Tennis can be a bit self-centred with all this singles play. You need to feel part of a team still. Just enjoy the doubles. I want them to be fun for you both. Absolutely no stress! Just have a go. And my top piece of advice is," he added with great seriousness as pulled into the driveway and turned off the car, "try not to hit each other with the ball when one of you is at the net!"

The next morning, they left early so they could have a warm-up together before their first matches. Jenny had opted to stay home again because she was busy packing and sorting things to take to Winjarra. Jack was first up, and he was up 5/3 when Tim was called for his match. Tim went to Court Seventeen as directed and was surprised to see more than the usual handful of spectators gathered. Assuming this guy had lots of relatives and friends, Tim thought nothing more of it.

He'd been stretching while he watched Jack's match, so he was feeling relatively relaxed and ready, his nerves under control. He felt himself swinging much more freely at the ball even in the warm-up. This time his opponent was quite powerfully built, and far stronger than his last two adversaries, with a boomer of a serve that either kicked out wide or up high. His forehand shots could go like a rocket but luckily, despite being fast, they were also flat and predictable.

Once Tim learned to stand back and take his serve late, after the sting was out of it, he had little trouble returning serve. The hard, fast balls he sent down were just like returning Jack's balls in practise. It was a hard-fought set though, and there were many long, grinding rallies. Tim was so focused that he was slightly surprised when the umpire called, "Match, 8/4, Anderson," and it was over. He was even more surprised when the majority of the spectators clapped him as he walked off the court, and he smiled sheepishly as he nodded thanks and acknowledged their congratulations. Maybe they weren't relatives of his opponent after all: but, if they were, they were certainly not biased, he thought.

It was not long after this game that the brothers lined up for their first game of doubles. The doubles were being played in a round robin format, which meant they would get a chance to play each team in turn, instead of the knockout matches in the singles. They were in luck. Their first opponents were two mates who had entered more to get some good tennis than with any expectation of winning. While they were no slouches, they were nowhere near as consistent as Tim and Jack. The competition was strong, but there were plenty of laughs and a bit of banter that was definitely absent from the intense singles matches Tim and Jack had experienced so far.

Despite getting in each other's way a few times, they managed some very good points, and finished comfortable winners. They had enjoyed it so much they were almost sorry to play the last point.

As they shook hands together at the net, their opponents were generous in their praise. "You two should go well. Good luck in your next match," said one of them.

"Thanks. Good luck to you, too," replied Jack.

Gathering their bags from the side of the court, Jack said, "That was great! I had no idea doubles was so much fun."

"It was awesome!" exclaimed Tim, genuinely thrilled. "And we did okay, bro. High five!"

Their next doubles match followed quickly and wasn't quite so easy, but they still managed to scramble a win. With no prior experience they had to rely on instinctive play, and their intimate knowledge of each other's game. They knew intuitively which shots they could trust each other to get, and when they needed to chip in to help each other out. Trusting each other was what kept them in the match until they won 8/6. They were very pumped up this time as they came off the court.

"That is so much better than being on the court on your own, Dad! I am so glad you put us in doubles," enthused Tim after they had won their second set.

"Yeah! I love it!" agreed Jack. "I mean, we can talk to each other, and it's so good. Like when Tim starts losing it, I can settle him down, and get him back on track," he joked and then flinched, saying, "Ouch!" as Tim flicked him with his handtowel.

"Hey! I think you were the one losing the plot with three forehands out in a row! You were so lucky I was there to smash away the next winner!" said Tim, dodging quickly out of the way in advance of any retaliation.

"Hey, steady on, you two. You're supposed to look after each other, now you're partners," laughed Mark. "And I have to say I've enjoyed these matches too. They are fun to watch. You need to rest now because you've both got singles coming up in the next hour. You should eat something and hydrate."

"Gee, Dad," complained Jack with a grin, "talk about cracking the whip!"

Two days later, Tim walked out onto Court One for the Under 18 boys' final at the same time that Jack walked out on Court Three for the Under 16 boys' final. Jenny had come to watch this time because Mark couldn't be at both courts at the same time. Besides, she was keen to watch them play after hearing about nothing else all week.

As Tim took his position on the court, he took a few moments to glance around, taking in the larger than usual crowd in the temporary stands.

It seemed that every time he played the crowd had gotten bigger. He squared his shoulders and breathed in and out slowly. Since his first foray into competitive tennis against Bernie, he had become much better at conquering his nerves. It had been a week saturated in new experiences and his learning curve had been steep. Mark had prepared him for this match, and the added pressure, and they had discussed several possible scenarios in depth. He knew he had caused a bit of a stir not only beating Bernie in the first match, but by going on to win every match since. Tim was aware of the curious eyes following him all week, which he had wisely decided to ignore, but this time the crowd was significant.

"Use the crowd to your advantage," Mark had advised him. "They'll keep you sharp because you know they're scrutinising everything you do. You can't expect any easy points anyway, and the crowd and the opposition will make you earn them. And when you do put a good shot away, and they clap, then you deserve to get the reward, so enjoy the applause."

"And what if I hit a bad one and they clap the other guy?" Tim asked quizzically.

"Well, then you know you weren't good enough and you need to sharpen up. Either way, it's good for you." Then, placing his hands on Tim's shoulders, he said sincerely, "And,

I wouldn't say this if I didn't believe it. I know you can win this, just play your own game." And he enveloped Tim in a big hug.

Putting the crowd to the back of his mind, Tim let himself enjoy a moment of satisfaction. He had come so far in a week. He'd played better than in his wildest dreams and his game had stood up to all sorts of attacks. One more match, he told himself. Just one more match.

The finals were being played as best of three six-game sets. This was another new experience for Tim. He'd watched plenty of three-set matches on TV, but he had never played one. This would be a step-up; he was playing the Mornington Tennis Club junior champion, Ben Tate, and this was his home court. As well as that, Ben was a left-hander, a totally new experience for him. Even in the pre-game warm-up, Tim sensed that this would require some adjustments to his own game.

Three games in and Tim felt like he was wading upstream through deep water. Ben's left-hand shots were tricky, and Tim relived some of the panic of his first few games against Bernie. But experience is a wonderful teacher and, this time, he composed himself. Instead of giving in to his fears, he forced himself to breathe and slow down his frenzied negative thoughts. Tim went down 6/3 in the first set with a fairly dull performance, but it gave him the chance to adjust to Ben's game and valuable time to settle into his own game.

More focused, he started the second set remembering his strategy was to send his returns deep into the right-hand court. The intention was to force Ben to play backhands, then surprise him with a shot to the opposite side of the court, hoping to wrong-foot him. It didn't work every time, but it did help take some of the sting out of Ben's attacks. Mixing up his shots, Tim moved to the net as often as he could. He was blessed with long arms, and he used them to his advantage. Quick on his feet, he covered the net well, keeping himself in the rally and taking winners when he could. Tim's long reach forced Ben to attempt risky, low-percentage shots, and he began to make some unforced errors that were to Tim's advantage.

While the lawn courts of Mornington—with their occasional unpredictable bounce—should have been an advantage to Ben as the local, the times spent playing on uneven surfaces as Tim and Jack had first honed their skills on the rough surface of Pa's farm now produced gold. It was second nature for Tim to watch the ball with hawk-like intensity, and he reacted quickly to each bounce. Tim was in his element, trading shots with a truly worthy opponent. The challenge had sharpened his game rather than overwhelming it, and he felt he was seeing each ball as clearly as if it were in slow motion. Tim won the second set in a tie breaker. One set each and the match looked very even, with every point hard-fought.

As they battled a particularly long rally in the third set, Ben sent a wide ball to Tim's forehand that hit the grass in a dead drop and bounced low. Scrambling a hasty return that he just managed to reach, he lobbed the ball high to the back of the court on Ben's forehand. Miraculously, it bounced inside the line, and Tim recovered quickly, racing back into position to be ready for the smashing return he expected. However, instead of a return flying past him for a winner, Ben miscalculated, and Tim watched it land uselessly into the net. A bonus point!

Both boys were beginning to tire. They'd had a long week of tennis and the mid-summer conditions had been particularly challenging. The third set was fairly evenly poised at 3/2 to Ben when Tim set-up to serve. He faulted his first serve, and his second serve was lucky to land in. Ben placed a short, choppy shot just over the net that Tim raced to return. He barely managed to get to it, scooping underneath it and lobbing it high, so there was very little pace on the ball that luckily landed, as before, just inside the baseline. Once again, Ben put the ball into the net. Tim walked back to the service line, his mind racing furiously. Was this an Achilles heel?

A few points later, Tim got another chance to play a slow-paced lobbed ball on the backline. Again, he won an easy point. Tim began to look for the opportunities to exploit this weakness in Ben's game. It didn't always work, because if he played the slow-paced ball and it wasn't deep enough, Ben pounced on it and put it away. Ben was also strategically more defensive in his game, not allowing Tim to do as he pleased. But as Tim dug in, continually probing his opponent's weakness, he eventually broke serve and went on to win the last game. When the umpire called, "Game, set, and match to Tim Anderson, 4/6, 7/6, 6/4," Tim slumped forward, his hands on his knees, and allowed himself a solitary joyous moment of victory. What a week it had been! He took in several deep breaths as he gathered his scattered wits and met Ben at the net.

Ecstatic, but mindful of the etiquette required, he shook his disappointed opponent's hand and congratulated him on the game, as Mark had drilled him to do. He thanked the umpire and then shook hands and accepted the congratulations of the tournament referee, who was courtside. Then he looked around for his family. Jack was waving wildly at him, standing with his parents who were still clapping as he reached them.

"You little champion!" said Jenny, unaware of the irony of that statement as she reached up to her tall son to give him a kiss and a hug. Mark was also in a hugging mood.

"Well played, mate. I watched the first set and I thought that left hand was going to trouble you. Then I had to leave to watch Jack storm his way through two sets, 6/2 and 6/0, and I was almost too scared to come back. You played so well! We're so proud of you! Did you realise you were on the court for over two hours? Jack's been finished for ages."

Tim shook his head in disbelief and exhaustion suddenly overwhelmed him. "Well done, Jack! Only gave away two games! That's pretty fantastic," he gasped, greedily gulping down more water.

"I think I was lucky. My guy was having an off day, but that Ben Tate guy, he was awesome. But not as awesome as you." Jack put Tim in a brotherly headlock that Mark moved quickly to disengage.

"Okay, cut that out. You two need to look after each other. You have the doubles final this afternoon, and presentations look like they're starting now. Have another drink, Tim, and tidy yourself up a bit. I want to take a photo when you get your trophies," said Jenny with authority. Taking over, she produced the camera from her bag, and shooed them both together so she could take a photo. In the end, Mark took the photos because Jenny was too busy crying happy tears to capture the moment.

There wasn't much time at all before they were called to play their doubles match. Tim was really beginning to feel both the effects of his recent match, and the week of tough, unfamiliar, and stressful tennis. Neither of them was exactly match-fit. However, Jack's relatively quick match was a bonus for their doubles team. He had energy enough for two and he had been looking forward to this doubles match as much as, if not more than, his own singles. Again, they faced a three-set match.

Compared to their opponents, who were fresh and hadn't played in a singles event just an hour before, the odds were against them. However, despite Tim's weariness, they went into the match relaxed and happy. On a high from their respective wins, they couldn't help but feel that anything was possible.

Their cockiness was short-lived though, as they lost the first set, both struggling to refocus after the adrenaline rush of their recent wins.

At 3/4 down in the second set, and with their games just ordinary at best, Jack stopped Tim in between points, as he moved to the net. "C'mon, mate, stuff this! Time to use our brains. Let's play our game. Remember?"

Tim nodded. They were better individual players than the team they faced; however, their opponents were certainly the better team at the moment. Once again, they painstakingly worked their way back into play. Hitting exclusively against each other for so long had given the brothers an inside edge, and finally they made good use of it. Anticipating each other's shots and moving to backup or close out a point saw them take the second set, and the third. It was a complete turnaround and a polished performance. Few spectators would believe that they had only played their first doubles match five days earlier.

Jack and Tim were on a high as they walked back to the car. As they got there, Mark quietly passed the keys to Jenny and sank gratefully into the front passenger seat. Tim looked closer at his dad. Exhaustion lined his face. Tim caught Jack's eye, and imperceptibly flicked his head towards his father. Jack nodded silently. It was a reminder of just how fragile their father's health still was. As Jenny pulled out of the carpark and turned onto the highway leading home, the boys were considerate and unusually quiet, reflecting on their wins and giving Mark some peace and recovery time. What a week it had been! Jack gave Tim's arm a gentle push to get his attention. He grinned and held up the trophy he had won. A silver figure of a tennis player, atop a timber stand: the date and "Mornington Junior Classic Under 16 Age Group Champion" engraved on it. It was identical to Tim's, except for his Under 18 engraving. Suddenly

Mark turned around from the front seat. Slapping their knees like a drum roll, he made them jump as he yelled in triumph, "First step accomplished! We're right on target!"

CHAPTER 11

"Spot on, Tim!" called Jack.

Tim prepared for a forehand top spin again as Jack returned the ball, landing it just inside the line. They were finishing off a late practise session on their own with a drill that involved hitting back and forth but only using the width of the tram lines on the court. They played for "Bits" and, so far, Tim was four Bits up overall. Despite the coolness of the evening, both boys were sweating and tiring fast. At 5.35 pm Tim called time. He had study to get started, and he wanted a shower before dinner.

They were training on their own tonight, which was rare. Mark was in the city for a couple of days for work and it was Tuesday night staff meeting for Mr Mac. Even Karen had not trained because she was busy with schoolwork, and Tim was feeling guilty himself for not hitting the books yet. Year 12 had been constant, and the exams were only a few weeks away.

So far Tim had coped better than he had expected, and he knew, if he could keep it up, he was on his way to get a far higher result than he'd ever anticipated. He felt that this was the first year that things had begun to gel for him. Not ever having put in much effort before, he had thought he was only capable of average results. But this year by working hard, studying, and following up with questions to his teachers, he had achieved some very creditable results.

It helped that his mates Nick and Tony had a good work ethic and weren't turning up at odd hours to distract him like his mates in the city did. And he'd been very easy to distract, he had to admit. Tennis had kept him busy as well as motivated. It gave him a physical outlet after a day in class, but it also allowed for a social life as he trained with Karen and some of the other kids in Mr Mac's squad. Jack had also thrived at Winjarra High and topped most of his classes. Although he'd always been strong academically, there had inevitably been someone smarter in his big high school in Melbourne. For the first time, everyone looked up to him as the smart kid. Moving up to Winjarra had worked out pretty well all around.

Mr Mac had brought a whole new dimension to their game. He was an excellent player still, often playing himself in open tournaments, so he had a great deal to offer them as a coach. Not only that, but after Easter he formed a mixed tennis team consisting of himself, Tim, Jack, and Karen, Mrs Mac, who was also a strong player, and Ms Tonkin, another lady teacher from school who had been a strong junior in her day. They had played a hardcourt A Grade winter competition in Bendigo every Saturday afternoon, taking out the finals as undefeated champions.

It was a strong competition and they played four sets each for the afternoon, consisting of two doubles, another mixed doubles, and one singles. Tim and Jack played together, but more importantly they got to play with Mr Mac, who taught them both a great deal about how to play doubles. Tim usually played the mixed with Karen, and Jack played with Ms Tonkin, who was also his English teacher.

Initially Jack found this slightly awkward but Ms Tonkin was way cooler out of school than in class. Mr Mac taught them not just to divide the court in half but how to move smoothly together, covering the court and backing each other up. He gave them the skills they needed to risk both of them being simultaneously at the net: how to communicate on court, to be patient, to wait for the right ball, and when to hit your winner.

"Matches are won the same way in doubles as in singles: good shot selection, percentage tennis, and exploring your opponents' weakness." By the end of the season, Jack and Tim could say it backwards. Saturday was fun even if Karen was the only other teenager in the team. They certainly played against lots of other teams just like theirs—a mix of ages—so they still made lots of friends and had a chance to hang out with kids their own age, even if they were their opponents.

Most Saturday nights they would meet at someone's place, which made up for the lack of entertainment available. There was no bowling rink, cinema or disco in town, and they were mostly too young to be able meet at the pub. However, there were plenty of parents who allowed low-key gatherings, and somehow there was always somewhere to go

What Tim did wish for was the spare time Jack seemed to have, compared to him. Tim's life was a fine balance between friends, fitting in tennis, and keeping up with a constant stream of study, assignments, and exams. It wasn't just an old saying that that the year was speeding by. It really was. No sooner had he gotten used to frosty mornings replacing the hot, dry weather when spring arrived, with the promise of another warm summer.

Walking home together in companionable silence, Tim contemplated what he would need to study for that evening. Jenny was sitting happily at the kitchen table with a glass of wine and some schoolwork she was busy marking. As they came in the door she looked up, saying, "Glad you guys are back. Dinner's not too far away."

"Great. I need a quick shower and then I have to study because I've got a topic test on maths tomorrow," said Tim, already pulling off his shirt as he headed to the bathroom.

In the shower, Tim let the hot water run down his back and soothe his muscles. He actually had muscles now, after Mark had added a circuit weight training session to their routine, developing their strength and flexibility and quick, explosive moves. He and Jack had never been this fit, even after a season of gruelling footy training. He did miss footy slightly, and he often found himself envious of his mates' camaraderie after a Saturday that he had spent playing tennis, while his mates had their footy match to talk about. He didn't miss the injuries though, and he knew that he wouldn't give up tennis for anything. No matter how hard they practised, they still had so much more to improve on.

He enjoyed the squad training sessions with Mr Mac and Dad. Even Pa was part of the coaching team! He didn't come every afternoon because the farm kept him busy, but it seemed all the squad lifted a bit more when they saw him arrive.

Pa had a few words of wisdom he liked to impart to anyone who would listen. "The game isn't over till it's over," or, "It's not losing that's a crime, but low aim."

Pa was surprisingly perceptive, and he seemed to know just when one of the squad needed some praise to lift them, or some sage advice to help out their game. He didn't give praise easily, but he unerringly knew just when it was needed, which was almost more important. He helped Tim and Jack believe in themselves, understanding their self-doubts, and anticipating when a quiet word of support was required. Mr Mac and Dad were more focused on their technique and fitness, so they didn't always see that the boys' confidence and morale needed nurturing as well.

Jack didn't suffer from self-doubt as much as Tim did. He was born optimistic and was prepared to look for the positives, not the problems. Tim lacked Jack's natural confidence and had a much more introverted personality. Jack had always been drawn to people, and he was a risk taker even as a kid. The toddler Jack would wander off from their parents, happily smiling and engaging with strangers, whereas Tim had always stayed close by his parents' sides, safely watching from a distance. Their dispositions reflected in their tennis.

Tim was typically more cautious, relying on steady, consistent play, going for the percentage shots. Jack, while steady, was more prepared to take risks and go for his shots. Tim would stew over a loss, critical of himself and revisiting his errors, trying to learn from his mistakes. Jack hated losing as well, but he didn't stew over it endlessly like Tim. He would quickly work out what went wrong and what he should have done, and resolve to be better next time. Then he moved on.

They had played in a few tournaments after their first foray into competition at Mornington. Most of the time they reached the semi-finals or finals in age-group tournaments, and they had moderate success in open competitions. With Mr Mac's help they were learning which tournaments would be the most advantageous for them to enter. There were lots to choose from, but only certain age-group events offered points that would go towards their ranking in the state.

Likewise, for the open events, they entered some just for the experience, but others offered ranking points that would allow them to enter satellite tournaments later on. There was no shortage of young guys just like themselves, chasing dreams of tennis greatness and needing those points to move up the ranks. The competition was fierce enough in the age groupings, but the open rankings were full of seasoned players who had more than one trick up their sleeves.

Tim had discovered this the hard way at a tournament he'd played in Geelong over the Easter weekend, several months earlier. His opponent, Jon Talbot, was twenty-two, and running out of time to make his mark in the tennis world. The Geelong District Easter Championship was quite a prestigious event, attracting many of the top-ranked players across the state. It had significant prize money of $5000 for the open men's singles. Tim had won all his matches and made the cut-off for the quarterfinals.

Jon had been a highly ranked junior who had let his chances slip. He was inclined to be a bad-tempered loser and he had even been suspended for several weeks after a display of bad sportsmanship—reported to have been throwing his racquet at the umpire's chair. Luckily for him he threw it after the umpire had already left the court, or the penalty would have been much more severe. With that penalty hanging over his head, Jon knew he needed a win. He was experienced and canny and he summed up Tim's inexperience in a flash. As they met at the net for the toss he remarked casually, "Oh. You've got one of those Prince Arrows they brought out last year. I thought they took them off the market? It doesn't bother your serve?"

Not waiting for Tim's answer, and having won the toss electing to serve, he walked straight back to the baseline and stood there impatiently bouncing the ball, ready to start the hit-up. Tim was reluctant to say anything, but the umpire seemed busy writing things on the scorecard, so he realised it was up to him to stand his ground and tell Jon he was at the wrong end.

"Hey, mate, no worries. I don't mind. But are you sure you want this end?" he quizzed.

Switching ends, Tim tried to let it go and concentrate on his hit-up. But Jon didn't follow the etiquette of the pre-game warm-up. When Jon took his place at the net Tim affably fed him some volleys to put away. But when Tim took his place at the net, Jon ignored him and began serving balls down to the forehand court. Even when the umpire called time, Jon managed to fit in a couple of extra serves. Tim hadn't had the warm-up he expected, and it left him feeling cheated and unsettled.

Already unnerved, Tim found it increasingly difficult to concentrate when Jon kept making unnecessary chummy remarks after points Tim lost. He also questioned the umpire on any close point, knowing just how far he could push him. In just over an hour, he succeeded brilliantly in totally upsetting Tim's game, defeating him 6/2, 6/1. Tim was furious with himself for being so naïve and so easily manipulated. The sour taste of defeat stayed with him for some time, and it took a long talk with Pa before he really came to terms with the fact that not all games are won with a tennis racquet. It was a lesson he learned well, and he was never conned so easily again.

Reflecting on the year as he stepped out of the shower, Tim knew that he and Jack had been more than successful. They had earned respectable ranking points, and they often received invitations from various club officials asking them to play in their upcoming tournaments. Tim and Jack Anderson were no longer seen as newcomers and they had an enviable reputation as seriously good competitors, particularly in men's doubles. Jenny's voice calling from the kitchen switched Tim out of his musings and back to reality. Maths! He needed to study. The lasagne Jenny had made smelled delicious. Perfect study and tennis fuel, he thought.

Jack was already at the table, eating as if it were his last meal. With a mouthful of food, he gestured to a large yellow envelope on the table, and said, "Look what arrived today for us. What do you think? Will we be able to play?"

As Tim ate, he skimmed through the contents of the envelope. It was an information package, and an invitation to play in the first Victorian satellite tournament of the season, on November 19, two days after his last exam. He had biology on November 17. Winking at Jack, he said, "I'll be finished at 11.30 am on the seventeenth. So it looks like we're a goer. What about you though?"

"Mr Mac said I can get special permission for something like a satellite tournament. It's like a national level competition. I just need Mum and Dad to sign a form."

"Oh, your father would never agree to something like that," said Jenny, trying to look stern but laughing anyway. "Dad will be so excited about this. It's such an opportunity for you both, I can't believe it myself. Let me read what it says."

Jenny began to look a little concerned as she perused it. "But, Jack. This will take you out of school for the week, maybe more. How will you fit in your last exams and assignments? This is fantastic but schoolwork should still be a priority."

"I might have to work out if I can sit exams early or something. But honestly, I think I've done so well this year that they are certainly not going to fail me. I might miss some of the stuff they do though to prepare us for Year 11, but probably not. And it only gets to be a problem if we keep winning anyway. If we bomb out in the first satellite, we won't get asked to do the next one," shrugged Jack pragmatically.

"Hmm. All true," reflected Jenny. Then, looking up from the paperwork to her sons, she asked them, "Hasn't this been an amazing year? I'm so glad we did this, and I know your dad has loved it. But what about you guys? Has it been good for you?"

In between mouthfuls, Tim grunted what sounded like a "Yes," while Jack nodded enthusiastically, neither prepared to stop devouring the tasty lasagne. Jenny allowed herself a smile of satisfaction.

"You have both been just wonderful, you know. I'm so proud of how hard you've worked at school this year, Tim. Your attitude has been such a turnaround. And you, Jack! You've been fantastic too. The move hasn't held either of you back. But you know, the part I love best is how you've been happy to hang with Dad, not just with tennis, but ... everything." She shook her head and got a bit teary as she stood up and gave each of them a big hug in turn.

"When I think how close we came to losing Dad, it scares me. It will be sad in so many ways to be heading back to Melbourne next year, but Brian has handled the Melbourne work on his own for long enough. Mark needs to get back and pull his weight. And the council offices are really quite stunning, aren't they?" Jenny continued, dabbing at her eyes. "And everyone loves what he did so that will help with more work eventually for the business. I know your dad is very proud of them, and the sports centre as well, which is coming along beautifully. With any luck that will all be finished by the time we have to be back in Melbourne in January."

Tim finally swallowed the last of his lasagne and was ready to agree with Jenny. "It's been a huge year, and yes, Mum, it has been fun all of us here together. I'm glad we came. I don't reckon I've missed much in Melbourne at all. And," he picked up the letter from Tennis Australia, shaking it for emphasis, "here I am in the top ten in the state, and Jack is as well for his age group. And we're even higher ranked in doubles!"

"Yeah, I'm with you, Tim. I've got some great mates here, and everyone in Melbourne is just doing the same old stuff. It'll be good to get back, but there's lots I'll miss here as well," said Jack, helping himself to more lasagne. "And I think your cooking has improved, Mum. This is yum."

"Well, I haven't had much choice in the matter, have I?" replied Jenny, laughing. "There are no takeaway options here, and that's something I definitely won't miss when we go back."

"And Dad loves that he can walk to the pub, and that everyone wants to talk to him about the new council buildings. Between that and our tennis he's in his element. He'll hate going back to those fussy home builders he usually has to deal with, won't he?" asked Jack.

"Well, he's done such a great job on these two projects that the firm has been getting lots of interest in their commercial designs. Fingers crossed it all leads to more big projects. So, yes," Jenny smiled, "it has been a good year."

Much later that night as Tim was getting ready for bed, he re-read through the accompanying details for the entry forms. He knew that he and Jack had to play the qualifying rounds first before they would play in the main draw. This was also an internationally ranked tournament and the best players from Australia would be there, as well as some international players. This was the only way the lower-ranked players could break into the professional events, and the ranking points offered were almost as valuable as the prize money.

It was a long shot to even have a go at getting into the satellite tournament, but Tim had been hoping the offer would come. At the last competition he and Jack had played, in

September, they had met Fred Elkes, who coordinated the satellite circuit in Australia. He had come up to them after they had won the men's doubles and introduced himself. He said he'd been watching their results for a while and was impressed with how they played. Neither Jack nor Tim had even noticed him among the few spectators, but Mr Mac came up to them while they were all talking together, and it was obvious the men knew each other well.

"I've been having a nice chat with your boys, Paul. I agree with you. They do play a great game and they combine very well. Most impressive."

"I'm glad you had a chance to see them, Fred. Have you met Tim and Jack's dad, Mark?" said Mr Mac, making the introductions. Jack and Tim were awestruck. Fred Elkes had been a noted Davis Cup player in his day, so they knew they were in the presence of someone who really knew his stuff, and they hung on every word.

"I think you boys should give yourselves a shot at the satellite tournaments over the summer. It would give you enormous experience to play at that level, and you know I don't think either of you are that far off the level required."

Looking back at Mr Mac he continued, "You know they need a bit more variety in their serves, and I'd like to see more strength in their backhand volleys, but they hit a very consistent ball, and they move exceptionally well around the court for rookies. There's a lot that I like about these two."

Mr Mac and Fred went on to discuss a few issues in general, which were not really relevant to Tim and Jack, but they listened politely anyway. Before he was called away, Fred said, "Leave your address at the tournament office for me, and I'll send you an invitation to enter the first satellite qualifying tournament in Melbourne. It's at Flinders Park, the new tennis centre. And well done on your win today."

Tim smiled, remembering the excitement in the car driving home as he and Jack talked about the possibility of playing in such a prestigious competition. From then on, they had stepped up their practise even more. Mr Mac had also spent hours changing their serving style and forcing them out of their comfort zones so that they learned more ways to attack as well as defend. During some of these training sessions they had felt totally confused, but as they worked at the new strokes, after a while, what had felt so strange eventually became muscle memory and added more depth to their games.

Tim also wondered, as he settled in his bed, if Karen had received an offer as well. He hoped she had. Karen had been such a part of all their training and competition, it would feel strange competing without her. He was fairly certain she was due to finish exams earlier than him, so study wouldn't be a problem. Maybe they could actually go out somewhere on their own instead of always being in a group. Although they spent so much time together, they were still just good mates.

Tim really liked Karen, and he wanted to be more than just good friends. If they were both in Melbourne for the tournament and were knocked out, then the consolation prize just might be some time together when they didn't have to rush off to study or face each other on the opposite side of a tennis net. Tim also knew that it was well and truly time to find out if Karen actually fancied him, before someone else snapped her up. The thought terrified him.

CHAPTER 12

"Time! Pencils down, please."

A groan and a collective sigh went up at these words. One by one, pens clicked down against the hard plastic desktops, and seats scraped on the timber floor of the high school hall as students slumped back in their seats. A lone whoop went up, which caused a few laughs. Any further writing was futile. If it wasn't down on paper now, it was too late.

"Close your exam booklets, please. Check that you have your correct number on the front, and place them here in a pile as you leave." The supervisor stifled a yawn. The students weren't the only ones relieved that the ordeal of the last three hours was over. Tim sat for a few seconds longer, taking in the significance of the moment. He had just finished thirteen years of school, and his final Year 12 exam! Shuffling slowly to the front of the room, he placed his biology paper almost reverently on the pile with the others. He couldn't quite feel anything yet. Was it all really over?

Immediately behind him, Tony grabbed Tim by his shoulders and, reading his exact thoughts, said very slowly, emphasising every word, "It's over! It's finally over!" Outside they filed into the courtyard, and the noise grew. The girls were hugging each other and squealing, and everyone was talking at once. A few teachers poked their heads out of their rooms to see what the disturbance was, but wisely just pulled their doors closed.

Despite looking forward to this moment when the last exam was over, the Year 12s were suddenly at a loose end. They milled around talking for a while until, eventually, in pairs or groups they drifted away. It was a gorgeous, sunny afternoon, and the now ex-students had it to themselves, to do whatever they wanted with it. For some that would be just going home and chilling, others would meet up at the pool or the waterhole, and some would aimlessly wander the streets together.

Tim and Karen were due to meet at the courts at 4 pm after Jack got home from school for a low-key practise session. Karen had received her invite for the tournament at the same time as Tim and Jack. She had also managed to juggle study and tennis by sacrificing her social life. It had been a huge commitment by all three. They were leaving for Melbourne the next day in preparation for the satellite qualifier on Saturday. The hard work had already been done, so this session was just aimed at hitting confidently and talking through a few things.

Mr Mac had already warned them and spoken in depth about handling the increased pressure. "There will be plenty of age-group players, just like you, competing. They will all have impressive achievements, and they'll want to win, just like the three of you. Quite a few will crumble under the pressure. Don't forget that. There will also be players trying to use this to break into the professional ranks. Time is running out for some of them, so they'll be very focused on winning, and they are used to this intensity. They face it every time they get on a court. You need to get used to the pressure and make it work for you."

In their lead-up training sessions, he had taught them several mental strategies to keep their nerves under control, including breathing techniques, and visualising before the game how calm they were going to be. Probably the advice that resonated most with Tim was to believe in himself and trust his shot making.

"You've played these shots over and over. Your body knows what to do. Just let muscle memory take over, and relax." These were Mr Mac's final words as they finished up that evening. "And one more thing. Don't be out too late tonight or have more than one or two drinks," he added, eyeballing Tim and Karen. "I know everyone will be celebrating but you guys have worked too hard to blow this chance by being hungover and tired tomorrow."

The Year 12s had a party planned at Snake Gully, a picnic and camping spot just on the outskirts of town that was relatively easy for everyone to get to. Its bonus was that they could stay all night and camp, but it also wasn't unrealistic to drive back into town if need be. And, at this time of the year, it was somewhere they could all let their hair down without bothering anyone else. Karen had planned to stay in town at her friend Susie's. Tony was going to pick up Tim and Nick and the girls and drive them out to the party. Tony and Nick had stuff to camp the night, but the girls and Tim were planning to head home by midnight, which was boring but necessary.

The party was just getting started when they arrived at six-thirty. There had been several early starters who had arrived there late afternoon, so the music was blaring already. A couple of barbeques were going and there was an unending supply of sausages, hamburgers, and buns. Tim was happy to do barbeque duty because he had to limit himself to a couple of beers anyway. Karen soon joined him, and they made a good team as they served up a constant stream of food.

"Check out those dance moves," laughed Karen as she pointed out some of the boys' more enthusiastic efforts. "I definitely think Tom Rogers should stick with his plans of being an engineer because joining a dance group is not going to happen!"

"He's in need of some practise, that's for sure, before he lets himself loose on any discos or clubs in Melbourne next year," agreed Tim, laughing. "But I probably need some dance practise too. C'mon, dance with me." Tim put down his barbeque tongs and started moving to the beat. Karen needed no second invitation and joined him, and they danced together as they continued to turn sausages and flip hamburgers. At one stage Tim grabbed Karen's hand and they had a go at a jive, but when Karen went twirling too close to the hot barbeque plate, Tim had to pull her close into him for safety. Laughing, she collapsed into his arms as she got back her breath.

When Karen moved to draw away, Tim pulled her back in close. Karen's first instinct was to pull away, but as she laughingly looked up at Tim, she noticed a new look in his eye. Tim's heart skipped a beat. He began to move closer to her, his lips almost touching hers, when he was suddenly interrupted by a group of Karen's friends demanding sausages.

"C'mon, youse two. Don't you see each other enough on the tennis court?" slurred Karen's friend Anna. "This is no time for kissing, there's food to be served," she said, and stumbled slightly as she gestured around them.

"No tennis and no kissing! That's the rules!" agreed Nick as he came up behind them. "Just because you've been wasting time all year hitting tennis balls instead of making out doesn't mean you can do it now. Put down those tongs and come out here and dance!" Nick grabbed Karen and Tim and swept them away into the melee of dancers. Tim had barely a second to register his disappointment at being thwarted—just when he had finally built up the courage to kiss Karen—when his mates swamped him and kept him dancing until everyone was exhausted. He and Karen met several times in the middle of the ever-evolving dance group, but there was no moment for conversation and anyway, the thumping, loud music well and truly drowned out any chance to speak.

Eventually groups of kids not intending to sleep the night began heading back into town. Tim hitched a ride back in with a mate from his maths class, and Karen and Susie went home with Susie's mum who had volunteered to pick her up at eleven-thirty if she hadn't heard from her by then. Tim crept back into the house, trying not to wake anyone, at around midnight.

Just as he closed the back door, his mum called out from her bedroom, "Is that you, Tim? I'm so glad you're home safe. Was it fun?"

"Yes, it was awesome. Night, Mum."

"See you in the morning. You can sleep in a bit tomorrow."

A sleep in! Tim wasn't sure if he knew how to sleep in anymore. He fell into bed, exhausted by an emotionally draining day. It was almost too much to take in. He pushed any nagging thoughts of the last exam out of his head. There was nothing he could do about it now. He felt light and free, knowing there was no more study or school, and a whole summer stretched ahead. Then there was that moment with Karen. He was sure she was ready to kiss him. Maybe she didn't just see him as a mate or a tennis partner after all. And then he contemplated the tournament, and these thoughts chased each other around his head until he fell into a deep sleep.

By the time he woke the next morning his mum had already left for school, and Jack and Dad were packing the car.

"Hey, sleepy! I was just about to wake you. Mum's made you some pancakes and you've got about forty minutes before Pa gets here and we leave."

Tim shook his head in disbelief that he had slept so long and headed to the shower. Later, as he looked for his promised breakfast, he found a note from Mum on top of his pancakes. It read: *Good luck for this weekend and if all goes well, I'll come and watch you in the finals next weekend. Xxx*

On cue, Pa arrived at ten, and they set off for Melbourne. Karen and her mum were driving down themselves later in the day. Mr Mac would leave for Melbourne after school was finished but stay just until Monday when he had to go back. Pa and Dad were to be the backup coaches for all three of them. Mark had invited Karen and Clare to stay with them at the Melbourne house, but Mr Mac was staying with a friend.

There was plenty of room if Jack bunked in with Tim, and Pa could have Jack's room. Karen and Clare were in the spare room. It was an arrangement they had done before on their odd competitions in Melbourne, so everyone was comfortable with how it worked. They were missing Jenny this time, who was usually in charge of food and logistics. But she had to stay in Winjarra to work, so they would have to manage themselves. Another consideration was the uncertainty of playing at this level. They could all be finished by Sunday night and on their way back to Winjarra unless they managed a few wins.

Tim and Jack had the afternoon to themselves. Mr Mac had said no tennis, but he did have a gentle fitness and stretching workout for them to do. Jack managed to meet up with some mates after school, and Tim did the same, catching a couple of friends who were not working yet at holiday jobs. They had instructions to be home for an energy-replenishing pasta dinner, which Clare provided.

The adults sat long over dinner, drinking wine and discussing things while Tim, Jack, and Karen watched a movie and tried to relax. They couldn't help but feel a bit nervous about the weekend ahead. Tim was very much aware of Karen next to him on the couch. At one point her fingers found his and curled into his hand, letting them rest there for a while before giving it a squeeze and letting it go. Jack didn't notice anything.

The next day they left for Flinders Park Tennis Centre in two separate cars. The new centre was spectacular, and the facilities for players and spectators were world standard. Their excitement was palpable as they met up in the tournament office to check out the draw. Doubles were not on until Monday, which suited them as they had singles to worry about first.

Scanning the draw quickly, Jack grabbed Tim's arm and hissed, "We're on separate sides!"

This was always the first thing they looked for when they were playing in an open format. They hated having to play against each other unnecessarily and if they were on separate halves of the draw they wouldn't meet until the final, if at all. Tim's match was first, and he found he was more fired up than nervous as he took the court. He took in some deep breaths, repeating his dad's last words to himself like a mantra. "Be calm. Be patient. Percentage shots. Play your own game."

Tim was so focused on every point he hardly knew the score. At one stage he noticed Jack and Mark get up to leave, and he realised fleetingly that Jack's match must have been called.

He did a silent whoop to himself when the umpire called out, "Game, set, and match to Anderson, 6/1, 6/3."

Tim had won and was on his way to the next round.

As he shook hands, Tim felt his opponent's disappointment. Relief that it wasn't him feeling disappointed flooded through Tim. This was a knockout format, and the best of three sets, so there were no second chances. The standard was as high as they expected, but they were well prepared. By the end of the weekend, all three of them had won through to the qualifying draw. They were eligible to play in the main event.

Late on Sunday afternoon, as Tim and Jack waited to see the draw for the next day's competition be posted, Fred Elkes came over to congratulate them. Rubbing his hands together he said, "A wonderful effort, Tim. Great work, Jack. It's no small thing to be accepted into a satellite tournament, you know. You're already winners. And I can't wait to see how you go in the doubles as well. This is such a wonderful opportunity, so make the most of it and enjoy whatever happens. You can't buy the benefit this experience will bring to your games."

His enthusiasm was catching, and Tim and Jack grinned broadly. They listened carefully as he went on to describe some of what they could expect to happen over the week if they managed to continue winning. In his day, Fred told them, he would have had to go overseas to get the sort of experience they would get this week. There had been nothing available for aspiring players in Australia, outside of state championships and the Australian Open.

It wasn't until 1983 that Australia finally had their own series of satellite tournaments, and while young Australians still went overseas chasing experience and ranking points, they could now at least get their feet wet before they went. And it strengthened the Australian competition, as players came from all around the world to play in the Australian tournaments in the lead up to the Australian Open. Importantly, for once, the Australian players had the home-ground advantage.

This was nothing new to Tim and Jack, but it did reinforce how lucky they were to get this chance. Now circuit points were within their reach, dangling enticingly before them. Circuit points converted to ATP points, the Holy Grail for aspiring young players. With so much at stake they knew very well that they would have to perform above their best. Tim had noted that he wasn't in the youngest cohort playing. Even Jack looked older than some of the other competitors. This was confirmed when Fred began discussing some of the extra coaching options they could apply for next year. There was specialised coaching for talented juniors but Tim, who was almost nineteen, was already too old.

Tim was quiet on the way home. He had known the truth of this already, but hearing it from Fred, and seeing for himself just how many talented kids his own age were out there, was confronting. This tournament was more than a great opportunity, it could very well be one of a dwindling supply of opportunities for him. He loved the buzz of winning and he knew he was improving all the time. It would be so cruel if this all came to an abrupt end just because he had started too late.

Jack had another year or so to reap the benefits of being a promising junior. But Tim was a late developer, and he knew if he didn't keep winning, he might forfeit his slim chances of becoming a professional. And he knew this was what he wanted. His resolve increased as they trawled through the peak-hour traffic home. He knew his parents expected him to go to uni, but what he wanted was to play professional tennis. It was a dilemma that bubbled away in his mind.

Karen was in great spirits that evening because she hadn't dared to get her hopes up. Animated and buzzing with excitement, she chatted happily about everything that had happened so far. The women's draw was always tough and, unlike the men, the women tended to be older, stronger, and more experienced. Her achievement was significant, and she was pumped for the next day.

Jack was also over the moon with anticipation. If either of them were aware of Tim's subdued mood, they didn't mention it. Mr Mac dropped in to give them a brief pep talk before he left for Winjarra. He made them promise to ring through with the results as soon as they could.

His parting words to them all were, "I wouldn't have let you enter this comp if I didn't think you could win. Your games are as good as anyone playing here. Don't let their experience scare you. In the end it comes down to who wins most of the points, so just do that. Win as many points as you can, and you'll do well."

The tournament sheet for the men's first-round matches showed 128 names. This comprised players like Tim and Jack, who had gone through the qualifying rounds, and players who had earned the right, by virtue of their ranking points, to play. There was a similar draw for the women, and Karen. Points were only awarded if you made it through to the third round. Matches were to be the best of three sets. Tim drew a player from the US for his first round, and Jack drew a Kiwi. Jack's match was first up at 9.30 am.

The Rebound Ace court was as familiar to them as a home court could be after their year of training sessions in Winjarra. This was almost like a home-ground advantage, and Jack moved smoothly across the surface. He lost a serve in the first set with an uncharacteristic moment of nerves. Jack's opponent was good and pressured Jack, trying to make the most of his lead, but Jack steadied and won the first set at 7/5 in a tie breaker. When Tim left to start his first match, Jack was playing solid shots and making the most of his chances.

Tim met his opponent at the net, feeling confident and calm. He stole a quick look over at Pa, who was his support person for this match, with Mark keeping an eye on Jack. Pa gave a thumbs up and nodded, a quiet gesture that said, "You've got this." Tim won the toss and began to serve. For the next seventy-three minutes he concentrated on playing steady, high-percentage tennis. Keeping the ball deep, he gave nothing away easily. It wasn't a performance to set the world on fire, but it was the kind of tennis that wins matches. Tim's strong point was his consistency. He had a great eye, and he rarely misjudged the way a ball would bounce. With good coordination and reflexes, he could quickly adjust to variable shots, and still make the return. Patient and prepared to rally, he had the composure to wait for his chance to play a winning shot.

Jack undoubtedly had more flair than Tim. From the first day they picked up the old wooden racquets from Nanna, Jack could produce a shot out of nothing. Tim had dominated Jack for a while with his strength, but as Jack had grown in height and muscle, so did his game. While Tim had enormous reserves of determination and a killer instinct, Jack really did have the flashes of brilliance that make up a true champion. Tim's strength of mind and consistent play, combined with Jack's ability to produce the unpredictable brilliant shot, was what made them such a formidable doubles pair.

That week they both played some of the best tennis of their short careers. Mark was ecstatic every evening as they made the trip home. He and Pa talked about every detail of the games they had watched, savouring each and every victorious point like a good wine. Not that Tim and Jack minded. They were also fired up by their wins and discovering so much about this level of competition. Karen had some success as well, but she only made it through the third round before losing in the fourth to a first-class player from Sweden. She did manage to win her share of games though, so she wasn't too disappointed with her efforts.

When Tim and Jack made it to the third round, they began to attract attention. As they finished their doubles match that afternoon, they were stopped by representatives from two rival clothing brands, who gave them a couple of tennis shirts and shorts for free. Jack, who was confused about whether or not he was supposed to pay for them, was about to say no, when Pa stepped in and thanked the reps. After chatting with them for a while, Pa even managed to get some socks for free, which totally embarrassed Jack.

"It's okay, Jack," said Mark, reassuring him. "These guys want you to be seen in their gear because you are playing so well. It's a compliment to you, and it's free advertising for them. If you guys win, and someone takes a photo and you're wearing their brand, then it's as good as an ad in the paper. It's of mutual benefit, so enjoy it."

"And the best thing about it is that I don't have to wash out the one set of tennis gear every night ready for the next day," added Pa. "I can have a rest tonight!"

Over the next two days, Tim and Jack's run of luck came to an end. Tim played a rangy Queenslander with a big serve and an even bigger backhand. Despite Tim's best efforts, this guy was playing the game of his life and he won in three sets. Jack lost a little quicker the next day in two sets.

"He kept pushing me deep and I couldn't attack the way I wanted to," complained Jack. "Next time, though, I reckon I could work him out."

There wasn't much time to mourn their losses because the men's doubles finals were scheduled for the next day, Saturday. Mr Mac, Jenny, and Nanna had come down to Melbourne to watch, and while this was the biggest crowd they had had to play in front of so far, at least they had several familiar faces cheering for them on the sidelines. Both Tim and Jack were still smarting from the defeats they had suffered in the singles, so they didn't need much motivation to get them pumped up for the doubles final.

The brothers combined beautifully from the first ball and, being an Australian pair against a combined pair from the UK, they had the support of the small crowd as well. Jack said later he didn't even hear the applause because he was concentrating so hard, but Tim could hear it and felt the crowd support definitely helped him. Their prize money for winning was $500 each. More significantly, the twenty-five circuit points they received gave them automatic entry into the next satellite tournament the following week. They were on a roll. It wasn't a bad effort at all, considering they had started out as long shots to even qualify for the event.

CHAPTER 13

The second satellite was held at Wodonga, which was right on the Murray River, on the border between New South Wales and Victoria. At this time of the year, it was much hotter than Winjarra, and by the time they got there after a long drive, they were ready for a swim. Following the tournament in Melbourne, everyone, with the exception of Mark, had returned to Winjarra. Jack was due back at school, and Jenny and Mr Mac had to teach, while Tim planned to give Pa some help on the farm for the week. Karen and Clare had also gone home after the doubles final had been played, but only after they'd had an extra day's shopping in Melbourne.

Practise that week was low-key because they needed to taper after playing so many matches in the lead-up tournament and the main competition. Mr Mac decreed just a few gentle hit-ups, with an emphasis on flexibility training and fitness. Only Nanna and Clare could come with them this time. Mr Mac, Jenny, Mark, and Pa would make the trip on the weekend.

They all stayed together at a motel close to the river. The motel had its own pool, but it was more fun to take the short walk to the river and swim from the pontoon there. Jack, Tim, and Karen made a dash for a swim as soon as they unloaded their gear, while Nanna and Clare rested up with cups of tea. Huge red gums lined both sides of the banks, majestically casting shadows on the sandy bush scrub that lined the river. Thick grass grew further out away from the river's edge, offering a softer option that they could lie on to soak up the last of the day's hot sun.

The water was freezing at first, but they were all so hot they soon dived under and swam out to the pontoon. Jack climbed up onto the pontoon, diving into the water several times, but Tim and Karen were content to float and talk. They hadn't seen much of each other during the week, and since Karen had driven up with Clare, and they had driven up with Nanna, they hadn't had much chance to catch up.

"So, how good was winning the doubles last week?" said Karen, after coming up from a duck dive. "You guys played so well. It was just amazing."

"We did, didn't we?" laughed Tim with absolutely no modesty at all. "I couldn't believe how many of our shots came off. And Jack! He was sensational with some of those winners on the net."

Wiping her eyes and kicking lazily on her back, Karen agreed. "I know we've talked about this with Mr Mac, and he keeps telling us we're good enough, but it really was such a blast to make it into the satellite in Melbourne. And now this one! I didn't do nearly as well as you two, and I'm still thrilled just to be here."

"Yeah. It makes all those afternoons after school worth the effort, doesn't it? And how good is no study? I'm still getting used to the fact I can watch a TV show without feeling guilty," exclaimed Tim, swimming over to the pontoon to hang on for a while.

Karen joined him, saying quietly so Jack couldn't hear, "But I kinda enjoyed all those practise sessions with you."

Tim looked at Karen. Her wet hair clung to her cheeks, and she was smiling at him. Feeling uncharacteristically emboldened, he gently shifted the strands of hair from her face, saying, "So did I," before bending forward to kiss her. Karen responded just the way he had hoped. For once there was no interruption. Jack was busily swimming on the other side of the pontoon, and they kissed several times until, becoming aware of Jack splashing closer, they quickly broke apart. Tim dived under the water, while Karen climbed onto the pontoon before diving back in the water. As Karen surfaced, she called out that she was heading in to lie in the sun. Tim and Jack swam for a little longer, enjoying the novelty of a river swim, and then they all returned to the motel to shower and change. Clare and Nanna had planned an early dinner so everyone could get a good night's sleep, ready for the next day's competition.

At 9 am the next morning, they arrived in convoy at the lawn tennis club, parking in the dusty, crowded car park behind the courts. Typical of the country towns along the Murray River, Wodonga's grass courts were the envy of many a city club. The modest clubhouse, on the other hand, was a reality check after the magnificence of Flinders Park, and on approach, its cream brick construction appeared stark. However, as they rounded the corner and gazed on row after row of immaculately presented lawn courts—thick, green, and cut low—their spirits improved. The courts were in spectacular condition in readiness for the tournament.

"Fantastic," breathed Jack. He couldn't wait to start. For the first three days, Clare and Nanna were their managers, coaches, and cheer squad, reporting faithfully back to Mark, Mr Mac, and Pa. Despite the different venue, they recognised many of the same competitors they had seen in Melbourne, and this time they were not so overawed by the competition.

Fred Elkes was there as well, and they often spotted him on the sidelines watching their matches. Tim and Jack missed having Mark there, but when Pa arrived midweek, that helped make up for it. They checked in by phone with Mr Mac each night and he usually had tips on what to look for in their opponents the next day. Tim was constantly impressed by what Mr Mac knew about the competition they faced. He had clearly done lots of homework on their behalf.

The courts played as good as they looked. Grass was a more unpredictable surface, but all three of them were well used to it after the grass courts in Winjarra and other places they had played. Grass wasn't everyone's favourite surface, and not all the international players liked it very much. Jack especially thrived on it. He loved the greater choice of shots he had, and was totally in his element, whether the ball kicked up suddenly or dropped sharply. Whatever the bounce, he moved swiftly, with a tiger's instinct, to cover it.

This time Tim and Jack were both on the same side of the draw, which meant one would have to knock the other out. They didn't meet until the quarterfinals, and the match was tight. Quite a crowd gathered to watch the two brothers compete against each other. Both boys were in great form, and they fought it out over two and a half hours. It was an absorbing and gruelling battle, and Jack eventually won a tie breaker in the third with a fantastic ball down the line, completely out of Tim's reach. A puff of white dust marked the spot where the ball just caught the line before bouncing away to the right.

It was clearly great entertainment for the crowd who cheered and clapped both boys as they met at the net to shake hands. Despite the closeness of the match, it was played in very good spirits, and while neither gave the other any quarter, they did manage some brotherly banter that kept the crowd amused. Pa, Mr Mac, and Jenny had arrived from Winjarra for the weekend, and Mark had driven up from Melbourne. They made sure there was equal cheering for both boys. Karen made it to the quarter finals before being beaten, and she was elated at going one round further this time.

After several days of playing in such hot weather, Tim was drained. There hadn't been a day under thirty-five degrees that week, and the conditions had certainly taken their toll. Tim and Karen had a chance to rest after being knocked out, but Jack had to play his singles semi-final. Tim was almost relieved it wasn't him lining up for singles again.

The final of the doubles was due to be played on Saturday afternoon, giving Jack a couple of hours' rest, depending on how long his semi-final went for. He somehow managed to produce excellent tennis again on Saturday morning, and won in two sets, giving himself the maximum time to recover before the doubles were to be played. It was always going to be a tricky balance while they continued to enter both competitions.

They were still on a winning streak with their doubles matches, and again they had a loyal band of supporters, with Karen's family also arriving for the weekend, in time to see the match. Jack and Tim started slowly, dropping the first set. They were down 0/3 in the second before Tim won his serve convincingly and the boys found their rhythm. Pairing at the net and hitting deeply into the baseline, they went on the attack and won the set 6/4, only dropping one more game. The final set was more textbook tennis, and they won comfortably in three sets.

Jack needed to draw on all his fitness and stamina when he turned up the next day for the men's final. Again, the weather was stinking hot, which certainly was to Jack's advantage. His opponent, from Sweden, was drained by the relentless heat and humid conditions throughout the week. He played well, but his game was just a fraction off, and Jack made the most of every opportunity. He closed it out in three sets and was totally spent at the end of it.

While the families got together to celebrate, Karen and Tim headed down to the river with Karen's two little sisters. Jack was happy just to lay around the motel pool, flopping in the water when he got too hot. His legs were not going to take him anywhere unnecessarily. Mark kept him company, managing to fall asleep within minutes of spreading out his towel on a deck chair. Jack wondered briefly at his tiredness.

Karen and Tim had fun watching Karen's little sisters, Meg and Charlotte, charge in and out of the river on their boogie boards. Tim had to complete one rescue when Meg, the youngest sister, lost her board after jumping off the pontoon. Otherwise, he and Karen had a rare chance just to spend some time on their own, sitting in the shallows and talking about their plans for the coming year.

Karen was sure she would be at uni studying physiotherapy, but the next year was a great unknown as yet for Tim. His uncle Bill had studied commerce and seemed to enjoy his job working for a large financial planning firm, so he had toyed with that idea. He knew Mark secretly hoped he would be an architect, but he just felt he didn't have the creative streak to do that, while he was more than sure Jack would thrive on the challenge. He really just wanted to play tennis, but he was still reluctant to admit this yet to anyone. Karen was content just getting to play at this level. She held no ambitions for making tennis a career choice.

"I can let you in on a secret," confided Karen. "While we were watching Jack play, Fred Elkes came up to Mr Mac and asked if he'd decided about the offer for next year."

"What offer?" Tim was immediately curious.

"Well, it sounded like he'd offered him some sort of state-level coaching role at the tennis centre in Melbourne. And not that I know exactly everything, because I couldn't hear it all, but it sounds like Mr Mac is going to do it."

"Which means he'll have to move to Melbourne," said Tim triumphantly.

Karen nodded. "So, you'll still have Mr Mac to coach you, as well as your dad. Your tennis is pretty much all sorted for another year at least."

"Whoa!" said Tim, hugging Karen with the sheer joy of new possibilities. Maybe he didn't have to choose between uni and tennis at all just yet.

"Hey! I'm telling Mum you were hugging Tim!" called out Meg.

"We don't care," yelled back Tim before kissing Karen. Meg and Charlotte squealed with delight and shock until Karen broke away, breathless and laughing.

The third tournament was two days later in Ballarat. It was closer to Winjarra than Wodonga, but all the same it was a two-hour drive each way to get there. Again, they opted to stay at a motel nearby. This was the last week of school, so Mum and Mr Mac were unable to be there, Pa was committed to the farm, and Mark had to work for at least a couple of days in Melbourne. He decided to start the week in Ballarat and do the hour commute up and down to the Melbourne office from there.

Nanna and Clare would again be the backup team for the week. Tim and Jack had done very well so far, but Mark already had his eye on a tournament in Sydney in a couple of weeks. The Sydney competition was an invitational championship satellite tournament, gathering together the top twenty-four players at the end of the three satellite tournaments in each state. Jack and Tim had a better than average chance of making the cut-off.

The boys were getting accustomed to the tournament routine, recognising many familiar faces as they played their way through the opening rounds. By now they had earned the respect of many of their competitors, and they enjoyed getting to know them and hearing their stories. They all shared a love of tennis, so it was easy to develop a sense of camaraderie. However, while they made lots of good friends, there were also some players who were insufferable tossers. The same as anywhere, thought Tim philosophically, keeping his distance from the few that stood out as difficult.

Tim was still hoping to make a singles final. Once Jack had been successful, they had both readjusted their own evaluation of where they stood in the pecking order of the competition. Although they had had only a fraction of the experience of these other guys, their games clearly stood up to the test. Ballarat was proving to be a particularly tough competition, however, because there were several additional ranked players arriving from international events, all hoping to pick up a few more points before the limited Australian circuit began in January. This time matches would be played as the best of five sets.

Jack, who was aiming for another final match, had his hopes dashed in the quarterfinal when he came up against Alberto Ipano, a powerful Argentinian. Alberto had been ranked in the top one hundred earlier in the year and after recovering from a knee injury was back playing some strong tennis. Jack didn't handle his wide-swinging serve at all well, but he also didn't play anywhere near his best, and looked hesitant, unlike his usual confident game. It was a disconsolate Jack who walked off the court at the end.

Tim learned from his brother's tentative play and notched up his best win to date. He faced Paul Taylor, who had been ranked as the top Australian junior only a few years ago. Now just twenty-one, Paul was on the international circuit, but had so far failed to live up to the heady promises of his junior days. Despite this, he was known as a tough competitor and expected to win through to the finals. Fully aware he was the underdog, Tim attacked from the very first point, managing to dictate the play, and forcing Paul to chase and run down every ball. Mixing up his shots and playing very smart tennis, Tim had him constantly on the defensive and, despite Paul's superior experience, Tim never gave him a chance to establish any rhythm to his game.

While Paul may not have been in his best form, he was still a very strong player and he faced Tim's aggression with tenacity, never giving away an easy point. When Tim won a long match of lengthy rallies, after forcing several rare errors from Paul, you could hear Jack's and Karen's cheers five courts away. Tim's euphoria was short-lived though. In his next match, he lost in four sets to a lesser-ranked opponent, lacking the concentration that had gotten him through so many tougher matches. This was probably a far more valuable experience for Tim than his creditable win against Paul Taylor. It was a painful lesson, and the sting of a defeat due to his own fault stayed with him for a long time.

The brothers were both beginning to feel the effects of the intense competition of the satellite circuit. With so many players—like themselves, desperate to win—Tim thought the major tournaments surely couldn't be much harder. Playing doubles together continued to be their break from the stress of singles. Together they talked tactics, encouraged, and settled each other down, sharing the load. It suited their temperaments. Both of them were well used to team sports and doubles was simply an extension of that team spirit and purpose. They played better together because they played for each other.

By the time they had finished the satellite competitions, they hadn't lost a doubles match. Jack was ranked third in singles, and Tim in the top ten. They had been given more free tennis gear and, even better, several free racquets to try out and keep. The Prince gear, similar to what they already had, continued to be their favourite, and extra racquets certainly helped validate their image. Every player at this level needed at least two spare racquets in their bag in case they broke a string. They couldn't believe their luck to be given new racquets for free!

Karen had won through a couple of rounds but hadn't made it to the quarterfinals. She had stayed on with her mum until the end of the week to keep Nan company and support the boys. They had been on their own most of the week. Mr Mac couldn't make it over for the finals, but he had rung through and given them a pep talk before both the semi and the final.

Mark had not made it back to Ballarat after the first two days of driving up and back from Melbourne. The original plan was that he would be there as support on the weekend of finals. He had been quite vague when he had rung through to the motel room from Melbourne. He didn't quite say what the issue was, but it sounded like work was too busy and he couldn't get away.

They had missed him courtside, but having Karen, Clare, and Nan cheering them on had helped. Karen was waiting for them outside as they collected their things and left the locker room after their doubles win.

"Another fantastic win. You guys just get better and better!" she said as she hugged them both. "And I've been asked to tell you that your biggest fan, Fred, wants you to call in and see him in the tournament office before you go."

"When are you leaving?" Tim asked Karen, putting his arms around her. "Nan's decided to take us down to Melbourne now, because Dad didn't come back up. So we aren't heading back to Winjarra just yet, and I'm not sure where we'll be for the next few days. We'll have to go to Winjarra at some stage to pack up the house, but I don't know when."

Jack was a few steps ahead, so Tim pulled Karen towards him and kissed her goodbye.

"We don't seem to get much chance to see each other unless it involves tennis," said Karen, smiling ruefully at Tim.

"I can't wait for next year. We'll both be in Melbourne. It's going to be so much fun. And maybe we can finally do stuff together," replied Tim before kissing her again.

"But first we have to get our results," reminded Karen, breaking away as she saw her mum's car back out and head towards them. "You have to ring me when you get your results. No matter what they are," she instructed firmly as she waved goodbye and ran back to the car.

Oh, jeez! thought Tim as Clare drove off with a toot and a crunch of tyres on the gravel. Exam results! Now tennis was over for a bit there was no avoiding it. The exam results were due in the next couple of days. Tim felt slightly apprehensive as he thought of them.

"Well, it's good to see you and Kaz are finally on kissing terms," said Jack, as Tim gazed vaguely into the distance.

Tim came back to reality. "What?"

"I think everyone could see, with the way you were constantly mooning after her, that you were clearly infatuated."

Tim gave Jack a brotherly shove.

"I'll admit I like her. Everyone likes Karen. But I wasn't 'mooning' after her. That's ridiculous." A pause. "Was I that obvious?"

Jack nodded sagely. "Yep."

Further discussion was halted as Fred Elkes came around the corner of the building looking for them. "Ah! Just the two chaps I wanted to see. I was hoping to catch you before you left. I missed your dad this weekend. I hope everything is okay. It's not like him to miss one of your matches."

"He's fine, I'm sure, Mr Elkes," answered Jack politely.

"I think it was a problem at work," Tim said helpfully, but also considered for the first time that maybe it wasn't just work that had prevented Mark from driving back up to Ballarat. In fact, he'd complained about being tired, hadn't he? Tim had a sudden sinking feeling that he did his best to ignore while he tried to concentrate on what Fred was saying.

"I know I've already congratulated you boys in public, but I wanted to make sure you understand just how impressed I am by the way you two are playing. I like to think I can take some of the credit for at least putting the idea in your heads to have a shot at these satellite tournaments." He beamed at them both as they nodded and smiled their thanks. "Now, I had a word a while ago to your dad. Has he mentioned anything to you yet about next month?"

The boys looked at each other and shook their heads.

"No. Unless you mean the invitational in Sydney coming up?" queried Tim.

Fred looked at each of them in turn. "Hm. Yes and no. I don't want to pre-empt any discussion he might want to have with you, but I'd like to put an idea forward for you to think about. You will need every day to prepare if you decide to go ahead. And I'm only mentioning it because your dad was keen on the idea."

By this stage the boys were intrigued.

Fred looked around as if to check anyone was listening in. "What do you think about having a crack at the wildcard tournament for the Australian Open?"

He had their attention.

"I'm not telling you anything you don't know when I say it's a long shot, at best. And I can't guarantee that you would be accepted, even if you do well in Sydney. And yes," he answered Jack's question before he could ask it, handing them both an envelope, "your invitation to Sydney is here, especially since you did so well again this week. A fabulous effort."

Jack and Tim grinned from ear to ear. They did make the invitation satellite in Sydney! Tim couldn't believe his luck at making the singles, especially since his record wasn't as strong as Jack's. But, he thought, trying out for the Australian Open, even if it was just a lead-up elimination tournament? Surely that was a stretch?

"But we're way off even thinking about the Australian Open. We couldn't do that! Could we?" Jack blurted out, incredulous at the thought. He'd been thinking it would be nice to get tickets this year to watch it. But play in it? That's crazy, he thought.

"Well," Fred put his hands up to ward off further questions, "I know what you're thinking, and it may be impossible: in fact, normally I wouldn't even consider suggesting it to you yet, but there's a couple of things in your favour this year. For a start, the South African Tennis Federation has offered some very lucrative prize money and intend to run their tournaments in January, at the same time as the Australian circuit. Which means they have set themselves up in competition with the Australian Open. They know they won't attract the top-ranked players, but they may attract quite a few of the lesser-known professionals who may decide to have a go at bolstering up their prize money in a few tournaments that they know they'll have a better chance of winning."

Tim shook his head slowly, still trying to absorb the suggestion.

"And the other reason is that you are both playing amazing tennis. I've watched you two improve out of sight. Every time you get on the court you seem to raise the bar just a little higher. And you've earned your place in the top ten of players in these satellite competitions. That's as singles players, and no other pair has even come close to you in doubles. Now, if you play well in the invitation satellite—and you'll be up among the best of the satellite players, from all over the world," Fred warned, "that is, the players who choose to play here in Australia, as opposed to South Africa," he added with a conspiratorial wink, "then you just might be eligible for the Open qualifying competition. That's where players can earn a wildcard entry to the Australian Open."

"Wildcard entry?" asked Jack, confused.

"It's much the same as the process you went through in Melbourne that gave you access to the first satellite. They have the main draw of seeded players, then there are a number of spots open to the Tennis Federation to nominate players that may not be seeded but who they think have the ability to play at the highest level. For example, they might give a wildcard entry to someone who has been a seeded player but is coming back from injury or has been out of form. But they also use this qualifying tournament to let players fight it out for the chance of a wildcard entry. And that is what I think you should aim for. You have as good a chance as anyone else to make it through, and you're playing your best tennis and getting better. This is a rare opportunity. I think it's worth a shot," he concluded.

Fred turned to go with a promise that he would be in touch, and a good luck wish to them for the Sydney tournament. As Fred walked away, Jack turned to Tim with raised eyebrows.

"What did you think of that? Can you see yourself at the Aussie open?"

Shaking his head, Tim said, "Personally, I think he's nuts! Especially in singles. But he might have a point about the doubles. We could just give some of those guys a shake. He's right that we keep getting better. I can feel it. Each time we play, we improve. But even so, it would be still way out of our league. Surely he's not serious?"

Jack nodded. "I'm not surprised Dad hasn't mentioned this crazy idea to us yet."

Nanna beeped the car horn to let them know she was waiting. They grabbed their bags and walked quickly to the car. It was almost eight o'clock, and getting dark, by the time they got back to Melbourne. Jenny's car was there as well, which was a surprise because she had previously said she wouldn't be down until the next day. When they came into the kitchen Jenny was there, ready with a late dinner for them, and it felt just like the old days before they moved to Winjarra.

After the initial greetings and short discussion about the traffic that had held them up, Tim, more than a little curious, asked, "Where's Dad?"

"He's in bed, actually," said Jenny. "That's the reason I decided to come back a bit earlier. He finally confessed to me that he's been feeling exhausted and sick, so I am worried about him." Then looking at the immediate horror and distraught looks on the boys' faces she quickly added, "No, don't think that! I'm hoping he's okay, but he has lost weight and he doesn't have any energy, so we need to find out what's happening. I'm sure it's not the cancer back," she finished softly, keeping her voice low. "But I am going to see that he has a blood test tomorrow, just to make certain."

She gave them both another kiss and a hug, and then Nanna hugged Jenny, murmuring in her ear, "Oh, you poor darling."

A tearful Jenny said, "Go up and see him. He'll want to know all the details, and he's fine just resting in bed. It won't hurt him. And don't make a fuss about him being sick," she whispered to them as they headed up the stairs to their parents' bedroom.

Halfway up the stairs Tim turned to Jack and said quietly, "Let's not say too much about getting into Sydney next week."

Jack nodded his agreement. Both of them knew that if their father was sick, going to Sydney would be out of the question. If the cancer had returned, they couldn't even start to imagine the future.

So, instead of telling Mark about Fred Elkes's crazy idea for them to try out for a wildcard entry to the Australian Open qualifier, they gave a detailed, blow-by-blow description of their winning doubles matches and their losing singles efforts, updating Mark on everything he had missed. Jenny brought them up bowls of pasta so they could all eat dinner together.

Mark had initially protested that he could go down to the kitchen, but he was quickly overruled and accepted the pampering with quiet gratitude.

He did look tired and unwell. Both Jack and Tim noticed it and couldn't believe the change in him from earlier in the week. He declared that he was fine, that he just had a virus he couldn't shake, saying that Jenny was dramatising what was a simple case of the flu. However, he was visibly different from just five days ago, and it bothered them both.

"Now, did Fred Elkes catch you at all? I thought he might have a word with you, especially after you won the doubles again. Did he talk to you about the Australian Open wildcard tournament idea?"

Jack froze, and Tim looked like a rabbit caught in the headlights.

"Well, yeah, he did. But I think he's lost the plot," Tim answered, gathering his wits. "I mean, how far-fetched is that idea! They don't just hand out invites to the Australian wildcard qualifier to anyone," he laughed wryly.

Jack joined in laughing but Mark was serious. He sat higher in the bed and looked at them both. "Not so stupid at all. Fred and I had quite a long chat on Monday about this. You've got enough points already to be eligible. And if you play well in the Sydney comp, which you should, then you could be asked to play in the Open qualifier rounds. It's not as crazy as it sounds. You're not giving yourself enough credit for how well you've done these last few weeks." As he finished saying this, Mark had a huge coughing fit that left him gasping and out of breath.

Slightly alarmed at how much toll the conversation seemed to be taking on their dad, Tim quickly responded. "Of course, we'll have a go if we can, but we might not do as well in the

Sydney comp. There's going to be lots of interstate and international players who are way more experienced than us."

"Anyway, I'm going to bed," yawned Jack. "I've had it. It's been a big week."

"Same," said Tim. "See you in the morning. Sleep well, Dad." They each gave Mark a kiss and, avoiding further conversation, escaped downstairs.

"Whew," breathed Jack, following Tim into his bedroom. "What's happening?"

Tim shook his head as they both settled down onto the carpet for a quiet talk. "I don't know. But he does look crook, doesn't he?"

"He does! We can't even think about going to Sydney if he's like this. Mum will never let us go alone, and Nan and Pa have got the harvest going on. And I don't want to go off, anyway, if Dad is sick. It's not fair on Mum either."

Neither of them even felt the slightest disappointment about not going to Sydney. They simply didn't have the stomach for it if Mark was sick again. Instead, they decided to wait and see what the next few days would bring. Between them they had already dismissed the idea of playing in the Australian Open pre-qualifying tournament as just too far-fetched. Even Tim with his secret ambition of playing professional tennis felt this was too much too soon.

Both boys were late getting up the next morning, and the rest of the family were already up having breakfast when Tim stumbled into the kitchen in his PJs.

"Good afternoon, sleepy head," said Nan, finishing her cup of tea and standing up. "I'm glad you're up. I'm about to head off back to Winjarra."

"I can't believe how well I slept! I don't think I moved all night."

"Well, you've had a big week," said Nan. "And good luck for Wednesday. I'm sure you'll do well."

Tim made a face. "I can't believe I keep forgetting results are due this week. Thanks, Nan, and thanks for looking after us in Ballarat."

"No worries at all, but I must be off. Pa is flat out cropping this week, and I have to be there to cook for the workers."

"Tim and I will come up and help later in the week, Nan," promised Jack as they walked her to the door. "I know you'll be up as soon as things get sorted here," said Nan. Looking at Tim and Jack, she added quietly, "Look after your mum. She's going to need lots of support if the news is bad."

They both nodded and after hugs all round, they waved her off in the car. When they returned to the kitchen, Jenny was just finishing a phone call to the doctor's surgery to make an appointment for Mark.

"All good. He'll see you today, Mark, at ten-thirty, so we better get a move on. I'm so glad it's finally school holidays, and we've got time to do this together."

She smiled at Mark. Then turning to Tim and Jack she picked up her notepad and tearing a piece of paper off it, said, "No holidays yet for you two, though. I have a list of things for you to do!"

CHAPTER 14

Mark had his doctor's appointment and went back home to bed. The doctor had sent him straight off for blood tests, and the effort of it all exhausted him. He did get up later in the day and, after making several calls to clients and the office, headed to his drawing board in the study. Tim and Jack worked methodically through the list of Jenny's jobs.

They mowed the lawn, put through loads of dirty washing from a week of tennis clothes, and even went to the supermarket to get a long list of groceries. It was just under a week until Christmas, and the supermarket was crowded with shoppers. The plan had been for them all to be in Winjarra for Christmas, but now Tim and Jack weren't so sure. Much would depend on what happened with the results from Mark's blood tests.

The next forty-eight hours were a waiting game. The family waited on the test results and Tim waited on his exam results. By Wednesday morning Tim was edgy and tense. The postie wasn't due until 11.30 am, so he decided to go for a run.

He hadn't picked up a tennis racquet since his doubles match with Jack on Sunday, and he needed the distraction of physical exercise. He and Jack planned to see if they could still use the local church court later that afternoon for a hit. Ridiculously, the mail had arrived in Winjarra early that morning, well before the city posties had made their run. He'd already had phone calls from Karen and his mates. Karen received a 96.4 and she was elated. That would be more than enough to get her into physiotherapy at Melbourne Uni. Nick got an 89, and he was happy with that. Tony got 87.2, and he was ecstatic. Tim was hoping for something over 90, but he just wasn't sure that he'd done well enough.

He was recovering from his run, catching his breath at the front gate, when the postie cycled into his street. Handing the distinctive yellow envelope to Tim, he winked knowingly and said, "Good luck, mate."

Taking one steadying breath, Tim tore it open and scanned through the figures to see the one that counted. He read it twice and scanned it all again before he turned to Jenny and Jack, who were waiting anxiously at the front door.

"94.2!" He rushed back into the house, whooping with joy. "I can't believe it! 94.2! I'm so happy!" Grabbing Jenny, he gave her a big celebratory hug, lifting her off her feet in his excitement.

Jack slapped him on the back and hugged him as well. "Hermano! You did it!"

"I know! I'm sure it gets me into commerce at Melbourne!"

"I'm so proud of you," said Jenny, chuckling as he finally released her safely to the ground. "Go and tell your father."

"I've heard the good news already," laughed Mark, coming out of the study where he'd been working. "That's fantastic and so well deserved. You put in the hard work, and you've got your reward."

Just then the phone rang. Jenny answered it, still smiling, but they could all tell as her face went from smiling to frowning

in seconds that this was the phone call they had been waiting
for. The little family went silent and watched Jenny's reactions
carefully.

"Yes. He's here, Doctor, I'll put him on."

Mark took the phone and all eyes switched to him. Jenny
stood stoically close by with her arms folded across her chest.
Mark was noncommittal, but continued to say, "Okay," several
times before agreeing to be at the surgery later in the day for an
appointment.

He hung up slowly and, turning back to the family blew out
a long, slow breath. He looked visibly shaken by the phone call.

"Bad news, I'm afraid. The cancer is back."

Jenny rushed to embrace him, as did Tim and Jack. They
stood together silently, just taking in the dreadful news, their
heads spinning.

Finally, Mark gathered himself together, saying, "Come on.
Let's sit down and we'll talk about this." Making a wry face, he
continued, "It's actually not all doom and gloom. Let's have a
cup of tea. There's a bit to take in."

Jenny looked too shell-shocked to move, so Mark guided
her to the table while Tim put the kettle on, and Jack put out
the cups. The phone rang but everyone ignored it, despite its
shrill insistence, letting it ring out.

"This is too much," said Jenny, her tears falling freely as
she sank down on a kitchen chair. "I thought we had put the
cancer behind us. This is obviously why you've been unwell.
I'm so sorry, darling." She put her head on Mark's shoulder and
cried quietly. Mark soothed her and waited until the boys had
sat down with them.

Taking a sip of his tea he began slowly, saying, "Well, the
bad news is that, unfortunately, the cancer cells have
reappeared: but then I have to admit that Dr Thompson always

warned me that this would most likely happen. I suppose I should have been more honest with you all as well, but … I just didn't want to think about it, and I've been feeling so well that I thought I could beat the odds." Mark's voice broke a little before he steadied himself. Tim's knuckles were white from clenching. Mark reached out and gave them a gentle rub. Then he put a hand on Jack's knee, which was jigging up and down uncontrollably.

"I'm really not explaining this well," sighed Mark, "and I'm sorry I didn't always give you the full story. But there is good news in all of this. For a start, the prognosis is actually positive." He gave them all a reassuring smile. "The cell count is fairly low, which means the leukaemia has been mostly knocked out, and with more treatment I should get full remission. Apparently, this type of cancer can recur, but the fact that I've gone over twelve months before that has happened means I have an almost certain chance of eventual recovery. Of course, that is after I've gone through more chemo, which I'm not exactly looking forward to. And there will probably be more than one lot of chemo, over the course of the year. But then— fingers crossed—that should be the end of it."

"This is so unfair, Dad! When do you have to start?" said Jack angrily.

"Oh Mark! Not two lots of chemo!" sympathised Jenny, knowing full well the toll it had taken on Mark the last time.

"Unfortunately, yes, but Dr Thompson promises me the sessions won't be as intense as last time, so I shouldn't feel quite as nauseous, and there will be two-week gaps between each treatment." Shrugging his shoulders, Mark made a grimace before managing an upbeat grin. "It is what it is. And the other good news is that we don't start until next year. He is completely relaxed about the time frame, within reason. He wants me to get over this virus first, which will take a while because, of course, the old immune system is down again because of the cancer."

Polishing off his cup of tea, he went on, "So, we are going to think positively. This is just another setback. We need to forget about it and celebrate Tim's fantastic results, and we need to think about heading up to Sydney next week for that tournament. Nothing has changed. I'll just have a few more trips to the outpatients' again next year."

The phone rang again.

"Answer it, Tim. It's probably one of your mates wanting to know how you went. Might even be Karen," he winked.

Reluctantly Tim answered it. It was Karen, wanting to know if Tim had gotten his results. After telling her about his marks, and letting the family hear her excited screams, Tim took the phone to his bedroom for some privacy. He really wasn't in the mood for much chat, even with Karen. And he certainly wasn't ready yet to tell her about his dad, until he had a chance himself to absorb the devastating news. And it was devastating news for him, no matter what positive spin Mark had tried to put on it. Karen talked enthusiastically for a while about how much fun it was going to be next year. Luckily, she had loads of gossip on everyone's plans to celebrate over the summer holidays, so Tim didn't have to contribute too much to the conversation.

"What are the plans for Sydney? Tell me everything. I'm so excited for you and Jack."

"I don't know if I'm that excited at the moment. Maybe I've just been playing too much tennis, but I'm feeling a bit flat."

"What? But it's your big chance! What's happened? I know you. Tennis is everything."

Tim explained to Karen about his dad's recent exhaustion and illness, leaving out the details of the cancer recurring.

"I think it's probably too much for Dad at this time of the year. He's keen to go, but Jack and I aren't so sure."

"But you can go on your own, can't you?" Karen suggested.

"I'm sure we could. We could catch a train or fly up, and we don't really need anyone with us. We'd be fine. It's just that Jack and I know that Mum and Dad would both worry, and they just don't need anything extra at the moment."

"That's such a shame though," sympathised Karen. "I understand what you're saying, but your dad knows how hard you worked for this chance."

"Look, its only one tournament and we probably wouldn't have done well in it anyway. I mean, some of the best players in Australia would be there, not to mention the international players. It would probably be a waste of time, and there are other competitions coming up over summer. There's always next year, and we might have a better chance then."

Changing the subject, Tim said he hoped to get up to Winjarra before Christmas and suggested they could go out somewhere together.

"You mean go to the pub for a counter meal and be seen together on a date?" Karen teased. "We would be the main topic of conversation for the town until the New Year."

"That's a deal then," laughed Tim. Then, feigning that Jenny was calling him, he said goodbye, promising to call her again later. When he returned to the kitchen, Mark was back in the study working, and Jenny was making sandwiches for lunch.

"How is Karen?" she asked, as if nothing had happened. "Did she stop squealing eventually?"

"What do you mean, 'How's Karen?' How are you, Mum?" asked Tim with genuine concern. He looked quizzically over at Jack, who shrugged his shoulders in response.

"I'm okay. Dad's news has certainly rocked me, and I need to make sure he is absolutely telling us everything this time. But I'm going to be positive. We've been through hell already and I thought, I hoped, it was all over; but we just have to keep going a little longer. Take it one day at a time, as they say. He told us when you were talking to Karen that he intends to keep working as much as he can, and that he doesn't want much to change."

"But he's not serious about going to Sydney after Christmas? It's only a week away? Surely he can't manage that?"

Jenny motioned Jack over and, checking to see the door to the study was closed, she spoke quietly to them. "I actually agree with you, but I think it will be good for him. The last thing we want is Dad sick and depressed again. I still shudder at those days. Let's try it his way. He wants life to go on as usual, so we'll do it his way as long as it's possible. What do you think?"

The click of the study door opening ended the conversation. Nodding, Jack and Tim agreed.

That afternoon, at Mark's suggestion, they headed over to the church court to see if they could have a hit. They asked at the manse this time before they took the court. Their old friend the minister was there and only too delighted to walk them over to the court himself. In their absence he had taken to locking it, but once he heard they were back he gave them a spare key and told them he would be only too happy to see them use the court.

The court was definitely a step down after the beautiful lawn courts of the last few tournaments and the Rebound Ace courts they had been using in Winjarra, but they enjoyed being back on their old court, despite its imperfections. Very quickly they settled into their training regime, and the odd difficult bounce kept them well and truly on their toes.

By the time they returned home, feeling pleased with their efforts after a three-day break from training, they found their parents in a more cheerful mood than they had been that morning. Mark, accompanied by Jenny, had been to see the doctor. The consult was in the car park because the doctor didn't want Mark being exposed to any more potential germs with his current lowered immunity. Dr Thompson had talked to them through the open car window. Jenny was able to ask a few questions of her own and she couldn't help but be reassured by Dr Thompson's positivity.

Consequently, when the boys arrived home, they found the kitchen table strewn with maps as Jenny and Mark planned a few days' holiday at either end of the tournament in Sydney.

"I'd love a couple of days in Canberra on the way up," Jenny was saying. "Then we can go back home by the coast and maybe stay in a unit near the beach? That would give us all a great break."

Mark nodded. "I totally agree. We can't book just yet because we don't know how long the boys will be playing in Sydney. But I guess it won't matter. A few days extra in Sydney wouldn't be such a bad thing." Then, noticing the boys had returned, he beckoned them over to look at the map.

"We can make this a real holiday. It's about time we all did something together. This will be fun." Mark pointed to the coast below Sydney on the map and continued, "A few days at the beach would be great, especially in New South Wales. We haven't been there for years. Remember that holiday we had in Merimbula, Tim? That was such a good spot."

As the rest of the family made plans and talked enthusiastically about the family road trip to Sydney, Tim hid his reaction behind a bland face. He thought they were all mad. How can you go from, "Dad's got cancer," to planning a holiday, in the space of an afternoon? Instead, he decided to leave them to it and made plans to go out and celebrate his good marks with some school friends.

CHAPTER 15

"Don't be too hard on yourself," said Mr Mac, patting Tim on his back in consolation. "There is no disgrace in being beaten by a player ranked in the top fifty. You were unlucky he's even playing in this tournament. I don't think he would normally bother with this level of competition, but he's coming back from an injury, and I'd say he's after some extra matches to play himself into form before the Open."

Tim was disappointed in his own efforts, despite Mr Mac's words of support. Gathering his racquets and zipping them into his bag, he asked, "How about Jack? How is he going?"

"I think he's struggling as well. The last time I checked he was two sets down. Not much joy for the Anderson boys today, I'm afraid." Just then, to confirm Mr Mac's prediction, Jack and Mark rounded the low stands on the other side of the court, their body language telling the story. Jack put his thumb down and pointed hopefully to Tim, who also replied with a thumbs down. Frowning in sympathy, Jack just shook his head. There was no doubles competition at this tournament, so any chance to redeem themselves was gone. They had no more matches. Mark gestured towards the cafe area, suggesting they meet there. As Mark and Jack walked away, Tim collected the last of his gear and followed slowly with his coach. He felt disturbed and frustrated at his loss.

Turning to Mr Mac he asked, "Do you think I should just give up? I was a long way off today. Am I kidding myself I'll ever be as good as these guys?"

Mr Mac stopped. Steering Tim over to the side of the court he motioned him to sit down. "Let's talk."

Mr Mac waited patiently for Tim to start. After a few moments of soul searching, Tim gestured around them and began. "Look at these guys. I'm almost the same age as most of them and they've been playing since they were kids. How can I compete with that? You know I was even thinking of taking a gap year next year, and just playing tennis, which is pretty dumb anyway because I don't have any money. I was hoping that I would go well in this tournament, and that would convince Mum it would be worth doing. But I can't see her agreeing now. And is there any point to it if I'm never going to catch up?"

"Whoa! You have got some negativity happening there. Okay. First point. Yes, I do think you, and Jack, for that matter, are good enough. I haven't changed my opinion on that since we had those first training sessions in Winjarra. You were late starters, but you've got bucketloads of natural talent and you've worked hard to get this far in such a short time. I can only guess how many hours you've put in going over drills and skills, but I'd put my money on the two of you not being too far behind most of your competition, in terms of time spent training."

Paul tapped Tim's knee for emphasis.

"Second point. One loss doesn't mean it's all over. You were flat today. You're allowed an off day. Even the best of the best lose matches, and that gives someone else a moment of glory. Otherwise, it would be a very boring sport. And that brings me to the last point. The last few weeks have been huge for you and Jack. We expected a lot of you both, and you've really been outstanding. Don't forget you've virtually gone from the strictly amateur ranks to this semi-professional level—and managed some wins and very creditable performances along the way. Added to this you've had some new issues with your dad and his health … I know that's a worry for you."

Tim nodded.

"That alone is a fair bit to deal with. I also know Fred has been putting pressure on you to qualify for the lead-up tournament for the Open. He is right. You are good enough, but I'm not as convinced as he is that this is the right time. Of course, if you get in, we'll have a go, but his theory about a lack of interest this year from the South African players is not one I share. What do you think?" He chuckled ironically, referring to the fact that it was a player from South Africa who had just beaten Tim.

"But we'll talk more about that later because I've got some more ideas I want to share with you and Jack, and I think you need to hear them together. Okay? Have I convinced you to keep going?"

Nodding, Tim managed a smile. "Thanks, Mr Mac."

"Right! Now let's find Jack and Mark because they'll be wondering what we're up to."

Dodging past groups of spectators, Tim and Paul made their way to the cafe. Mark had ordered a coffee for Paul and a chocolate milkshake for Tim.

"I thought you guys had gotten lost. I was just about to tackle your milkshake, Tim," threatened Jack, pulling it towards himself briefly. Then, seeing Tim's devastated face, he swiftly changed tack. With the disappointment obvious in his own voice, he said, "Tell us about your match? What happened? You couldn't have been as bad as me. I was spectacularly hopeless."

"I must have been," replied Tim. "I just didn't get going. I couldn't find any rhythm. I had no consistency." He shook his head, still glum over his defeat, despite Mr Mac's pep talk.

"Well, it's actually not so unexpected that you've both had a loss. It isn't easy to turn up week after week at this level and continue to play your best tennis. I think you are both lacking match fitness—or I should probably say, match toughness," remarked Paul, looking at each of them to make sure they were listening. "I know you are both fit, but match fitness and match toughness are another level. Just remember how tired you were after the three satellite tournaments in a row. You were fit enough, but it still exhausted you. Playing a match at this level requires a great deal of mental acuity and concentration, on top of the physicality required. Quite frankly, you're not yet match hardened enough to turn up week after week and continue to win at this level. But the good thing is, we can work on it, and with more experience, you'll both be fine."

"But we didn't play or train much last week! We had Christmas and a few days off, so we should have been rested, shouldn't we?" queried Jack defensively.

"I think that's what Paul's trying to say," Mark noted, understanding the point the experienced coach was making. "This game isn't just won by physical competence. It's more than that. You have to be on the top of every aspect of your game, especially the mental side of it."

"Exactly, Mark. You guys have been incredible, but it takes practise and experience to keep playing at an elite level. We'll get there, I have no doubt. And we'll build up those skills and mental toughness over the year, which brings me to something I want to discuss with you all. Next year."

Before he could begin though, Jenny appeared. She had watched Jack's match and knew Tim had lost as well. Knowing that they would be hungry, she had gone to the car for the lunches she had made that morning. As the boys unwrapped their sandwiches, she gave them both a kiss, saying consolingly, "Never mind. I know you both thought you'd make it further than the second round, but this is a tough competition. You should still be proud of yourselves for even being here."

"Very true, Jenny. They shouldn't be too hard on themselves. I've just been telling them that. I'm glad you're here though, because I've got some thoughts on this coming year, and you might have an opinion."

"Go ahead. I'm listening," she said, sitting down on the extra chair Mr Mac had pulled up.

"You know I've been given the head coaching position at Flinders Park. This means that we will continue to have access to the best facilities and, more importantly, that we can keep working together, which is perfect. It's going to be an exciting time, and I have great plans for the boys, but I also know that Jack's in Year 11, and will have limited free time. Tim will face the same time constraints at uni. Making time to train together will be a challenge. However, now you're in Melbourne, there are also plenty more training partners and squads to train with, and that variety of competition will be a bonus. Now," Paul paused for effect, "I'm proposing that Tim drops back his university commitment to part-time, which takes some of the pressure off him. As an elite athlete and semi-professional, which he is now, he can do that. It means he can keep up his training commitments without having to take a complete gap year, which I know you aren't exactly keen on, Jenny." Paul raised his eyebrows questioningly at Jenny.

Nodding her head slowly, she agreed. "No, I wasn't keen on the gap year just yet, but I can't argue with that. It sounds like a great idea if it's possible. Not a bad compromise."

"And I think we can also work with Jack's school, and his timetable, so that he can either start late or leave early on certain days, to accommodate his training schedule. What do you think?"

Jenny looked at Mark, who was nodding his approval. Feeling a tad manipulated, she nevertheless saw the sense in all of this. It was not going to be an easy year ahead with Mark's chemo treatments. Tennis was not just a distraction anymore for Tim and Jack. They were deadly serious about it, and she knew she would lose if she insisted that they choose study over tennis. Hopefully this would work and make all their lives a little less stressful.

"What do you think, Tim? Would that suit you?" she asked, already knowing the answer.

"I love the idea!"

"What about you, Jack?"

"Perfect. I won't waste any time when I could be training."

"Okay then," said Jenny, "I can't see a problem with any of it. Let's give it a try and see how it works."

Paul looked pleased. "I think it will work, but we can tweak it as the year goes by. And we can be flexible, so that if you're going through a bad patch, Mark, or whatever, we can adjust the schedule to suit."

As they discussed some of the other ideas Paul had for his two young protégées, Tim felt the disappointment of his defeat ebb away. He began to get caught up in Mr Mac's excitement and enthusiasm about his plans for the year ahead. Jack's demeanour also lifted as Paul outlined plans for competitions and training. Mark was positive and fired up with the possibilities ahead. Catching each other's eyes, Tim and Jack shared a small smile. This was going to be an awesome year.

Finally, Paul stood up to leave. "At least you guys can have a few bonus days here in Sydney before heading home. Enjoy the trip and stay safe. We'll see you all back in Melbourne."

Waving goodbye, he made his way towards the administration centre, where he had a schedule of meetings to attend.

"Okay then," said Mark. "We shall do what the man says and have a holiday. Let's get out of here!"

CHAPTER 16

Mark didn't begin his chemo treatments until late February. The first time he was diagnosed Dr Thompson had been keen to start treatments as soon as possible. This time he was far more relaxed. Mark had a low-grade infection that lingered for several weeks and, until that was clear, Dr Thompson was loath to start treatments. Jenny was concerned at the delay, but she was constantly reassured that the cancer cells were reproducing very slowly this time.

She was relieved all the same, as were Tim and Jack, when the chemo treatment finally commenced. This course of chemo was, as promised, far less aggressive than the first round of treatment Mark had endured. The schedule was for one treatment a fortnight, with a course of six treatments over three months. The unexpected upside for the family, especially for Mark, was that he suffered far less. Apart from the seventy-two hours following his chemo, when he felt some nausea and tiredness, Mark was able to go about his life as usual. He continued working, even going into the office on most days. Just as he had over the last year when he had become so involved in their lives, he attended as many tournaments as he could, seeming to thrive on their successes. Their fitness program was devised by Mr. Mac, but Mark remained proactive, stepping in to supervise their training sessions with the same enthusiasm as before. Taking his role as fitness coach very seriously, he proved a hard taskmaster even when he battled nausea. There was no sign of the depression of those early days returning, and Tim, Jack, and Jenny's relief at this was tangible. It was obvious in the regard they showed Mark, and in the consideration and various little acts of kindness they performed to ease his bad times.

When the first course of chemo finished at the end of May, the test results were very promising. The second, and hopefully final, course would commence in September, concluding at the end of November.

Tim felt he had the best of both worlds. He enjoyed his time at university—although he wasn't entirely convinced that he liked studying commerce. That was something he needed to work out for himself. His heart not really in it, he nevertheless managed to scramble passes, putting in just enough effort to get through exams and assignments. It did give him an experience of uni life, but it wasn't quite the same, living at home and going to uni. He envied his mates from Winjarra who lived on campus and could enjoy all the freedom and fun parties. He kept up his social life by staying with Karen or bunking in with his mates on nights he had no commitments, but he was aware he missed out on heaps. Karen understood more than anyone else just why he was still so tennis obsessed, which helped. She no longer had the commitment required to play seriously herself, but she was still interested and keen to hear about the details of his training and competitions.

Mr Mac continued to inspire and challenge them. There were several other strong players, male and female, in Jack and Tim's training squad. Most of them were a bit younger than

Tim, at around sixteen, but there were a couple of other guys his age and older. Twenty-one seemed to be the cut-off age for this hand-picked squad, which made Tim feel he was still on track. Some of the guys had cracking forehands or serves that skimmed across the net with incredible speed. Others had drop shots to die for, or backhands that could cut right across the top of a ball and send it spinning in any direction. There was no doubt though that Tim and Jack were the stronger and more consistent members of the group. They soaked it all up, learning something from them all.

Jack was able to make the majority of training sessions but he had to put school first, as did some of the other younger squad members. If they missed a session they could get together in another designated time, and Tim or another of the older squad members might fill in for Mr. Mac at that session. It was flexible and worked well. Over the course of the year, there were several tournaments, all at the satellite level and all offering points towards their rankings. Singles were available for everyone, and a few like Jack and Tim formed doubles teams. Jack wasn't always available to compete in the doubles, but whenever they did play together, they continued to win.

Mr Mac had also involved Tim in coaching, for which he was paid. Tim appreciated having some cash, but he also found it was something he really enjoyed and looked forward to. There were weekend clinics at tennis clubs all across Melbourne, working mostly with juniors, but sometimes with teenagers and adults. Tim felt he gained as much from these sessions as he taught. As any teacher knows, there's no better way to reinforce a skill than having to break it down and teach it.

Mr Mac didn't fail either on his promise to make them more match-fit and tough. Within the squad they played set after set, under tournament conditions. Five sets was always the minimum sets played in training, building and developing the concentration and stamina needed to repeatedly perform these physical and mental challenges. By degrees they became match toughened. Now, in competitions, when they had to backup and play another match with limited recovery time, they did it with confidence. Tim and Jack could feel the difference in their strength and endurance. Being match-fit had taken on a whole new meaning to them.

As the last chemo session was completed towards the end of November, the mood in the Anderson family was upbeat. Life was looking good, and everyone was feeling like a weight had been lifted. Tim's uni exams were done and dusted, as were Jack's school commitments. Released from study, they entered as many events as they could. This was the time of year when the international competitors began arriving in Australia, anxious to boost their rankings and earn those elusive wildcard entries to more prestigious events. Mr Mac entered them in interstate tournaments: Wagga and Goulburn in regional New South Wales, and Mt Gambier in South Australia. He was keen to seek out new competitors for them, away from just the Victorian circuit.

With newfound freedom, Jack and Tim drove themselves to each destination in Jenny's old car. Mr Mac had pre-arranged for them to be billeted in each town, with volunteer families who took them under their wings and generously fed and housed them. They had a wonderful time, loving the road trips and making great friends with the families they stayed with. Mr Mac kept in touch and managed to be a step ahead of every match, having researched their opponents on the tour; and, as usual, he always had at least one tip on how to approach the match. They made it to the quarterfinals in all three events, with

Jack, despite having less match practise this year than Tim, making it to the final of the Mt Gambier event before losing to a very talented Yugoslavian, Ivan Goric. In Goulburn they played each other in the quarterfinal. It was always a bittersweet win for whoever won these battles, and battles they were. Neither was willing to concede a point, and every game was highly contested. This time Tim, as the older brother, was determined to be the winner. He had lost the last time they played, and it still smarted. The word had gone around the Goulburn courts that the two Anderson boys were facing off in the quarterfinals, and there was an interested and noisy crowd there. More than a few players and coaches were curious to see the outcome.

Tim played his usual consistent tennis, managing to chase down enough of his brother's brilliant shots to edge ahead. The match went to five sets and into a tie breaker, but eventually a sweaty and ecstatic Tim clinched the set with a sneaky drop volley that caught Jack flat-footed on the baseline. Jack was crushed but good-naturedly hugged Tim at the net and congratulated him. The crowd had been neutral, cheering all points equally, and they gave them both a round of applause as they walked off the court. Unfortunately, Tim lost the semi-final in his next match, against the now-infamous Ivan Goric, who had dispatched Jack the week before in Mt Gambier. It was another close match, and Tim was not disgraced. When they arrived home after the final tournament, Mark was hanging out for all the details.

After rehashing events as best they could, including blow-by-blow descriptions of certain games, Mark was finally satisfied.

"I can't wait until the Sydney tournament. You'll be getting your entry for that soon, I imagine, and hopefully you can do a bit better than last year. I think you'll give a few of them a run for their money this time."

Mark, despite his physically weakened state after the twelve weeks of chemo, was optimistic and already looking forward to the boys returning to Sydney to compete their unfinished business. Fred Elkes had continued to keep in touch over the year and he hadn't lost his conviction that they could enter the wildcard qualifying event in January for the Australian Open.

"And I've got my fingers crossed Mum and I will be able to head up to Sydney with you. I should be feeling much better by then." Smiling widely, Mark went on, "And then we'll see if Fred is able to pull some strings and get the two of you an entry into the Open qualifier he's always talking about."

"I'd be happy with another holiday like we had last year," interrupted Jenny wistfully. "I loved the few days in Sydney we had." She continued in a firmer tone, "Now, Mark, these boys look absolutely done in. They've had a tough few weeks. No more tennis talk tonight. No doubt Paul Mac will be at you to start training in the next day or so, and you can discuss it all to your heart's content. This evening I'm declaring a ban on tennis. We can watch a family movie and I have Nanna's spaghetti and meatballs for you, and a chocolate cake. Agreed?"

"Okay. It's a tennis-free night. Anything for Nanna's meatballs," laughed Jack.

"I just had one more question," tried Mark, before being quickly drowned out by Tim and Jack yelling, "No!"

"Are you kidding, Dad? Meatballs win every time over tennis!" said Tim, holding up his hand to stop any further questions. Jenny's decree worked until the next morning, when Mark was again full of questions he had thought of during the night. It was almost a relief when he left for a blood test, the first one post-treatment. It was hopefully going to be a day of celebration when the results came in tomorrow.

Paul Mac visited later that day and he was delighted with their results over the last three satellite tournaments.

"They were great results, especially in the singles where the points count. You had some tough competition as well, so it was definitely worth the effort to go interstate. I've looked up the stats of some of those players. It's no disgrace being beaten, either of you, by Ivan Goric. He's highly ranked in Europe this year, and he's already played in several tour events. You both got some valuable experience there, without doubt."

"What do you think their chances are in Sydney this year?" asked Mark.

"Good. They should do much better. They've come a long way from where they were last year. It will be interesting, that's for sure." By the time Paul had left, tennis was again the main topic of conversation. Karen, Nick, and Tony were back in Winjarra for the summer, so Tim began making plans to go up for a quick visit before Christmas. Jack was also keen to get out and enjoy some time with his mates, whom he'd hardly seen since they'd finished exams.

The next day, Jenny went with Mark to Dr Thompson's. Tim and Jack waited at home, keen to be there when they returned with the results. They knew the news was good the moment they drove up and Mark tooted the horn all the way up the drive. Jenny got out of the car and was unable to contain her smile. "Tell them, Mark."

"I'm officially in remission, with over a ninety-five percent chance of it never recurring again! I'm as cancer free as I can get!" said Mark, raising his arms in the air in a gesture of triumph.

The boys whooped and cheered on the very spot where they had fought, almost three years earlier, as they came to terms with their father's illness. They moved into the house, everyone talking at once, and this time it was the boys who wanted to hear every detail.

"Not one cell detected," Mark explained, "and these results, combined with the negative results I've had since June, are very positive. The statistics are all highly in my favour, and Jenny heard them as well. Dr Thompson's very confident we've beaten it."

The boys looked at Jenny for further confirmation.

"It's all true, this time. Dad's all clear and Dr Thompson has assured me I can stop worrying about it." Putting the kettle on, she frowned for a second, recalling the doctor's final words. "But there is something else. We're not quite out of the woods yet."

"I'm not even worried about that, I'm fine," interrupted Mark.

"I'm sure you are, but I think we should take it seriously all the same. Dad's white blood count is very low, which means he is immunocompromised again, and he can't afford to get any infection. A virus at this stage could be disastrous, so we have to do our best to make sure he stays well. He needs rest and a diet high in vitamins. No going into the office, Mark, you'll have to work from home." Mark hung his head in a gesture of mock defeat. Warming to her plans, Jenny continued, "We should try to keep our contact with any germs as minimal as we can. No visitors to the house, and let's stay close to home as much as possible. No going to any places with crowds or big gatherings, which means, guys, no pubs and concerts."

The boys' faces fell.

"I know, I know," Jenny said sympathetically, "but it's just until Dad's white blood cell count goes up. Dr Thompson was firm on that point. It's crucial you stay well, Mark," she said firmly, cutting off his protests. "We don't want to go backwards now we're on the home stretch. And these guidelines come from Dr Thompson himself, so I'm not making up rules to make your lives miserable," she said, waving an information sheet in the air. As Jenny outlined a list of the dos and don'ts for the foreseeable future, it felt like some of the gloss had gone off what should have been good news.

"What about training? Can we still do that? And my trip to Winjarra?" asked Tim, concerned as some of the ramifications of the new rules began to occur to him.

"And the Sydney tournament is coming up? It won't make any difference to that, will it?" fired off Jack, also realising there were compromises ahead.

"I think tennis training is okay. You'll have to drive there and back together, no public transport obviously, but otherwise because it's all outside, it should be fine. Washing hands is the key, so just make sure you wash your hands frequently." Jenny knew how much the boys had already given up over the duration of Mark's illness. She didn't want to make this any harder on them than she had to. "I think though you'll have to rethink going to Winjarra, Tim. If you came back with any virus, it could be very serious for Dad. I'm sorry, I know you were looking forward to it," she said ruefully. "Sydney is still a couple of weeks away, Jack. Let's not stress too far into the future. Dad's white blood cells could be through the roof by then."

A few days later, Paul Mac came for a visit. He had heard the good and the bad news about Mark's test results from the boys. He was keen to congratulate him and also see how he was managing, and if he could help in any way. He and Mark had become close over the last couple of years. They sat outside while they had a coffee and talked things through. Paul thought Mark looked a little anaemic, but he assumed it was a lagging symptom from the last bout of chemo. The topic of the tournament in Sydney came up before long. The invitation had arrived earlier that week.

"Actually, I've got some ideas on that I'd like you to think about." Paul had their attention, although none of them was prepared for his next words. "I was wondering if you boys would consider skipping the tournament. I have an option for you that I believe will be far better for your long-term development as players."

"Skip it? You mean not play?" Jack exclaimed, leaning forward as if he hadn't heard his coach properly.

"Hear me out, Jack. You might like it." Pausing to choose his words carefully, Paul continued, "As you know, we have international and interstate players arriving over the next few weeks, all here to play in the Australian Open. The Rebound Ace surface is still relatively new, and they're all busting to be able to train on it. The very top players arrive with an entourage that includes their coach, physio, even a training partner. However, most don't have all that. They need to train against someone, and that's where you two come in. I could get you both two or three training sessions a day with some of the best players in the world. The opportunity to be able to hit with these elite players, returning shot after shot, playing rallies back and forth, is priceless. I'm convinced that it would be far more beneficial than playing in Sydney. Can you imagine how much you would learn, listening to their coaches and watching their technique at such close proximity? The inside knowledge and experience you'd gain would be simply incalculable!"

Mark put his hand up in a gesture of confusion.

"But the boys were hoping that a better result this year up in Sydney might get them into the Open qualifier. It would get them a foot in the door for future tournaments, wouldn't it? Should they throw that chance away when they've been working towards it all year?" asked Mark, voicing everyone's thoughts.

"That's true. It could put their chance of going overseas to compete on hold for another year, but this kind of exposure is rare. I wouldn't suggest it if I wasn't convinced it would be great for the boys. It's solid experience, against what is still only a chance. You could get to Sydney and in the first round go up against a world-class player, and then you're on your way home without any real benefit. There's no guarantee you'll make the quarterfinals where you could pick up points."

"Hmm," was Mark's noncommittal reply.

"There is a slight possibility that they'll still get into the qualifier even if they don't get any extra points. They're borderline entries at this stage, and you just never know your luck." Paul tapped the table for emphasis. "What I do know is that being able to trade strokes with players of this calibre would do wonders for Tim and Jack's development." Shrugging his shoulders, Paul hoped he had made his argument well enough to convince them. "What do you think, guys?"

Tim could feel another year of his life slipping away, but he had to trust the man who had done so much for his tennis. Breathing out, he said reluctantly, "I was really looking forward to Sydney, but if you think it's for the best, I'm in."

Everyone looked at Jack. "Okay. I suppose so," he said with obvious disappointment.

Mark looked at Jenny, who nodded as well. "Looks like you've convinced us all. I can see the benefits, and if it helps them strengthen their games, it's a no-brainer."

Paul looked pleased. "I'm sure you won't regret this, boys. Once you're trading forehands with some of these guys from the tour, you'll not even give Sydney another thought. I promise."

Despite Paul's optimism, it did take Jack and Tim a while to adjust to not going to Sydney. However, the Sydney tournament came and went, and life continued quietly in the Anderson household, albeit with few visitors or interruptions. Tim and Jack were booked up every day at Flinders Park, just as Paul Mac had predicted. They spent very little time at home in the hygienic bubble Jenny had tried to create for Mark, spending most of the daylight hours at the tennis centre. The unexpected side bonus was that they were also making good money, as they were being paid for their time. This was a dream holiday job. Tim begrudgingly overcame his disappointment at not being able to go to Winjarra, or Sydney because, exactly as Mr Mac had promised, he was learning so much every day. Jack was also quickly persuaded. Like Tim, he was on the learning curve of his life. The brothers became highly sought after as practise partners, for two reasons. The first was that they had the strength and consistency required for the tour players to fine-tune their own strokes: the second was that they weren't considered "on the tour" so they posed no threat.

Occasionally they managed to see their mates, but they were careful about their movements, only agreeing to catch-ups that were outdoors. The whole family washed their hands frequently and tried to follow the doctor's guidelines as closely as they could. Mark checked his temperature every day for signs of infection, and once a week he had a blood test. The whole family anxiously awaited the results.

While the white blood count had remained steady, it was still dangerously low and hadn't started to go up yet. Dr Thompson was confident that once the levels began to rise, they would replenish rapidly: but he did warn that, even then, Mark would need to remain vigilant. Jack and Tim continued to train together when they could, in between working as training partners for the ranked players. It was a quiet Christmas and New Year for everyone.

The boys had well and truly resigned themselves to not making the qualifying tournament when in early January, totally out of the blue, a call came through from Tennis Australia. They had both been put on the reserve list of players for the Australian Open qualifying event! This was a fantasy come true, and absolutely unexpected after they had declared themselves unable to play in Sydney. They tried not to get too excited over the following days, while they awaited the outcome. It was still a long shot that either of them would make the cut. Fred Elkes rang several times with updates. The first call was to tell them they had moved up the reserve list when one player pulled out, citing family reasons. Next call was to tell them that five of the top players had decided to go to South Africa to play, just as Fred had forecast twelve months earlier. They were edging closer to the cut-off. Then came the phone call they hadn't dared to hope for. Two players had pulled out due to injury. They were in!

Despite all the odds, Tim and Jack were now officially two of the 128 hopefuls who would battle out three qualifying rounds before the main draw of the Open began. The top sixteen would go into the main draw, and there would be eight additional wildcard spots available as well.

Fred Elkes and Paul came to the house to celebrate the fabulous news. Jenny apologised profusely to Fred that he couldn't come inside, but he understood completely. They had morning tea on the porch, well distanced from each other, while they discussed what would happen when the tournament started.

"And you'll earn some decent money as well," Fred told the boys, smiling. "You're in the big league now. They'll pay you to play. Even if you lose in the first round of the qualifier, which you won't, you'll be paid around $500. Sponsors fund the tournament at this level. Tickets are sold to paying public, and you get paid to play for them. If you make it to round one of the main draw, the loser still gets $4600."

"Wow," was all Jack could say.

"But we need you both to qualify into the main draw, because it will give you a better chance of being given a wildcard entry into the doubles as well. There are seven wildcards on offer for the doubles. The first fifty-seven spots are taken by the highest-ranked doubles teams, with the final spots left to the discretion of the organisers. As young local players with potential, especially with your satellite doubles record, you have a good chance of being offered a rare doubles wildcard. If you make it into the main draw as singles players, that will give you even more credibility, and they'll be more inclined to offer you a doubles wildcard entry as well.

"I really believe you've got a secret weapon in the way you combine together, and I can't wait to see what you can do at this level in doubles. The tennis fans will love you. There is nothing better for the game than to have a couple of locals do well," Fred enthused, beaming at them.

While the others continued to discuss the training schedule in the lead up, Jack zoned out into a mild sense of panic. He had gotten used to a few spectators, but they had just been hanging-around spectators, not people who had paid money to watch him play. That was a whole new level of angst to add to his already building nerves. He looked over at Tim who met his eyes with raised eyebrows and a wide-eyed look of his own. Jack wasn't alone in feeling the pressure.

Mr Mac, who knew them both very well, noticed the anxious looks they were exchanging. Before he left, he took them aside, reassuring them once again in his calm, perceptive manner, "Don't stress. This is still just a game of tennis. All you have to do is take one point at a time. One game at a time. Don't get too far ahead. I'll guide you through it and believe me, it won't be nearly as difficult as some of the matches you've already won in your satellite tournaments. You have progressed so much in these last weeks; you are absolutely ready for this. I wouldn't have backed you in this if I didn't think you could handle it. Okay?" he finished, looking them each in the eye in turn as he tried to settle them down.

They both nodded back, as always trusting him, and feeling slightly more at ease at their coach's words. These words became their mantra as they filled the days leading up to the qualifier with a regime of practise, fitness, and recovery sessions.

CHAPTER 17

Several days later, at Flinders Park Tennis Centre, Tim wished he could be anywhere else. Taking a deep breath, he repeated the mantra, "One point at a time. One game at a time." He flushed the toilet, straightened his shoulders, and opened the cubicle door. He gave a swift, almost furtive glance around before stepping out to wash his hands and splash his face.

It was his third trip to the toilet in half an hour, and he hoped no-one else was counting. He jogged lightly back to where his grandfather and Mr Mac were talking quietly. There were other similar groups dotted around the locker room, also waiting for their games to be called. Tim looked at their composure and self-contained demeanours with envy. His right leg jiggled nervously.

His grandfather put a hand on his knee. "Just relax! You're making me tired just looking at you," he smiled.

"A few nerves are a good sign," reassured Mr Mac. "When we were waiting with Jack, I thought he was going to pass out with the sheer terror of waiting, but once he got on the court, he took it all out on poor Vogel. It was a demolition." He shook his head, relishing the memory of Jack's win.

Tim took a deep breath in and a long sigh out. Jack's first-round victory did help settle Tim a bit. After all, if Jack could do it, so could he. He just had to shake off this feeling that he was out of his league. Stretching his arms above his head, he stood slowly and went once more through the pre-game warm-up routine that he and Jack completed before every match and every practise session. Not only had it so far prevented them getting an injury, but the familiarity of the routine also helped him control his nerves. He missed Mark at this moment, but he had Pa and Mr Mac, and he had spoken to his dad by phone that morning before they left for Flinders Park.

Yesterday, with impeccably bad timing, Mark's temperature had suddenly gone up. Dr Thompson didn't hesitate. Mark was immediately put into hospital, in isolation, with only Jenny allowed to visit, and only if she was in full protective gear. It looked like an overreaction, but they trusted Dr Thompson completely and complied. Jack and Tim had hoped that Mark would be able to make one of their matches, but with this new development it was looking unlikely. Pa was already the designated backup, and he was delighted to be part of the support crew. The crop was in, he had a young roustabout looking after the farm and the sheep, and he was ready to stay in Melbourne for as long as they lasted in the competition.

Tim's name was finally called, and he walked out to the court alongside his opponent, a guy from Western Australia called William Cole who, at sixteen, was their current state junior champion. He was also playing in the junior events, so Tim didn't feel too sorry for him when, after playing some flashy shots, William struggled to find his rhythm. Tim won relatively easily in the third set. Day one of the qualifier was over. Both Jack and Tim were into the second round.

Jack's win that first day had been significant and attracted some attention. Serge Vogel from Germany was returning to form after an injury that had sidelined him for eighteen months. He had been ranked in the top thirty before his injury and would probably still be given a wildcard entry, but he needed match practise, and had opted to go through the qualifiers to sharpen his game. It was expected that he would meet with little opposition, and no-one gave Jack much of a chance. However, Vogel looked rusty and lacked his old touch, sending several balls long. Even after Jack won in two sets, only conceding four games, people didn't give him full credit, calling it a fluke.

Jack's match on the second day brought a few more spectators. He drew Guy Longridge of England, who was two years older, experienced, and just as fearless as Jack. Their games were drawn-out and hard-fought battles, but Jack steadily won the points that counted and was the eventual winner in three sets. Tim watched from the stands and could only be inspired by his little brother's mix of brilliance and considered shot making. He was hoping to emulate him; however, in his second-round match he lacked Jack's assurance. Struggling to concentrate, his game almost deserted him, leaving him vulnerable.

Tim's opponent was Jake Rollins from the US, a skilful left-handed player who had Tim's measure. Mr Mac had worked on mental strategies as part of their preparation. Convincing them that feeling nervous was a positive, he talked them through ways they could use the added adrenaline to sharpen their focus and play with heightened awareness. Unfortunately, it didn't always work. Tim was aware that he took longer to settle into his game at the best of times than Jack did, and this time he lost the first set before he'd had a chance to think about focusing his energy. He knew he needed to find his rhythm and pace, and it took great deal of serious self-talk, after losing the first set too easily at 3/6, before he managed to get back into the game. The lead fluctuated but Tim finally found his confidence, making Rollins work for every point, keeping the ball in play and contesting long rallies.

This was when he played his best tennis: intelligent percentage tennis, keeping every ball in play, and letting his opponents make the unforced errors. When he walked off in three sets as the eventual winner, Pa breathed out a long sigh of relief. He felt like had had been holding his breath for two hours. Meanwhile, Jack and Mr Mac were grinning from ear to ear. Both boys had made it through to the third round, and Tim felt pumped and ridiculously proud of himself.

Every evening, when they got back from the tennis centre, Jenny would be home from the hospital and waiting for them. She listened eagerly to their blow-by-blow descriptions of each day's play, and in return she would give them news of their dad. They talked to Mark by phone but, as Jenny explained, he wasn't able to talk for long, on doctor's orders. It was great to hear his voice, at least, and they could tell Paul Mac was keeping him well informed, as he always knew in advance who they would face in competition the next day. Jenny had promised that once they had finished the qualifying rounds they could go to the hospital for a visit. They were looking forward to seeing Mark and telling him in person about the whole experience. Neither of them were unduly worried about their dad. He was still in remission, and his blood count had been down for weeks, so they assumed this was just a matter of precaution. No-one else seemed overly concerned. They both thought it was a bit crazy they couldn't visit him, but then they were so absorbed themselves with warm-ups, playing, and cool downs, that there wasn't much time to do anything other than eat or sleep.

Sunday was the last day of the qualifying tournament. The 128 players who started would be reduced to the final sixteen. This group would go through to compete in the main draw for the Australian Open, and the remaining wildcard spots were yet to be announced. Tim's match was the first scheduled game of the morning, so he was spared the long, anxious wait for his match to be called. The early start must have helped because he won his third and final round, decisively cruising through a two-set victory over Jim Waters of the US, a young guy from Destin, Florida, and a newcomer to the circuit. Tim commiserated with him at the net after crushing his opponent's hopes of making the main draw.

"Great game, mate," Tim said as they shook hands.

"No, great game to you, maate," said Jim, with an attempt at the Aussie accent. "Best of luck in the Open. I'll be rooting for you. If you win, it will take the pressure off me losing here for a start," he managed to joke, despite his obvious disappointment.

"Good luck on maybe getting a wildcard," replied Tim, high-fiving him before heading off to the practise courts where Jack was waiting. Jack had another hour before his final match, and Tim was going to hit a few balls with him to cool down while Jack warmed up. Several spectators stood by the court watching them as they hit back and forth. This was unusual attention for them but, as Tim said to Jack when they met at the net, it was all good practise for them to get used to a crowd watching.

Since Jack had beaten the highly favoured Vogel, he found himself being greeted by tournament officials and players by name, and he'd even had his photo taken with fans. When Tim made it through to the main draw, several officials and players had approached him offering congratulations. It remained only for Jack to win his final round and they would both be there. Jack's win was crucial. Their doubles wildcard entry was not assured, but doubles was where they knew their best chance of success would lie. They were counting on the Australian Open selection committee to decide that if they were both good enough to make the singles, they were also worthy of a doubles entry.

Not long after his warm down, Tim sat, still in his tennis gear, in the players' section seats of the main outer court, with his mum, Pa, and Mr Mac, watching intently as Jack walked on the court for his final match. He was relieved to be the one watching on and relaxed for a change, but he felt for Jack who was under pressure at the moment.

Jonas Schnook from the Netherlands awaited Jack, his six-foot-two frame looking athletic as he hopped lightly from one foot to the other. He was a burly blond giant and he greeted Jack with disarming friendliness and impeccable English, making Jack feel slightly inadequate because he could only speak English. Jonas had also won his previous matches with relative ease, and he was looking confident and in control. The weather had been slowly warming up for several days, and by early afternoon it was already hitting thirty degrees.

Jonas had the advantage of being far more experienced. He had competed in qualifying tournaments such as this all over the world, only recently losing his 105 ATP ranking after taking time off with a couple of injuries. He was definitely a player on his way up.

Most of the time, Tim and Jack knew very little about their opponents. Mr Mac, as always, was their scout, gathering what information he could pre-match about their style of play.

However, it wasn't always easy to find much, especially against their international opponents, so they had to work them out as quickly as they could in the first few games. While the brothers never dared to underestimate an opponent, their rivals inevitably did fall into the trap of underestimating two unknowns who, along with Flinders Park, had Winjarra Tennis Club listed as their home club.

Jack won the toss and served first, winning it in textbook fashion. In the next game he took Jonas by surprise with some strong returns, breaking his serve, and then quickly winning his own next service game. Jack was 3/0 up before Jonas realised the quality of his opposition. He should not have been so complacent in those crucial early games, because he allowed Jack to gain his confidence. Finding his rhythm early, Jack won the first set. Jonas quickly changed his style of play and settled into some strong rallies, hitting deep and keeping Jack on the defensive.

As the match progressed, the conditions on the court became quite stifling. The Rebound Ace could get very hot underfoot, but this was something Jack was prepared for, with thick, absorbent socks that added an extra layer of coolness. He was also well used to playing in a cap, which helped keep the sun off his head and out of his eyes. In the hot climate of Winjarra, there was no way you would play sport in the middle of the day without a hat, and wearing a cap was now second nature to Jack. The European players, having honed most of their tennis skills indoors, were sometimes disadvantaged by this, and the Dutchman favoured a sweatband rather than a cap. He had no relief from the blazing afternoon sun, which was getting into his eyes and bothering him.

At the end of the second set, Jonas had clawed his way back into the match, winning it in a tie breaker; but he was clearly succumbing to the Australian heat far quicker than Jack. It was time for Jack to make the most of the hot conditions and use it to his advantage. He noticed the big Dutchman liked to hug the backline, preferring to move defensively from one side to the other. He seemed reluctant to go to the net, but once there, with his huge reach, he was more than capable of getting to most shots. Jack began taking advantage of his baseline defence by dropping balls short over the net where possible.

The short sprints to the net took their toll in the heat. Jonas began making more errors as his energy depleted, and Jack was able to step-up his aggression. When he won the third set comfortably, Jack's first reaction was pure relief. He sensed that Jonas was probably a far more talented player than himself, but he had managed to outsmart him, and he silently thanked Mr Mac for the time spent developing his fitness. Jack doubted, as they shook hands, that Jonas would make the mistake of underestimating the next unknown Australian he played in the sweltering summer sun.

Jack and Tim were feeling quite overwhelmed later that afternoon as they made their way out of Flinders Park. They had received so many congratulations from players and officials and, although it wasn't official yet, they been quietly assured by Fred Elkes of a wildcard entry into the men's doubles championships. Fred was nearly beside himself with excitement that his two protégés had performed so well—way above expectations, in fact—and he was keen to introduce them to everyone he knew. It had been difficult to slink away at the end of the day because their low profile was now in tatters. It had been a valuable shield from all the pressure of the last three days, and they were sorry to see it disappear.

Eventually they managed to escape, and Nan and Pa drove them straight to the hospital to see Dad. They were excited at the prospect because there was so much to tell him. They were totally unprepared for what they encountered. Their first indication that something was amiss was arriving at the entrance to the sterile ward and being asked to sanitise their hands and don protective gear over their tennis clothes and shoes.

Mum had warned them they wouldn't be able to go into dad's room because he was being isolated, and that they would only be able to see him through the observation window. However, once they saw him, it was clear that Jenny hadn't told them the full story. Their dad looked sick. Really sick.

Tim swore softly under his breath.

"Far out!" whispered Jack, drawing out each syllable.

Noticing them at the window, Mark instinctively smiled, brightening his features and making him appear slightly better. But Jack and Tim had already seen his unguarded face, grey and exhausted by illness, and immediately unwelcome memories of three years ago had come rushing back. Jenny was with him in the room, gowned like them, but also with a facemask, surgical cap, and gloves. She had been at both their matches earlier that day, but she had taken her own car and had left as soon as Jack's match finished.

The thumbs up from Mark told them that she had already passed on the good news of their wins. There was a phone connection into the room and one of the nurses set it up so they could have a three-way conversation with their dad. He was far more ill than they had expected. With his immunity once again compromised, an infection was running rampant through his system. He looked dangerously weak, and the boys noticed what an effort it was for him to talk.

The nurse murmured to them not to tire him out, and they were mindful of this as they gave a quick rundown of their games that day. They already knew the details of the draw for their respective first matches in the Open, and they discussed that quickly. Mark wished them luck and told them yet again how proud he was of them. He pointed to the television in the room and said he would be watching every match, hoping to get a sight of them. Then they waved goodbye and left, trying not to show just how shocked they were at his decline in three or four days.

It was unlikely their matches would be televised, but it was good to know their dad would be watching the telecast and listening for any mention of them. It rattled them to see him so desperately ill, especially since, only a few days ago, he was only slightly unwell with a raised temperature. Once again, he was seriously weak, confined to bed, and hooked up to any number of tubes and intravenous fluids, while machines constantly monitored his wellbeing. In contrast to their earlier elation, it was a very subdued pair that met up with Nan and Pa a short time later in the hospital car park.

Jack collapsed into Nan's waiting arms, needing a big hug. Pa put his arms around Tim and squeezed him tightly. They had known how sick Mark was, and they had felt terrible keeping it from them.

"What's happening, Pa? We didn't know Dad was this bad! I thought he just had a high temperature and they had to be careful of germs. He looks awful," Tim exclaimed, thinking of that first vision of Mark—pale, sweaty, and dozing—before he rallied on seeing them.

Nan was brutally honest this time. "Let's go home and talk about this. But it's time you knew everything. Your father is gravely ill. Dr Thompson says this could go either way. Mark's immune system needs to start working, and soon. He's been given another transfusion to top up his white blood cell count, but his own body needs to start making white blood cells, if he is ever going to fight the infection he has."

Nan's words were sobering. They got into the car and headed home in a strained silence, each with their own depressing thoughts. Nan gave them time to take in the news she and Pa had known for days, before adding, "On the positive side though, your dad is young, and before all this cancer started, he was a healthy, strong bloke. I wouldn't give up on him so quickly. They have to prepare us for the worst, but, you know, I just feel he'll be okay. And I've been praying hard for him to get well, and so has your pa. It helps, you know, to send up a few prayers."

"We can't keep playing tennis with all this happening," said Jack, totally devastated.

"I don't want to even think about tennis now," said Tim dejectedly. "I can't get that image of Dad out of my head."

"I know, Tim. We saw him quickly last night and he looks terrible. It is confronting, and scary, how quickly the infection has taken hold. His immunity was obviously dreadful, and we're just so lucky they put him straight into hospital, or who knows what might have happened." Jim paused for a few moments. "But this doesn't let you two off the hook. The possibility of watching you boys play tomorrow and the next day is a huge motivation for him. It's going to be very important in his recovery. He'll be shattered if he thinks you gave up this fantastic opportunity, one that you have worked so hard for, because of him. Hearing about how well you played is like a tonic for him, and even if it seems impossible right now, you need to get out there tomorrow and play the best tennis of your life."

"I know," replied Tim without enthusiasm.

"It's a tough ask. We all understand. But we'll be there with you, and you know your dad will be listening to every shot on the radio as well. Maybe he'll even get to watch it on TV. I'm sure the ABC radio will cover any local matches the TV networks can't. And what would you achieve by pulling out? The hospital won't let you in to see him. Jenny is the only one allowed in. The best thing you can give him is the thrill of knowing you are playing in the Australian Open. That's priceless medicine for him that no doctor can provide," said Jim firmly, trying to encourage them.

Tim and Jack had nothing to say. Tim nodded glumly and Jack wiped away a tear. This was surely asking too much of them.

As they pulled into the driveway, Nan said practically, "You need to ring Karen and tell her family that you've both made it through. I promised Clare we'd let them know as soon as possible."

Karen's was ecstatic when she heard the news. She knew more than anyone just how hard Jack and Tim had worked to get to this point, and she had been a large part of it all. She screamed out the news to her parents and sisters, who came rushing to the phone with congratulations and questions. It was quite a commotion for a while and it made Tim smile, in spite of his worry about his dad.

"We're coming down tomorrow, Tim. We were just waiting to hear the news before we confirmed it. We'll be there for every match, cheering you guys on. How's Jack? I can't believe he's going to be first up tomorrow. The town will be gunning for him for sure. And for you, of course! When I get off the phone, I'll let everyone know."

"I think he's a little nervous. His first match is against Chris Walker of the UK. I think he's ranked in the top eighty, and poor Jack's not going to have much time to relax. At least I have one day off before I have to play."

"He'll be fine. He's used to playing daily matches in the satellite rounds, and he always had the best match fitness of all of us."

Tim agreed, then said, "Karen, Dad's in hospital."

Immediately there was silence. Karen knew as much as Tim did about Mark's illness. She realised instantly this meant a serious change in his health status and listened intently as Tim poured out everything that had happened in the hospital and his confusion about even playing tennis at a time when his father was literally hanging between life and death.

"It's exactly what you have to do," she replied firmly. "How could you not play? This probably means more to him than it does to you. Remember it got him out of that slump he was in after chemo. It gave him something to live for, and it was a road back to health for him. Coaching you and Jack gave him back his spark. You can't give up now when he needs something more than ever to distract him."

"I know you're right, and that's what Nan and Pa have said to us. It's just so overwhelming. I can't even think straight at the moment. And when I start to play, I know I forget everything else, and that makes me feel guilty. I hardly gave Dad a thought today while I was playing, except to remember a coaching tip or two. The game was all I was thinking about, and all the time Dad was getting sicker and sicker."

"That's exactly the way it should be and, trust me, that's exactly what your dad wants you to do at the moment. And I'll be there watching to make sure you concentrate entirely on tennis. Give your dad our best wishes and we're all sending get well vibes to him. And by the way, I miss you."

"I miss you too," replied Tim before hanging up.

Tim did feel more at ease after talking to Karen. He was still feeling shell-shocked though, and he and Jack talked things over for a long time before they both agreed that they were doing the right thing by playing. It was impossible to reconcile all the emotions they were feeling. But it came down to one thing: the realisation that Mark would be devastated if they didn't give it a shot. Neither of them wanted to cause him unnecessary grief by not playing. Reluctantly, but united in their conviction, they made a pact to go out, all guns blazing, play their best tennis, and not leave themselves wondering what could have been.

CHAPTER 18

Tim sat in the players' seats the next day with Pa, Mr Mac, Nanna, and Karen and her family, watching Jack, feeling relieved that it wasn't him out on court. They had arrived three hours earlier at Flinders Park, and even at 8 am there was a different tempo to the day. This time, parking spots were scarce, and Pa needed to use a player's pass to get through the gates, allowing him access to the players' entrance. Yesterday, for the last qualifier, the crowd was minimal. Today there were queues to get into every turnstile, and the atmosphere was alive with excitement. The paths to and from the outside practise courts were lined with spectators trying to get a glimpse of their favourite players. Jack and Tim were awestruck as they saw, close-up, several of their tennis idols going through their practise routines on courts adjacent to them.

As Jack's allotted warm-up time finished, and he and Tim began gathering their gear, the next practise pair walked onto the court. They acknowledged Jack and Tim briefly before going immediately into their obviously well-rehearsed warm-up routine. The boys did a double take as they simultaneously recognised Anders Johannson from Sweden, the world number five, as he took to the court. They had watched his matches often with Mark, dissecting every detail and trying to learn from them. Now they were in the same draw as him and sharing the same practise court!

They managed to keep their cool, walking as nonchalantly as they could towards the locker rooms and out of earshot, before Tim exclaimed, hissing under his breath to Jack, "Whoa! I'm only going to say this once, because I have to, and then I'll never say it or think it again because Dad would kill us for saying it. But what the hell are we doing playing in a tournament with the best in the world?"

"Jeez, I don't know either, but I'm going to blame you for it," replied Jack, seeing the funny side of it, and laughing at the sheer craziness of it all. Then in a serious tone he continued, "I'm absolutely terrified, but there is only one way and that's forward, and we can't exactly pull out, so this is it. We play the best damn tennis we can!"

"Yeah! You are so right. And we earned our spots in this tournament the hard way, so we deserve to be here," Tim reminded Jack.

"And remember …" they finished the mantra, their heads close together, "it's one point at a time, one game at a time."

Tim put his arm around Jack's shoulders, squeezing him in a brotherly hug before he left him to get ready for his match. "You can do this, bro. I know you can."

Jack's first match was on an outside court, normally quiet, but today packed with spectators. He wasn't a name player, but because he was an Aussie, a Melbourne boy—a local, no less— there were plenty of fans there to support him. *The Age* and the *Herald Sun* newspapers had both run articles on the two brothers, previous unknowns in the tennis world who had won through the qualifying tournament to earn a place in the draw for the Australian Open. A sportswriter in *The Age* had written a background story on them, how they were Melbourne boys, and brothers, who had competed well in recent satellite tournaments. Consequently, there were lots of tennis followers who were keen to watch them play.

It had been a long time since Australian tennis players had dominated the rankings, and there was great interest to see who the next young upcoming star might be. Who could fulfil their dreams of another Aussie champion? There were several Australians in the draw, but the idea of two unknown brothers playing made great newspaper copy. Added to this was their entry into the doubles as well as singles. The wildcard entry promised by their guardian angel, Fred, had indeed come through. He had predicted correctly that the selection committee would be well aware that giving an Australian pair a wildcard entry would be popular with the public. Popular decisions aside, they had in any case earned the right to play the hard way, on their own merits.

Halfway through his match, when the parochial cheers of support became louder and more animated, Jack had to suppress a grin. Having such vocal support from everyone in the crowd gave him an added boost, and he drew on it for some inspired shot making. His English opponent, Chris Walker, was an accomplished player and, as his ranking of eighty-two suggested, he was completely at home in a major tournament. Under normal circumstances he should have wiped the court with Jack, but this was the Australian Open, and not everything goes to plan. Jack's almost reckless style of play, combined with his speed around the court, paid dividends. Chris was also facing a completely unknown quantity in Jack, and he had no answer for Jack's "I'm putting everything on the line" style of play. When he demolished Walker, in four very entertaining sets, the crowd stood and clapped loudly to show their appreciation. Jack acknowledged them all with a wave and a clap at the end, appearing very composed. The fans had a new star to champion.

Before he could complete his warm down with Tim, Jack had to attend his first obligatory press conference. There were lots of questions, and they came thick and fast.

"How happy were you with your game today, Jack?"

"Did you give yourself a chance before the game?"

Jack looked like a deer in the headlights for a few seconds, and then he answered, with great poise beyond his seventeen years, "I was hoping to play well, and I was lucky that some of my shots came off. Chris is a really strong player and he made it very hard for me out there. He was just unlucky, I think, and the crowd support was awesome and really helped me."

"Who is the stronger player? You or your brother?"

Tim was watching from the side of the room, and laughed as Jack said, deadpan, "I am, of course, but don't tell him I said that because he thinks he is."

The reporters loved it, and after a couple more questions Jack was able to escape, escorted off by one of the officials to make way for the next conference where Anders Johannson was to be centre stage after winning his first round. Once Jack had a chance to collect his gear and they had made their way through the bowels of the tennis centre to the exit, Jim picked them up and they went straight to the hospital.

This time they were emotionally more prepared, but unfortunately Mark was so fatigued that he barely acknowledged them before closing his eyes and seeming to fall back asleep. Tim thought his dad looked worse, if it was possible. While they were gowning up, he had asked the charge nurse how Mark was. She had said not to worry that he was tired because that was normal, and that even though there was no significant change for the better, he also hadn't deteriorated any further, and this was a good sign. In short, they were more hopeful today that his condition would improve.

His white blood cell count had remained steady overnight, not dropping any lower, and this was seen as a positive by the doctors. It gave them some indication that his body was beginning to develop antibodies to counter the infection. Mark had listened to the match on the radio with Jenny, and she told Jack that he had really wanted to talk to him about it, but he had exhausted himself just listening to it. When Jack heard that Mark had sparked up visibly during the match, it made him even more determined to play well. They stayed a while talking to him, although his eyes stayed closed the whole time. However, when they said their goodbyes there was a slight smile and a wave of his fingers, so perhaps he had been listening after all.

Mark still looked dreadful. They could only imagine how miserable he was feeling. Jenny stayed at the hospital that night, but she was back in the morning to wish Tim good luck before he left for the tennis centre.

Day two of the Open, and it was Tim's turn. As they sat together in the locker room before the match, Pa talked quietly to Tim about the possible crowd noise and distraction. Jack's win had made the back pages of the paper, and there had been a brief mention that his older brother, Tim, was in action at Flinders Park the next day. Tim had mentally prepared himself for a crowd.

"Is it going to be a worry for you?" asked Pa.

Tim shook his head. "Once I start playing, I'll be alright. It's just this waiting that's the killer. Jack and I finished on the practise court at ten, and now it's after eleven, with no word of a start time. I'm more worried I'll get cold."

"Cold! Its thirty-five degrees out there in the shade! How on earth can you think about getting cold?" laughed Pa. "It's stinking hot in here! I'm wilting!"

Pa's usual pragmatism and dry humour helped lighten Tim's mood. As a lower-ranked player, his match, like Jack's, was also to be on an outside court; Centre Court and the other main courts were reserved for the top seeds that always drew a larger crowd.

Summer had finally arrived in Melbourne, and this was the third day in a row that the temperature had soared well into the thirties. The more enclosed main courts and Centre Court, despite their open roofs, were legendary for the heat that reflected off their surfaces. The temperature was artificially cooked up well into the forties as the hot air had little escape. It was a bonus over the long two weeks of the competition if players could avoid that sort of energy sapping experience.

"Anything else you've got on your mind?"

"Can't I just pull out of this? I feel a bit weak."

Pa's blue eyes narrowed at Tim.

"This guy was playing tennis before I could tie my shoelaces. I've watched him on TV. He's ranked at fifty-two!" Tim blurted out. "I'm out of my depth!"

"Rubbish. If your dad was here, he'd be disgusted. You have the talent, and you have the ability, concentration, and the skill to win this. You've hit balls with guys like him all summer. Your reflexes and shots are just as good as his. You just need the courage to be strong. When you get on the court you won't care that he's Roland Blass, because he's just another opponent. I know you. Your killer instinct will fire up and you'll give it everything you've got, because you like winning. I'm right, aren't I?"

Tim nodded. Pa was a perceptive old fellow and Tim knew he was right. He was going to love this opportunity to mix it with the best, despite his nerves.

"Now, remember what Paul Mac said. This guy Blass is a frontrunner. You saw him at Wimbledon. Once he lost the first set, his game started to fall apart. Attack his backhand with power right from the start, and you just might get the first set advantage. Lay it all on the line in the first few games, then dig in and hold on."

Mr Mac appeared at the door of the dressing rooms just as a tournament official approached to marshal Tim to the court. Tim looked over to Blass, who had been sitting with his coach and support staff at the far end of the room, and who was now gathering his things.

Tim was ready. He collected his bag, retied his shoelaces and, after a few last words of good luck and advice from Mr Mac and Pa, joined his opponent for the congested walk through the crowds to the court. Tim kept his head down much of the way, while Roland was frequently stopped for autographs. Roland had a clothing deal from the European clothing brand Sergio Tacchini, and Tim had to admit he looked great, especially since he was also ridiculously good-looking. Tim felt a little dull in comparison in his mismatched tennis gear, all of which had been free.

As the two players arrived at the court and were introduced, there was brief applause, and the crowd began to settle themselves for the match. Tim searched the faces to find his small band of supporters and support staff: Grandpa and Nan, Mr Mac, Jack and Jenny, Karen and her family. He smiled at the sight of Karen's flaming, unruly hair, squashed firmly under a sun hat, and he took another calming breath. He hadn't expected his mum to be there, but that also made his spirits lift, thinking that it was a good sign if she felt she could leave the hospital for a while. The umpire signalled for the pre-game hit-up to begin, and Tim forgot everything else.

Roland had a huge serve that challenged Tim, stretching him to his limits. He had won the toss and elected to serve, and his first service game was a devastating lesson in accuracy. He got every first serve in while Tim struggled to make a return. Roland looked confident and composed as they changed ends for the first time. Tim was a bit worried, but he knew the law of averages wouldn't allow Roland to keep a start going like that indefinitely, and he fought back immediately with an excellent service game himself.

Roland continued to serve strongly, and the power he could generate on serve was easily the toughest Tim had faced in his short career. He had been well prepared for such a player though, by both Mark and Mr Mac, and now all those drills in which he had trained standing close to the service line to return Jack's serves at their most powerful point of impact proved their value. Even so, he was constantly pushed to find a way to get a racquet to the ball.

Tim's tenacity in returning many of Blass's winning serves gradually wore away at the German's confidence, and he began to show frustration as Tim scrambled back some of his best serves to keep them in play. You could also sense his growing irritation as the pro-Australian crowd clapped wildly at every point Tim won. Roland was used to being a crowd favourite himself, but he was too experienced and too professional to let that disturb his game, and he maintained his focus.

Tim matched him game for game until it was six games all, and the crowd loved it. Both players knew this was a vital moment in the match. So far, Tim had been trying, when possible, to attack his opponent's backhand, with little success.

According to Mr. Mac there was a weakness there to exploit. He took a punt after winning a point when Roland handled a high backhand volley awkwardly. It was never an easy shot, but he wasn't under pressure at the time, and he'd had a realistic chance to put it away for a winner.

On his next return of serve Tim held back and, driving the ball deep, forced Roland over to the forehand court. Popping the next shot across court and high to Roland's backhand, Roland was caught out of position and his volley fell short, allowing Tim to make good an easy passing shot. He repeated the high ball to Roland's backhand at the next opportunity, and this time had the satisfaction of Roland over hitting the return volley. It was risky play though, and the next time he tried, Roland moved swiftly to take the volley on his forehand. By then, however, Tim was up 5/2 in the tie breaker and, despite Roland winning two points in a row in his next two serves, Tim managed to win his serve, and hung on to take the first set.

Tim knew the match was far from over, but he had managed to shake the German's confidence just a little, and better still Tim began to really believe he could win. However, Roland Blass hadn't won three European titles to be beaten by a guy barely out of the junior ranks, and he rallied to win the second set 6/4.

Surprising himself most of all, Tim was not at all fazed by this. He felt strong and determined. He knew he was playing good, percentage tennis, and although Roland had played some amazing shots to win the second set, Tim could sense that he was wearing him down with his dogged consistency. He continued to attack.

Roland's backhand hadn't faltered despite Tim's constant probing, though he moved quickly to cover it when he could. At 4/3 in the third set Roland mistimed a relatively easy backhand shot that landed midcourt, sending it wide. Tim felt a familiar little shiver at the base of his neck. Was this a possible chink in Roland's armour?

Keep mixing it up and you can win this, he told himself.

Relentlessly, he kept probing and pounding away at Roland's backhand, varying the speed of his shots and their depth. Roland still managed to win points from his backhand returns, but the odds of him making an unforced error began to move in Tim's favour.

It took five punishing sets before Tim won, but he didn't doubt for a minute that he could do it. As the umpire called out, "Game, set, and match to Tim Anderson of Australia," Tim slumped forward, his hands on his knees, with sudden exhaustion.

A very subdued and dejected Roland murmured, "Well played," at the net as they shook hands. With great sportsmanship he also clapped Tim, while the crowd stood and cheered them both. At 7/6, 4/6, 6/3, 4/6, 7/5, it had been a thoroughly entertaining match. Tim acknowledged the crowd and the umpires before making a quick dash to where his family and friends stood, still jumping up and down with excitement and hugging each other.

Karen gave him a big hug, as did Jenny, Pa, and Jack, who managed to ruffle Tim's sweaty hair, before he had to gather his things and exit the court with the tournament official assigned to him. Together with Roland, Tim was then shepherded to a press conference in one of the interview rooms set up for the media in the bowels of Flinders Park.

Tim also handled his press conference reasonably well for someone with no prior experience. Luckily for him, most questions were being directed at Roland who was obviously, as a higher-ranked player, a surprise first-round knockout. It gave

Tim a chance to catch his breath and his wits before the media turned their attention on him. Roland was clearly very disappointed, but was generous in his praise of Tim.

"How do you feel after defeating a player of Roland Blass's calibre in your first time at the Open?"

"Roland played some great tennis, I think I just got lucky out there today," Tim answered with genuine humility.

Most questions covered how he felt about causing an upset at this early stage of the draw. Tim made sure he gave plenty of praise to Roland and acknowledged that Roland may have been slightly off his game.

"Can you tell us some more about your brother, Jack? How do you rate his chances tomorrow?"

"I think he'll do well. He's playing some great tennis and he'll certainly be giving it his best shot."

"Can you tell us how you both prepared for the Open? I understand you train together?" asked a reporter from *The Age* newspaper, who looked like he already knew a bit about what he was asking.

"Yes. We always train together with our coach, Paul Maclaren, and we use each other as warm-up partners."

"You must get on well as brothers, then. No sibling rivalry in the household?" asked another reporter, who jumped in before the guy from *The Age* could go onto more detail.

Tim made a joke about not being able to get away from Jack, even at home, and time was called on the press conference. The next day when he read the newspaper, he breathed a sigh of relief. He hadn't come across too badly and, in fact, the story was more about Roland bombing out in the first round, rather than the unknown who had beaten him. So far, they had been let off easily from media attention.

When Jack went on to win his way into the third round the next day, by defeating another Australian who had been fancied as a chance to make the quarter finals, there was a much bigger headline: "ANDERSON BROTHERS LEAVE THE BUSH BEHIND".

It was rather corny, but Nan cut it out and pasted it in a scrapbook with all their other newspaper clippings.

Time was fast running out on them being able to stay under the radar of the press, who currently had very little information about them. They had only played in a handful of satellite tournaments, after all. This did not compare favourably with the majority of players, who came with a credible tennis resume of matches won or lost on tour, and at major events.

Mr Mac was their official coach, while Mark was named as manager. Mr Mac, as a former professional player on the grand slam circuit, gave them something to write about, and the enterprising journalist from *The Age* noted that their grandfather had been a country regional champion in his day. He also wrote a flattering piece about Mr Mac's skill as a versatile player while on the circuit.

Most reporters looked on them as an interesting sideshow and gave them little chance of continued success. It had all been seen before by the hardened journos: the unknown rookie who wins a lucky match and then disappears forever back to the lesser tournaments until they give up.

When Tim won his second match, following Jack into the third round, the media interest went up significantly. Tim's second match was a tough battle against another wildcard, Uri Danke of Russia, who matched him point for point as they slugged it out in four sets, in muggy weather and under a very threatening sky.

When Tim won in a tie breaker in the fourth, just before the rain came, he felt very lucky. He couldn't imagine having to stop mid-game, wait for the rain to stop, and then start again with the same momentum. This time the press conference was trickier. Danke's English was sketchy at best, and most questions were directed towards Tim.

"Tell us about your grandfather, Tim. Was it because of him that you began playing tennis? How old were you when you started?"

"Yes, my pa was a great player. He's been a big influence on us. Jack and I had a bit of a hit with Pa about three years ago and we liked it so much we didn't stop."

"Are you serious? Are you saying that you have only been playing for three years?"

Tim shifted uncomfortably in his chair. He hadn't meant it to come out like that, as if they had only just taken up the sport. Most people wouldn't understand how hard they had worked in that short time to get to this stage. He silently cursed his slip. Both he and Jack had vowed to dodge this question, because they wanted to be treated with the same respect that the other professionals were. They certainly didn't want to expose themselves as inexperienced to the other players. Thinking quickly on his feet, he chose his next words carefully.

"That is, I mean, we didn't get really serious about our tennis until three years ago. It's a bit of a different path, but it has been a great advantage to have each other to practise with, and our dad could step in as coach whenever Mr Mac couldn't be there. We both love playing tennis and we've worked very hard over the last few years to get to this level."

"What are your plans for the future?"

"What can you tell us about your next match?"

"What will you do if you have to play each other?"

"You have a wildcard entry into the men's doubles. Isn't this an ambitious workload for two rookies?"

There were so many questions being fired at him at once, but Tim wisely chose the last one to answer.

"Yes, Jack and I play our first doubles match on Friday. We were lucky to make the draw, and there are some really great teams in the competition, so we're looking forward to it."

"You have an impressive doubles record together. How do you rate your chances?"

Tim's mouth was getting drier by the minute. He took a swallow from his water bottle before he answered. "The blokes here are definitely going to test us. But we really enjoy playing doubles and we're looking forward to it."

There were a few more questions which Tim answered as well as he could. He managed to clarify that they had lived in Melbourne most of his life, apart from their recent time in Winjarra, which was why it was named as their home club. Then, mercifully, the time was up, the flashlights and photos stopped, and he could escape back to the players' locker room.

It was a relief for Tim to sit quietly on his own for a bit, a rare moment to reflect briefly on his win before heading to the hospital to see Dad. By the time he got there, Jenny and Jack had already been. The nurses were very strict about the length of visits, ensuring that Mark conserved all his strength to kickstart his immunity. This afternoon Tim was pleased to see he appeared a little better. At the very least he was awake, and up for a chat through the glass window of the isolation room. Mark had already seen the post-match press conference on television and was interested in the media focus on their upcoming doubles match. Tim wondered if they were losing the advantage they had as unknown players.

"Nonsense," said Mark, pointing a finger at him for emphasis, as they talked on phones to each other. "You still have an advantage. They are no doubt wary of you both by now. They know that you are tough competitors, but they still need to actually play you to find out how good you are. You, on the other hand, know heaps about your opposition before you get on the court. Now, tell me the plan for your next match. Do you know who you play yet?"

Tim sparked up as he contemplated his next match. "Yep. I play the American guy, Ty Douglass. He's got a wicked backhand and Mr Mac thinks I need to try to keep the ball low, so he doesn't get a chance to play the deadly flat dropshot he has. On my serve I'm going to swing him wide as often as I can and hit every ball with a hard top spin. He's had a couple of tough five-setters, and I've been volleying well, so I'm planning to keep him moving, tire him out, and wait till he pops up a short ball I can smash away for a winner." He put his hands out. "Simple, Dad."

Mark managed a wry grimace that vaguely resembled a laugh. "A perfect plan. I'm sure Paul will have a bit more to say to you than that, but if you can beat Roland Blass, why not this guy?" He took a deep breath, in and out. The effort of talking was beginning to take a toll.

"I wish I were courtside watching you, Tim. Enjoy the first doubles match. Hopefully you'll be able to enjoy that one. I'm so proud of you both out there, dishing it up to some of the best players in the world!"

"It's such a buzz when I win, Dad. But I still have to pinch myself that this is all happening. I wish you were out there with us."

Mark nodded silently back at him.

"How are you feeling, Dad? Any improvement?" Tim asked hopefully.

"The levels haven't changed much," replied Mark with a sigh of frustration. "But I think I feel a bit better anyway."

Just then a nurse entered, ready to do some routine observations on Mark, and gave Tim a look that meant it was time to go. He mouthed, "Love you, Dad," through the window, which drew a weary smile and a wink from Mark.

A disconsolate Tim wandered slowly back through the hospital alone. This was such an incredible time for him and Jack. They were doing what they had only dared dream about, and they should be delirious with the excitement of it all. Instead, this dark cloud hung over their lives. Their joy was muted and guilt ridden at best.

CHAPTER 19

Karen was waiting for Tim in the players' lounge after his media conference. The Anderson family, as well as Karen, all had passes to the players' facilities, making the long days at Flinders Park much easier for everyone. Nanna had probably made the best use of her pass, attending several Centre Court matches. Her time in the players' lounge had also made her the go-to person for all the latest player gossip. Karen smiled sympathetically as Tim walked slowly over to her, before giving him a big hug.

"That was bad luck. You played so well. It was a gutsy effort."

Tim sank down onto the chair beside her and put his head into his hands. "I know I shouldn't be disappointed. It's a fairy-tale to even get this far, but I am disappointed. A lot, actually. I was kind of getting used to winning. Especially after this morning."

They had won their first doubles match earlier in the day, playing on an outside court to little fanfare. Most of the spectators were keen to watch the singles matches, especially the matches that featured the top-ranked international players, so there were few fans watching. Their opponents were also rookies. They were certainly talented, but flashy and reckless, lacking in the discipline needed for doubles. Tim and Jack, used to playing as a team, had no difficulty disposing of them in two sets. In the early rounds the doubles matches, unlike the singles, were decided by the best of three sets.

Karen patted him on the back, giving him another hug. She knew he was disappointed but there was no shame in his loss. Making it into the third round of the Australian Open wasn't even on Tim's radar four weeks ago, so he had already exceeded everyone's expectations. Yesterday, Jack had won through to the fourth round beating Tom Murray from the UK. Murray was a journeyman of the sport, who had been playing for years. He was usually dogged and consistent, chasing every ball, but Jack had his measure. Playing him at his own game, running everything down and returning impossible shots, Jack kept the pressure on, chipping away, pushing him to the limit, before overcoming him in four sets. Tim had hoped he could do the same.

His loss today to Ty Douglass of the US was a bitter one, because he was a fellow unseeded player, although more highly ranked than Tim; but Tim had still given himself a good chance of winning. Despite playing well and trying everything he could, Ty proved the better player on the day with an impressive display of power.

"Where are the others?"

"Your pa and Mr Mac are with Jack, practising on one of the indoor courts, and then they are going to watch the match between Lindstrom and Clarke, to suss out who Jack plays next. Jenny is off to the hospital, and your nan and my mum are staying to watch the night session on Centre Court. It looks as though we are on our own."

"Okay then. Let's get out of here and chill. Why don't we go home and watch a movie and not think about tennis for a few hours?"

"What about your dad?"

"If Mum is there, that's probably enough. The nurses don't like if we all come at once and tire him out. I've got tomorrow off so I'll see him later." He didn't admit it but, still very raw from his loss, he just couldn't face another depressing hospital visit.

They had barely had a moment alone in weeks, so it felt good to just hang together for a change. There was always someone around and if not, Tim had a match to prepare for or warm down from. They took advantage of player privileges and asked one of the official tournament drivers to take them home, stopping on the way at the video store to grab a couple of movies. Having the house to themselves was bliss, and they were finally able to just be together.

Settling in front of the TV with popcorn, drinks, and a block of chocolate, they managed to forget about tennis for a while. Karen snuggled in close to Tim on the couch, and Tim felt the tension and disappointment of his last match fade a little as he let the movie wash over him. At some point Karen lifted her face towards him and they began kissing. At first, Karen's kisses were a sweet distraction but after one particularly long kiss, Tim stopped and rested his head on hers. There was so much on his mind and so many emotions racing around his head. Although he had missed having such a moment with Karen, he just felt drained.

"Okay. What's up? Tell me what is bothering you," said Karen gently. "I can see you've got too much going on in that handsome head of yours."

Tim paused the movie. "This has been such an insane week. I'm still coming to terms with even getting in to the Open, and then I win my first two matches! That is crazy enough on its own, but Jack does as well! And we're still in the doubles. Meanwhile, Dad is literally hanging somewhere between life and death, and this feels completely wrong. The last thing I should be doing is playing tennis, in a tournament I feel like a fraud for getting in to! And now I can't even kiss you properly because I can't get my head straight!"

Karen was a good listener and she let Tim rant for a while, mostly about how it was all too much to be even thinking he could keep playing in the doubles, and how no-one seemed to understand how hard it was to play. Then she said, "Now, tell me what is really upsetting you."

Tim gave a pent-up sigh. "I just don't know what to do if Dad dies." He put his head in his hands. "I just feel so scared that he won't get better. You should have seen him the other day. He looked awful, and even yesterday when he looked better, he still looked like he was on death's door. He just looks so weak and frail, it's déjà vu all over again, and it's happened so quickly. I don't know if I can cope with everything, I still really need him around. I want Dad in my life."

Karen held him close. She comforted him with kisses and hugs, and just let him talk. Listening with sympathy and common sense, she calmed his fears, telling him his dad was strong, and he was fighting hard. Gradually, Tim felt as if a load was being lifted from him. It was cathartic to finally admit to someone else all his worries about his father: words that he had been too afraid to speak.

Karen gave him hope and a better perspective, and he was glad he had trusted her. She was also touched and pleased that he had chosen to confide in her. Even though they had been a couple for the last year, they were both a little surprised by the intensity of their feelings for each other. The friendship bond they had always shared had deepened into something rare and precious. No matter what happened, Tim knew that he had Karen beside him, and for a while he could believe everything would work out. By the time Jack arrived back with Nan and Pa, Tim had regained his equilibrium. His little meltdown would be his and Karen's secret.

Jack had his next round of singles the following day. It had been a gruelling schedule. There wasn't much time between matches for him to rest, considering he had already played three tough matches in the qualifying tournament before the main draw had begun. Jack wasn't concerned. He had been working on his match fitness for months, targeting this very scenario. The last few weeks of being a practise partner had given him the added match toughness Mr Mac had predicted. He was ready. This time, because he was playing a seeded opponent, his match was to be on Centre Court. Tim was in awe of his brother as he walked bravely out onto Centre Court at the Australian Open, and matched the big Swede Pieter Lindstrom, seeded eighth, point for point. Tim wondered that he ever had the edge over Jack as he hit winners and chased down impossible returns.

Tim was restless and Karen fidgeted in her seat as they willed Jack on from the players' box, yelling out words of encouragement that Jack would never hear over the noise of the crowd. Jenny had opted to watch the match live, rather than from the hospital, and she looked pale and tense. Nanna clapped his every move. Mr Mac and Pa leaned forward in their seats, frowning and cheering in equal measure.

Lindstrom would normally be a crowd favourite, but this time the crowd was very much behind Jack, and they almost managed to cheer him over the line. Jack went down in four sets, but he was brave in defeat and put up a huge fight, earning high praise from his fans, who stood as one to cheer him off. At seventeen he had made it to the fourth round, gaining a multitude of fans in the process. Everyone was disappointed for him but so proud at the same time.

That evening, after all the fuss had died down and Jack had completed his warm down, Tim, Jack, and Jenny went to the hospital. The required press conference was luckily kept to a minimum, the sports journos being otherwise occupied with other more interesting interviews, so they left the moment they could. They were all tired after yet another gruelling day, and Jack looked out on his feet. There hadn't been a moment over the last few days when it was just the three of them, and it was definitely time for them to be alone. As they neared the hospital, the conversation was desultory at best. Walking into the isolation ward and down the passage to Mark's room, each of them experienced that familiar sense of foreboding. What fresh worry would this visit bring? The heavy atmosphere around them was almost tangible, and Tim put his hand on Jack's shoulder as a show of support. He suspected Jack was as emotionally drained by the culmination of the last few days' events as he was, and Tim felt for him, especially so soon after losing his last match. But his support wasn't needed.

Mark was sitting up, eating an icy pole. Jenny hadn't seen him eat anything since he'd arrived in hospital, and she gasped as Mark saw them and gave a huge thumbs up.

"Oh my God!" breathed Jenny as she grabbed both boys' arms.

The nurse in charge of the isolation unit came over to them, smiling widely. "Blood count has reached 1200 and rising. We think he may be over the worst. You'll still need to gown and mask up, and stay back from the bed, but you can all go in to see him tonight."

Jenny wanted to sink to the ground with relief. Instead, she hung on to Tim and Jack and just cried. Mark gestured for them to come in. He already knew the good news, and he waited impatiently for them to gown up and enter his isolation room. This was the first time they had let anyone in other than Jenny. They still weren't able to touch him, but at least they were all together in the same room for the first time in several days.

"I can't believe it, Mark," said Jenny, continuing to cry through her facemask. "It's such good news!"

"I know. They told me this morning and I couldn't wait till you guys got here. I wanted to see your faces myself when you heard the news. And Jack! I'm so sorry, but I'm so proud of you. I watched it on TV. You looked so good. The nurses here were all cheering, and you were just magnificent. I wish I could give you a big hug."

For the first time in ages, they were able to talk freely together with some hope and confidence. Such a wonderful feeling of relief washed over them all and, although they were only allowed to stay ten minutes with Mark, Tim and Jack left feeling euphoric. Jenny stayed another few minutes, while the brothers grinned at each other all the way to the car.

They were still grinning the next day as they walked out into the late afternoon sun onto one of the show courts for their second doubles match of the tournament. Tim worried that Jack would be flat after losing, despite his great singles performance the day before, but he didn't need to. Jack declared emphatically he was looking forward to their doubles match, and he was more than keen to play.

The crowd was reasonable, and greeted them with claps and cheers. They had woken that morning energised and relieved.

With the singles behind them, they could concentrate on their doubles, and playing doubles together was what they enjoyed the most. Mark's count had continued to rise and was tested at 1500 earlier that morning. They felt great, and ready for anything their fifth-seeded opponents could throw at them.

Tobias Rietman from the Netherlands and Paul Wright from the UK were experienced doubles players, and they were confident this would be an easy win for them. From the first serve, the pressure was on, and the brothers forgot about everything, their only focus hitting the ball and reacting to the game in hand.

The strategy was for Jack to serve first because he had been playing and serving so well. Their luck was in when they won the toss. Jack's serves kicked strongly and drove the receiver deep, while Tim hovered threateningly at the net, waiting for a loose ball to put away. Jack was on fire and managed to cover the net and the backline with devastating effectiveness. Initially, the games went predictably on serve as both teams probed to find a weakness in the other team. At 5/4 in the first set, the brothers still hadn't been able to attack with enough depth to break serve.

Rietman was serving to tie the set. He had a powerful first serve that was difficult to return and had them scrambling just to get it back. However, if he missed his first serve, his second serve was more conservative—a consistent hard and flat serve that was reliable. He rarely double faulted, but his second serve was an easy return and Jack and Tim were ready to pounce on it when they could. The first two points were long rallies with both teams fighting to keep the ball in play, while all the time searching for unforced errors. Tim and Jack were love–thirty down when Wright, trying for extra centimetres, overhit two balls in a row to give them the next two points. Thirty–all. Both teams knew the importance of this game. At one game up, it would give Jack and Tim the set.

Their chance finally came when Rietman, totally out of character, faulted his first serve. It landed long by a whisker. As he stretched up and hit his second serve, Jack moved quickly forward and returned early, thumping the ball down the tram lines and safely out of reach of Wright, who was caught wrong-footed on the net as he was moving to the centre to cut off the cross-court forehand. Rietman scrambled to cover it but had no chance of making the shot. Set point.

Tim knew this was the time to take a risk. As Rietman sent down a thundering first serve, Tim drew his racquet back as if to return a drop shot low over the net. Rietman was already moving forward, preparing to cut off the return when, at the last second, Tim dropped his knees and his racquet, and lobbed the ball high into the backhand court.

Rietman realised almost immediately what Tim was doing and stopped midstride to double back and cover the backline. He made it back to where the ball landed safely inside the line, but he was off balance, and it was an awkward return. Jack and Tim were already in position on the net, and as the ball floated high and short Tim pounced and snapped a winning volley away to win the first set, 6/4.

The second set went to a tie breaker with Jack and Tim refusing to budge. Over and over Rietman and Wright set-up winning shots, only to have Tim or Jack chase them down. The rallies were long, and the fans cheered everything. The tie breaker crept forward with each point going on serve. Finally, it was 5/5 with Tim on his second serve.

Steadying, Tim tossed the ball high and sent it at a dangerously sharp angle deep into the backhand court, barely grazing the service line. Wright, expecting a fault, was forced to hustle wide for it, but his return landed uselessly in the net. Six points to five. Victory was in sight. One more point. The brothers conferred.

"Just keep it in play!" urged Jack, making a show of communicating with Tim, who nodded confidently back as if they had come up with a plan.

Rietman to serve. The ball came down hard and fast. Tim stood firm and sent it back with a strong top spin. The rally continued, neither team willing to take a risk, until Wright slightly mis-hit a lobbed forehand that looked as if it would bounce high and slow near the backline. Usually, Tim would have moved forward to attack the shot with a volley but, trusting his instinct, he took a risk and let it bounce, watching as it landed just outside the line. Just as Tim prepared to return the shot, "Out!" came the late call from the umpire, and the ball bounced away to be scooped up by a waiting ball boy.

"Game, set, and match!" The crowd erupted as the local pair and crowd favourites jogged to the net to shake hands. Tim and Jack hugged each other, which the crowd also loved, cheering even louder. Everyone in their player box jumped up and down in excitement, celebrating the win with abandon. When the TV camera zoomed in on Jack and Tim as they left the court, they both turned together to the cameras and put their thumbs up as a secret signal to Mark, who they hoped would be watching.

Fred Elkes was waiting as they headed down the players' ramp towards the inevitable media conference. He was never very far away when they played their matches and, as always, he was full of praise for their efforts. He had spoken to Mr Mac earlier, and he knew the good news about their dad. Well away from any prying media ears, he managed to get them in a little huddle to the side, saying an encouraging few words.

"You can do this, you know. Keep this up and you can go all the way to the final. That match was an important win. Just stay steady," he emphasised, smiling broadly at them before disappearing into the media room to listen to their post-game interview.

The interviews were getting easier, but Tim and Jack were both still nervous and on high alert. They didn't want to say anything that would embarrass themselves, so they were very circumspect. There were the usual questions about how they felt, and how their opponents played. These were easy to answer, because of course they were happy, and they made sure they gave the opposition all the credit they could.

It was a little trickier when someone asked, "Do you think being brothers gives you an advantage in playing doubles?"

As Tim nodded wisely, Jack jumped in ingeniously. "Oh, it's definitely an advantage. We've played so much together we know each other's games as well as we know our own. We don't have to second-guess because I know exactly where Tim is going to put the ball, and he knows me just as well."

The headline over the short write-up about the men's doubles the next day read: "NO SECOND GUESSES!"

Tim was highly embarrassed, but the rest of the family thought it was a great joke.

Their third-round match was on an outside court, in front of a smaller crowd. They were fortunate to be up against a doubles pair that were strong singles players but relatively inexperienced as a team, having not played together before this tournament.

Tim and Jack didn't start well and played some very flat tennis, dropping the first set. They were thankful for the crowd's totally biased support as they clapped and cheered the two young Australians, even though they made a rusty start. It motivated them to do better, and during their three-minute break at the end of the first set they did their best to fire each other up. Pressing the reset button, they shook off their lethargy and by the time the umpire called for play, they were busting to get out there and make amends.

At last, they began to play the effortless team game they knew so well, winning the first four games in a row. Their New Zealand opponents suffered as Tim and Jack found form, and the vocal crowd grew more and more raucous. Buoyed by the crowd, Tim and Jack began to dominate the court, easily winning the next two sets. The papers the next day gave them a back-page headline: "BROTHERS CRUISE INTO THE QUARTERFINALS". There were no less than two photos to accompany the text, which read:

Yesterday, two local boys played like future champions as they won in two sets over their highly fancied Kiwi opponents. Tim and Jack Anderson continue to impress, playing well above what is normally expected of two young rookies to the tennis scene.

Coached by Paul Maclaren, one of Australia's finest before he was sidelined by injury, these two are swiftly beginning to make their mark on the tennis world. Playing exciting tennis, they manage to make it look easy as they backup and anticipate not only their own partner's shots, but those of their opponents.

Nanna was quickly filling up her scrapbook with the many accolades the press was showering on them.

Almost in sync with their tennis successes, Mark continued to improve. As his white blood cell count rose, he was allowed out of the isolation room and into a private room. It was still in the isolation ward, which wasn't much different, but it felt like a huge step forward.

Buoyed by the continued good news regarding their dad, the boys were feeling elated and almost invincible. It was such a relief when they saw him visibly recovering from one day to the next. By the time the boys were into the quarterfinals, Mark's temperature was back within normal range, and he was starting to get back some of his old energy and spark. He was keen to chat, and he didn't tire so quickly. No longer attached to an IV, he was able to eat small meals, and even have a shower. Dr Thompson declared him over the infection, but he warned that he was still very vulnerable. Having lost so much condition, he looked gaunt, but there was a spark in his eye, and it translated into optimism for everyone.

The quarterfinal match was played on one of the outside show courts and there was a large crowd present. The stakes were lifted much higher when Cardwell and Linton, two experienced American players specialising in doubles, seriously challenged them. The Americans also knew each other's games like their own, and they seemed to have all the answers to everything the brothers tried. There was very little between them, as both pairs seemed to gel perfectly together, and they slogged out every point over four close sets. Now they were in the quarterfinals, the matches would be played to the best of five sets.

The first set went on serve all the way to the tie breaker. The tie breaker went on endlessly, with the two Americans finally winning at 13/11, when Jack made an unforced error trying to get some extra power on the ball and hitting it long. The next point was a bonus point for the Americans as one of their rallies hit the tape on the net to dribble over the side for the winner. One set down.

The very pro-Australian crowd, however, was totally behind the Aussie duo, and they willed them over the line. The second set was, again, a marathon. Every point was hard-fought, and there was no chance of just making the return, because their experienced American opponents would put it away with ruthless professionalism. When Tim anticipated a passing shot on the net, volleying it away for a winner, they won the second set at 7/5. One set each.

They had played so much tennis over the last couple of weeks that Tim was really feeling the effects. He didn't want to admit it to Jack, but as he started the third set his legs were staring to cramp, and he was afraid he was going to have to call a medical timeout. Stretching in between points, he kept playing, and just managed to keep going until there was a break in play. When one of their opponents took an awkward twist returning a forehand shot, suddenly pulling up short, Tim couldn't believe his luck. The few extra minutes while a medical time out was called gave him enough time to stretch and hydrate, so that the cramps eased and his legs felt strong again. Tim again silently thanked Mr Mac for his exacting fitness regimes.

While the physio had massaged Linton's knee before strapping it heavily, Cardwell called for ice and extra fluids. It appeared their opponents were also feeling the effects of a tough match after all the tennis that had been played. While the short break worked in Tim's favour, their opponents didn't transition back into the game as easily. Linton could still run and pivot, but he wasn't quite as fluid and agile as he had been earlier. They made a few errors, including a double fault, which proved costly.

The crowd made it difficult for the Americans as they showed their bias. The set was gruelling with long rallies, and Jack showed flashes of brilliance to steal the points that counted. The brothers won it slightly easier in 6/4. Linton and

Cardwell continued to attack in the fourth set, setting up a 3/1 lead, but there was no doubt Linton had lost his edge. Tim and Jack kept their composure, winning the next four games in a row. The last game see-sawed until, at forty–thirty on his serve, a rejuvenated Tim, anticipating a return, surged to the net and put away an unplayable deep volley. The umpire's call of, "Game, set, and match, Anderson and Anderson," was drowned in an avalanche of cheering as the home crowd celebrated their victory. They were through to the semi-final! The roar increased even more as Tim grabbed Jack's head and kissed him firmly on the forehead.

It was always a little chaotic as a match was completed, but Jack and Tim were beginning to find the post-match routine less threatening. There were the usual formalities to go through, such as thanking opponents and umpires, and acknowledging the crowd. Then they needed to pack up everything and make an exit down one of the now-familiar tunnels that led to the players' and administration areas in the bowels of the tennis centre. Walking through to the applause of Australian Open volunteers and staff, they were directed to the media room, which was the one spot they still dreaded.

Jack, despite being a loose cannon, was probably the more relaxed of the two at answering questions. So far, they had been fortunate because the doubles didn't attract as much press as the singles. Now though, as local players making the semi-final, they were hot news. Today, it was their turn to be in the spotlight.

"You play John Adams and Pier Gustav in the semi-final on Thursday night. How do you rate your chances of winning?"

"You had a good lead going into the fourth set, why do you think you started it so slowly?"

"Your match on Thursday is scheduled as a night match. How will you go playing at night, under lights on Centre Court?"

They took turns answering, helping each other out where possible. They acknowledged Adams and Gustav would be hard to beat. Even though at this stage they actually knew very little about them, they were smart enough not to admit this. They credited their opponents with some great play, which was why they had dropped a few points in the final set. Then they lied completely about having played often under lights and said that they were looking forward to the opportunity.

Finally, a question was asked that would have had them floundering a few days earlier.

"Your dad is listed as part of your coaching team, along with Paul Maclaren who, as we know, was a great competitor in his day. We haven't seen your father in your courtside box. Is there a reason he doesn't like to watch you play?"

Jack looked at Tim and, in that moment, completely handballed the question to him.

"No, not at all. Dad is our step-in coach when Mr Mac can't be there. He usually does watch us play, and he knows we're in good hands with Mr Mac. He's just been a bit under the weather this last week or two."

Tim left it at that. It seemed to satisfy the punters for the moment and the media conference came to an end.

"Brilliant, Tim!" whispered Jack as they made their way out of the room. The last thing they wanted was any more attention on their lives from nosy journalists. They were already getting too curious and invasive with their questions; neither Tim nor Jack wanted their dad's health issues to be exposed. This was private stuff, and it was still too raw for them to be able to deal with it in the public eye.

They both felt they were balancing on a knife edge of good luck, and they hardly dared to hope for yet another win. Not only had they gone way further than they could possibly have dreamt of in the Australian Open, but their dad was finally beginning to recover. He'd gone from being critically ill to, unbelievably, producing the viable white blood cells that would save his life. It was too much to hope that this run of luck would continue.

As they left the room, their old friend Fred Elkes placed his arms around them both and drew them aside. "I hear your dad is starting to improve. That's wonderful news. Now, make sure you hydrate and rest up. The next couple of days will be tough, so remember: Look after yourselves. And give my best to your dad. We're all thrilled to hear the good news here."

With that he nodded to a security guard who took their bags from them and escorted them out a lesser-known exit to a waiting car, so they wouldn't get caught up with fans. In no time at all they were on their way home.

The next two days, they took things easy, only turning up at the tennis centre for a light practise session each day. Even conversations with Mark were over the phone; heading to the hospital was considered unnecessarily tiring. They were both exhausted and emotionally drained. The last few weeks had really taken its toll and they were feeling the strain. Now that Mark was getting better, it was such a good feeling that they began to drift into a state of complacency. Karen and a few other friends came over, and they had a rare break, chilling out, watching movies, and talking about anything except tennis.

The afternoon before their night match, they waited until Jenny had returned from the hospital, intending to leave for Flinders Park together. They had a warm-up court scheduled, and they had plenty of time to prepare for their semi-final match. Pa and Nan were already there, along with Karen. So far, no-one had actually worked out where she fitted in the support group, and she wanted to keep it that way. She kept a low profile in case she was spotted by any curious journalists, who loved to nab a girlfriend photo if they could.

When Jenny walked in, they were watching one of the singles matches currently being aired live on TV. She took one look at them lying prone on a couch each, their feet up, completely content, when she inexplicably exploded. "No you don't! You don't get to do this!"

They both looked up.

What on earth have we done wrong? thought Jack.

Tim sat up. "We're just watching the men's quarterfinal!" he protested.

"I can see it in the way you're relaxing there. You think you've done well enough and that it doesn't matter what happens now. You've made the semi and that's good enough?" she challenged. She didn't wait for the answer. "It's your father's dream that you make it to the final. He is so proud and amazed by you both. I just know that it's helping him get better." Turning off the TV, she continued, "But it's not just about him anymore. Don't toss away all the hard work you've done to get this far now. I haven't gone through all of this to see you blow your chances because you think near enough is good enough. Just because your dad is starting to get well again, it doesn't mean you can go easy on yourselves."

Jenny drew a deep breath and went on in a more conciliatory tone. "I know I'm sounding slightly crazy. I'm not sure I can even explain it to myself. I feel that this has been a gift to us. Tennis has brought all my boys closer together and that's why I was your number one fan. That's why I supported it even though it took up so much time and, quite honestly, nearly drove me mad.

"It was a lifesaver for your dad. Remember what he was like? It was just what he needed, to wake him up and see what he was missing. It brought him back to us. Now you owe it to yourselves to finish what you started. It might have started out as a fine motivation to play for your father, but now you need to play for yourselves. Don't you dare waste this moment!"

Tim and Jack tried to protest, but Jenny would not hear a word. She held up her hand. "Now, make sure you get your minds back into winning mode. This is the chance of a lifetime and you both need to step-up. You need to snap out of this self-satisfaction. You've done well—brilliantly, in fact—but it's not over yet!"

They drove to the tennis centre, Tim and Jack somewhat chastened, but jolted out of their complacency. Jenny remained feisty, with a pep talk that lasted the entire drive. When she said goodbye after parking the car, she could tell they were mentally back on track, and she gave them each a forehead kiss and a ruffle of their hair before letting them go.

"Good luck! Love you, Jack. Love you, Tim. Now, go play like the champions you are."

They won in three sets: 6/4, 6/3, 6/4, and never looked like losing. The final was in two days. The Australian media went into a frenzy.

CHAPTER 20

The men's doubles final was the curtain-raiser event for the men's singles final on Sunday afternoon. It was the last day of a competition that, for Jack and Tim, had started seventeen days earlier with the first round of the qualifier. Tim was nervous. Jack was fired up and ready to play.

Their names had been splashed across every back page in every newspaper in the country. The headlines varied but they all screamed with a degree of a nation's anticipation. *The Australian* went for: "ANDO BROTHERS READY TO PLAY", while the *Herald Sun* tried: "LOCAL BOYS ON WILDCARD RIDE". *The Age* settled for: "ANDO BOYS HIT WILDCARD HEAVEN".

Their lives were no longer their own. Neither Tim nor Jack had spoken much to the media, but it astounded them how much information they had researched about them. When they read the articles however, the answer was clearly in the quotes. Nanna. The article in *The Age* was the most detailed. It spoke about them being generally athletic and sporty, and mentioned that they had played in several local competitions for footy and cricket, even noting that Jack had won the Under 15 bowling averages for his club three years before, and that Tim had been in the First 18 for Deakin High when he was only fifteen.

Tim read an excerpt from *The Age* newspaper tennis writer out to Jack that morning over breakfast.

"The two brothers were late to discover tennis but once they found it, according to their grandmother Moira Jones, of Winjarra, they were totally hooked. She describes how they would play for hours, hitting balls against the wall of the back shed on their farm. This is indeed a remarkable journey from the farm shed wall to the glory of Centre Court at Flinders Park.

"The Anderson brothers have an enviable record so far in doubles, winning most, if not all of their matches since they started on the satellite circuit. However, it must be said that they have not been tested yet. They were fortunate in being placed on the opposite side of the draw to the top-seeded Todd Hunt of the US and Anton Illic from Yugoslavia. This will be the first time they face the number one seeds. Hunt and Illic have had a strong run into this tournament, on the back of winning three of the majors in the last twelve months. On any given day, they will be hard to beat.

"The Anderson brothers do have a secret weapon: their ability to know exactly where each other will move or hit to at any given moment. It is an experience to watch them anticipate each other as they move fluidly around the court. However, even at their very best, it seems to be too big of an ask for them to be able to upset the formidable partnership of Hunt and Illic, who play a delightful mix of intelligent, skilful, and powerful tennis. While we are one hundred percent behind our local boys, who it must be said also play an entertaining game of tennis, this will more than likely be a valuable lesson for them, early in their career."

"No comment!" replied Jack, grabbing the newspaper from Tim and tossing it away. "Don't read that crap. They don't know us. But," he grinned, "it is nice to hear we are 'entertaining' at least."

"Absolutely, don't read that crap!" interjected Pa crossly. "I thought you would have more sense, Tim. That's Nan's fault, buying up all the papers. She wants to collect every word ever written about the two of you, and herself, by the look of it! You can read as much as you want tomorrow about your win. Today, we stay focused."

Then, changing the subject, he asked, "Have you heard from Jenny yet? Did she say if she is coming to Flinders Park, or is she going to watch it with your dad in hospital?"

"At the hospital. They're hoping that Dad is well enough to watch it in the patient lounge where there is a bigger TV. I suppose that's at least something."

"It's such a shame they won't be there, but you know you'll have Nan and me, and Paul Mac. And Karen, of course," said Jim with a wink at Tim. "But finish up your breakfast. We need to get the pair of you to Flinders Park so we have plenty of time to go through your warm-up. We don't want to feel rushed today. You can give your dad a ring from the player's lounge before you play. I'm sure he'll want to talk to you."

Tim and Jack stood up from the table, stretching and moving slowly, their muscles stiff and sore from the punishment of the last two weeks.

Jim clapped his hands a couple of times loudly, as if to wake them up. "Come on. Let's do this!"

Three hours later they sat together with Mr Mac in the players' waiting area, underneath the Centre Court stands. They had had their last warm-up and had gone through their stretching routine twice. They were feeling supple and ready. A call to Jenny and Mark, confirming that Mark was continuing to improve, left them elated. The doctors were even considering allowing him home in the next few days, providing his results continued to be positive. This was such a turnaround in Mark's health from the beginning of the tournament, when everything had suddenly gone pear-shaped. Consequently, the conversation and mood was upbeat and hopeful.

Mark sounded better, his voice stronger and more like his old self. "I think it's an omen, boys. Not that I'm normally superstitious, but I can't help but feel that the better tennis you two play, the better I seem to get. So go out and enjoy yourselves. I'm well and truly on the road back. I feel great, so I reckon you've done your job at getting me fit and healthy. Now just have fun. Beat the pants off them. No mercy!"

"And we love you and we're so proud of you. We won't be there, but we'll be there in spirit. And we'll be cheering so loudly you'll probably hear us anyway. Go get 'em!" added Jenny before hanging up.

Paul Mac's final words to them before he made his way back through the labyrinth of tunnels underneath Flinders Park and up into the stands were clear. Calm as ever, he made it very simple. "Stay steady. Play your own game. Stay focused. Just win one point at a time and the games will come."

Tim knew there were some inspiring words in there as well, but he struggled to take in anything else.

"Tim. Tim! Are you ready?" asked Jack, breaking in on his thoughts. "Time to do this, mate."

Standing up, they clasped each other in a final hug, and began the long walk out, down the players' tunnel, past the waiting cameras, and onto Centre Court together. The crowd roared their support, and Tim hoped it was for them. When the top-seeded players appeared a few moments later on court, the cheering was enthusiastic but far more restrained. It was overwhelmingly a parochial crowd. He took a calming breath.

Jack looked up to the stands and spotted the familiar crew. Mr Mac, Pa, Nan, Karen, and Clare. Giving Tim a nudge, he nodded in their direction, so he would spot them. Karen gave a thumbs up to them both, and Nan cheered wildly. Mr Mac looked confident, and Pa looked as nervous as Tim felt.

In the stands behind them, higher up in the nose-bleed seats at the top of the stadium, was a very noisy group. Squinting to see what the fuss was about, Tim and Jack realised simultaneously that it was a group of their friends from Winjarra High, dressed in what looked like a mixture of the school's basketball and football guernseys. They looked at each other and grinned. It helped to have so many friends and family there.

Although they had tried to keep it quiet, once the news of Mark's cancer, remission, and recovery, along with his latest brush with a life-threatening illness, had reached the papers, the story had blown up. Their close friends had always known what they were going through, but obviously the tabloids had a field day with it. They also loved that two local kids had made it through to the doubles final. It was just the story they needed, especially when there wasn't an Australian left in the singles draw. Everyone was excited for them, and there were high expectations. The rookies were under enormous pressure. The final, played as the best of five sets, would test all their endurance. They had worked hard on match fitness and toughness. They hoped it would be enough.

All too soon the umpire called to start the pre-game hit-ups. Jack looked relaxed and Tim, although nervous, felt himself begin to loosen up as they went through their hit-up routine. The crowd seemed restless and there was a great deal of movement as people came and went and settled into their seats. Tim took it all in on some other level. He was feeling comfortable with his strokes, and he thought he was ready to play. The umpire called the one-minute time warning. Tim and Jack returned to their bench, took a drink, wiped their hands, and gave each other a fist bump. They were ready. They moved to their positions on the court, the crowd began to hush, and the umpire called, "Play."

Tim won the toss and as planned, was the first to serve. Usually steady and consistent, they were counting on Tim to make a good start. He had indeed felt steady until the moment came for the first toss in his serving motion. He tossed the ball too far out in front and, rather than hit it, he caught it, putting up his hand as an apology to his opponents. The crowd murmured. It was a shaky start, and he went downhill from there. His next toss wasn't much better, but he hit at it anyway, and sent it too long. Fault. Trying hard to get the toss right, he sent down a very conservative second serve that Illic pounced on, setting his partner up for a passing shot at the net, where Tim, caught flat-footed and slow, should have already been standing. Love–fifteen. Tim continued to struggle with his ball toss. He just couldn't find his rhythm, and it totally threw out his normally strong, consistent serve. He began to second-guess his moves, feeling out of sync and always a few milliseconds behind the other three players on the court. He tried to relax but he felt tense and tight. The harder he tried, the more he tightened up and the worse he played. He scrambled for balls he should have taken easily, and his timing was out. He lost his first serve, setting up an immediate break for Hunt and Illic. Tim and Jack were on the back foot from the start.

As they changed ends, Jack was encouraging. "Don't worry. We'll break back. Just relax!" Tim nodded, drinking water, trying desperately to steady the rush of nerves that had come, fast and furious, out of nowhere.

Tim managed to settle enough to return Illic's serve, but his returns were cautious and flat, and he failed to put the required pressure on his opponents. Illic and Hunt both won their first serves easily. Jack, playing brilliant tennis, won his service game with four perfect first serves, which was enough to keep them in the set. They were 1/3 down when Tim lined up for his second serve. The crowd cheered him loudly, trying to boost his confidence. Taking a deep breath, he steadied and tossed. Instinctively he knew this was on its way and, dropping his racquet head behind him, he stretched up to hit down strongly on the ball as it reached its zenith in the toss. Tim's rhythm, however, was just out. No-one other than Jack and Mr Mac would probably notice anything different, other than the fact that the ball kept landing just beyond the service line.

Frustratingly, he missed all his first serves. This was costly. It is very difficult to win games on a second serve alone, especially when playing the best in the world. Illic and Hunt were ruthless and made the most of every weaker serve. Jack and Tim hung on, chasing every shot down, and combining well with their usual instinctive play. When Tim lost his second serve, despite the lead changing at advantage several times, they were fighting to stay in the set. Jack won his serve easily, again playing outstanding tennis and almost single-handedly winning his service game, but both Hunt and Illic managed to win their serves. Jack was amazing. He had the crowd cheering his every move, and all Tim could do was follow his lead as best he could. Tim was beginning to play himself back into the game, but he was still edgy and everything he did felt unnatural and tight. They lost the first set 6/2.

The crowd was noisy during the break between sets. People called out encouragement and there was a raucous rendition of the Winjarra High School chant from the stands. Tim's head was down. He was trying to get in the zone by blocking out the crowd. Unfortunately, it was again Tim's turn to start the second set with his serve.

Jack tried to encourage him. "Don't overthink it, Tim. Just play. Just watch the ball and hit the bloody thing. You know what to do. You can do this with your eyes closed. C'mon. Just hit the ball."

They jogged back on court as the umpire called time. Tim selected the balls offered by the ball boys carefully. It gave him a few more precious moments to settle, and the adrenaline that had been surging through him began to ease. Deliberately slowing his breathing, he felt a degree of calm finally start to wash over him. He was ready to serve. This time the toss went exactly to the spot he wanted. He arched his back and served his first serve smoothly and confidently. It landed deep into the service court, close to the centre-line, forcing Illic to adjust his position quickly and take it on his backhand. They rallied back and forth, with Tim and Jack forcing their opponents to switch sides often, moving quickly across court as they chased every ball down. Finally, Tim forced an error from Hunt, who was caught at the halfway mark of the court and had no choice other than a risky half-volley that landed in the net. It had taken three service games, but Tim had finally gotten a first serve in and won his first point. It was a relief.

"Don't overthink it," Tim told himself. Serving on muscle memory alone, without second-guessing, began to feel natural and Tim stepped up at last, winning his serve. The crowd cheered loudly with several supporters even standing up clapping to show their appreciation. One game to love. A much better start!

However, Hunt and Illic were champions and more than prepared for Tim to finally settle into his game. They had never been complacent enough to think Tim would continue to flounder, and they continued to challenge their young, inexperienced opponents with every shot they played.

Tim and Jack stood up to the attack, making their rivals earn every point. Illic won his first serve, but they took him to advantage three times before he did. One–all. Jack was next to serve, and he didn't miss a beat. He might have been the youngest, but you would never have known from his professional composure on court. Towards the end of his service game, when the score was forty–thirty, Hunt hit a beautiful top spin on an acute angle that forced Jack wide of the court. Jack moved swiftly to cover it, making an explosive lunge at the end to stretch out and reach for it. Unbelievably, he made it, but as he returned the shot and prepared to move back onto the court, his right hip suddenly gave way and he fell onto his side, sprawling helplessly on the ground. There was a collective gasp from the crowd, then silence as Jack failed to get up. The umpire called an injury time out. The score was deuce, and play was halted.

Tim was quickly at Jack's side. "Are you okay? Can you get up?"

"Yeah. I think I can move. Just give me some help."

Tim was deeply concerned. Jack had gone deathly pale, and as Tim helped him to his feet, Jack winced in pain. The crowd murmured anxiously. The designated medical professional was rushed onto the court. A sports doctor, he watched carefully as Jack limped to the side of the court. He signalled to a waiting physio for assistance.

The doctor lay Jack down on a mat beside the court while Tim sat on the players' bench nearby, watching on. Looking up into the crowd, he searched for Paul Mac. Mr Mac nodded encouragingly, but his face reflected Tim's own concern for Jack. After a quick discussion with Jack, the doctor began pushing gently around Jack's hip, moving his leg and asking him how it felt. The diagnosis was swift. He had probably strained his hip flexor as he stretched for the ball. It was a painful injury and could inhibit Jack's ability to move dramatically. The physio began working on it immediately, trying to free up the tightness in the ligament and joint. He dug deep into his soft tissue and Jack went even whiter with the increased pain. They were allowed a fifteen-minute injury timeout, and they had already used up precious minutes. Jack lowered his head and suffered. The doctor gave him a high dose of fast-acting anti-inflammatory to reduce the swelling, and a strong paracetamol to help dull the pain. Ice was applied to the hip and his arm was dressed where he had fallen on it and taken some of the skin off. He had blood all over his shirt and shorts, and he looked a mess.

With two minutes to go, the umpire came over to see if the match would continue. Jack said an emphatic yes and started to his feet. The doctor and physio watched him move after his treatment and nodded that he was good to go.

As he packed up, the doctor, moving out of the line of the cameras pointed at him, said quietly to the boys, "I'm not going to suggest this won't be painful, because it will be. You're not going to be able to push off on this right hip as easily, but it is probably only a minor tear. I'm fairly certain that you won't cause too much more damage by playing. Once the tablets kick in, they will help take the edge off. Good luck."

Jack sat next to Tim on the bench for the last few seconds they had left. He looked crestfallen. "I'm sorry, mate. So clumsy!"

Watching Jack in obvious distress, yet ready to play through the pain, was the extra jolt Tim needed. Putting his arm around Jack's shoulder, he hissed in his ear, "This is not how it ends.

We are not going to satisfy all those critics who said it couldn't be done. We are not just two lucky kids who fluked their way into the final and then couldn't go on with it. I know I've played some ordinary tennis so far, but if you can just serve and return, I promise you, I will step-up."

Then, lowering his head further so the cameras couldn't pick up on their conversation he vowed, "These losers have no idea what is going to hit them."

Jack nodded and, taking a swig of water, looked up to the players' box, giving Paul Mac a thumbs up signal to say that he was okay. Mr Mac nodded reassuringly back. When he stood up, with his racquet in his hand, the crowd gave a great cheer and clapped him as he jogged back onto the court with Tim.

Every now and then in life there is a moment of clarity. This was one such moment, and Tim felt his emotions shift and click into focus. He felt strong. He stole a look at their support team in the players' box. They were silent, watching intently. He caught Karen's eye and, even though he couldn't see her expression, he could sense her eyebrows raise as she looked back at him. He shook his head, shifting the last of the fog that had enveloped him. He looked at the score.

What the hell had he been thinking? So far, he had left it all to Jack, cruising along as Jack did all the work. Now Jack was compromised, and he had no idea of the pain he was enduring, or even if he would be able to continue to play. His dad might be on the way to recovery, but this journey wasn't over until they won. For the first time since they had made the semi-final, Tim found a real desperation to win. He felt it right to his core, as if every game he had played before didn't count. He wanted it for his dad, and he wanted it for Jack. He wanted it for himself. Yet he had only himself to blame that they were a set down.

"Sorry, mate. I'm back. I can do this!"

Jack looked at him. "Okay, I think I'm good. I'm moving better anyway. We need to stay in the game and see where it takes us. We've got time. We can do this, Tim."

They punched knuckles as the umpire called, "Time!" and Jack jogged to the service line. His body wanted him to limp but, apart from not wanting to show weakness, he needed to know how much movement he could stand. The score was deuce. Jack served fairly well but not with the same depth he had managed earlier in the game. The ball fell short enough for Hunt to be able to send one wide of Tim on the net, and also wide enough on the baseline to make Jack have to run to it. The sudden movement had Jack pulling up in pain, and although he reached it, he was again off balance and couldn't return it with any power. Illic smashed a return back and to the opposite side, outsmarting Tim, and making it an impossible return for Jack.

"Advantage, Illic and Hunt."

Jack served again. Tim was able to cut it off at the net, but Hunt scrambled magnificently and made the return. Again, Tim managed to cover the net, volleying it straight at Hunt's feet. Hunt managed an awkward return, but it was a lucky shot, and effective, as it spiralled over Tim's head and landed on the baseline, well away from Jack.

"Game, Illic and Hunt. They lead, 2/1."

The tension grew around the court. Hunt moved through his service game with methodical and calculating play. Whenever they could, Hunt and Illic ruthlessly hit to Jack, placing everything just out of his reach. While Tim was competitive, matching them with every powerful stroke, they were controlling the game to their advantage. At 1/3 down, someone in the crowd called out in sympathy, just as the crowd quietened for the serve. It was like a foghorn in Tim's ears.

"No disgrace, Ando boys. Great job just getting here!"

It was Tim's turn to serve. He heard the comment but didn't acknowledge it. Breathing deeply, he steadied, bounced the ball a couple of times, and tossed it high. This time as he stretched into the motion of the serve, his action was fluid and strong. His feet left the ground as he powerfully drove the ball straight down the service line for his first ace. Jack turned back from the net and smiled in appreciation.

And again, thought Tim as he repeated the same to Todd Hunt, the rangy American at the other end. Hunt and his partner noticed the sudden step-up in intensity from Tim and spoke a few words of encouragement to each other midcourt. All they had to do was win three more games and they had a handy two-set lead. No need to panic.

Tim felt the adrenaline he had been missing course through him like a shock wave. He won his serve without dropping a point, and he continued to attack. Their usual roles were reversed. Jack went to the net as much as possible, so he would have theoretically less movement, covering all the loose balls that were in reach. He went for safe percentage shots, while Tim produced the flashes of brilliance that won points. Tim sprinted across the backcourt from one side to the other, backing Jack up on everything he missed. Their instinctive understanding for where each other would be took over, and they moved confidently to where they were needed. Point by point, they crawled their way back into the set. Jack became the older brother. He talked encouragingly to Tim between every point, steadying him and being positive.

In what had looked like an impossible task thirty minutes earlier, with Jack lying prone in the physio's hands, they won Illic's serve and then Jack's. Jack was beginning to move with more freedom. Tim could tell he was in pain, but he wasn't allowing it to dictate the way he played. Jack moved to the net as often as possible while Tim continued to roam the baseline, coming to the net when he could to finish off a point. The score was three games all.

The crowd had remained supportive of the local boys, despite the grim scoreline, but as Tim began to step-up the crowd hushed with expectation in between points. They could sense the beginning of something, and there was almost a collective forward movement as they strained to watch every ball. The next four games went on service and, at five–all in the second set, the stadium had become electric. This was a comeback from almost certain defeat a few games ago, and it took the umpire several warnings to settle the crowd after every point.

Hunt and Illic were not performing quite so effortlessly as they had at 3/1 up. They knew they had blown a winning lead, and they began to tighten up. They still only needed two straight games to win the set, and after every point they connected briefly midcourt to urge each other on. The atmosphere was charged and the next two games were critical. Jack and Tim either had a lifeline or they risked going down in ignominy after all. It was Tim's turn to serve again. He stretched his neck from side to side to loosen it up and tilted it back, taking a moment to glimpse the clear, blue sky above the retracted roof.

He served perfectly, landing every first serve in. Hunt and Illic stood firm and returned serve strongly, and the rallies were long and bruising. Jack remained at the net doing damage when he could. Tim ran everything down, attacking every ball, his play reckless or brilliant, depending on whether or not his shots came off. He played aggressive tennis. He threw up unexpected lobs as they charged the net, and he wrong-footed them at the very last second, sending them wide of the court where Jack waited at just the perfect angle to chop off their compromised returns. Tim won his serve, and the score was 6/5.

Then, annoyingly, Hunt served brilliantly, nailing three first serves in a row where Tim and Jack simply had no answer. At forty–love, Illic and Hunt had a new skip to their step. After high-fiving each other, Hunt set-up to serve

Disregarding the score, Jack and Tim remained cool. Missing his first serve by inches, Hunt's second serve was a wide, swinging ball out to Jack's right side; a ball that meant he would have to take off on his injured hip. Anticipating this, instead of waiting and stepping right, Jack moved forward and took the ball early, as it was in its most powerful arc. Using his knees to bend into the shot, Jack sent the ball straight down the tramlines, past Illic at the net, at such a speed that Hunt, who had been preparing for a wide return, was unable to get a racquet to it. Forty–fifteen.

Tim jogged lightly in his spot. Suddenly he was seeing the ball as if it were a soccer ball, and he returned Hunt's first serve straight back at his body before Jack cut off Hunt's clever backhand top spin shot, volleying it out of Illic's reach to the forehand side of the court. Forty–thirty.

Again, Hunt missed his first serve—this time by a fraction. The pressure was mounting on him. Jack moved forward to take the serve early, but this time Hunt and Illic were ready and steadied for a long rally. Tim had stayed at the back of the court and between them, the boys covered the court well, waiting for the inevitable drop shot that they knew would come. Jack was the one who moved swiftly to the midcourt, predicting Hunt's attack. It paid off. When it landed, he was right on top of it, lobbing it beautifully over Hunt's and Illic's heads as they scrambled to get back for the return. Deuce.

The final points were almost an anticlimax. Hunt served well but Illic, trying desperately to put away the winning shots, played two risky volleys, sending the ball long each time.

"Second set, Tim and Jack Anderson, 7/5."

One set all and the Melbourne crowd was on its feet. They had almost resigned themselves to disappointment, when unexpectedly there was still hope they would see a hometown win. The roar of approval filled the stadium.

At the break, Tim asked Jack, "How's the hip?"

"It's actually numb and painful at the same time, but it's not stopping me. I'm getting to most shots, but I'll stay near the net if I can."

Tim nodded as they sat together on the players' bench over the break. "It's working well so far for us. Let's not change a thing."

The next set see-sawed, with each pair winning on serve. Hunt and Illic regrouped at the break, settling in to some experienced and defensive tennis. They were prepared to wait patiently for their chances. Tim continued to attack, with some brilliant passing shots. At four–all, and thirty–forty on Todd Hunt's serve, Tim smashed a volley at an impossible angle, and they had the service break they needed. Jack won his serve and they took the third set, 6/4. Suddenly they were in the lead with two sets to one.

Hunt and Illic were frustrated. They went to the bench, conferring intensely. Jack and Tim used the break to recover and regroup. Jack was feeling better, and the scoreline was helping. However, Hunt and Illic were not inexperienced players from the satellite ranks, and in the fourth set they showed exactly why they were the number one seeds. They played almost textbook doubles tennis, with consistent and powerful shots. Jack and Tim were forced to play defensively, and luck wasn't always with them as a couple of important points sailed out by centimetres. They went down 3/6. Hunt and Illic looked energetic and revitalised.

The final set began to rousing cheers from the crowd, urging Jack and Tim on. The umpire called for quiet. Tim and Jack took a moment. "I know we can do this," said Jack with steely determination. "We deserve this."

"I'm with you. We play one point at a time," said Tim. With a knuckle bump to seal the deal, they jogged to their positions.

The first games went, again, on serve. At three games all, and thirty–all, Hunt served wide to Jack, sending him scrambling well out of court to reach it. It should have been a winner, given that it clearly hurt Jack's hip. Stretching out his arm, Jack managed the impossible by even reaching it, but instead of just popping it back to Illic, waiting like a spider on the net, he managed to flick it on an incredible angle behind the net post, before falling over again. The crowd gasped as Jack scrambled to his feet and the ball landed safely inside the court on the backhand side, well out of Hunt's reach and where he least expected it. A bonus point!

Tim hopped lightly from foot to foot, every fibre of his being sharp and steely, as Hunt went through his service preparation. He predicted the serve would come down the middle service line, and Hunt didn't disappoint. Cleverly anticipating the serve, Tim moved forward and took the shot early, putting plenty of top spin on it. He drove it deep into the backhand corner, pinning Hunt there. The experienced Hunt returned a slice backhand to Tim that was well out of Jack's reach on the net.

Tim watched the ball with acuteness worthy of an eagle, waiting until the last moment before disguising his shot and lobbing it offensively into the forehand rear court, forcing

Hunt to race to cover it. As Hunt adjusted to take the unwieldy lob, Tim and Jack both moved to the net, restricting Hunt's options to either returning a lob or aiming for the very narrow gap available. He opted for the lob, miscalculating by only a couple of centimetres, sending it long.

"Game; 4/3 to Tim and Jack Anderson."

The umpire had to call for quiet several times before a hush fell once again on the stadium. It was Tim's turn to serve. He tossed the ball high and, unexpectedly, everything felt off again. Stopping to let the ball bounce away, he again apologised to Hunt for the bad toss. He steadied, but this time he didn't overthink it, moving quickly into his routine. He would not allow his brain to go anywhere down the track of self-doubt with which he had begun the match. He tossed perfectly and moved into his serve with power and confidence. It paid off, kicking high and giving Hunt little chance to do much with it. They rallied back and forth for several exchanges, Tim looking for a chance to attack. With great self-control, he made himself play defensive tennis as the long rally continued, accompanied by murmurs from the crowd. Illic finally settled the point with a beautifully-placed ball that spun tantalisingly away from Tim's outstretched racquet. Love–fifteen. Illic punched the air and jogged back to his position ready to return the next serve.

Hunt nodded his approval and once more Tim began his service routine. His concentration was exceptional. Jack shuffled his feet at the net. Tim served effortlessly, all thoughts of wonky ball tosses forgotten. Jack, at the net, felt Tim's serve whizz past him. It hit the service line and slid down to nothing. Ace. Fifteen–all.

Hunt's eyes were like radars and never left the ball as it was tossed in the air before being torpedoed towards him along the centre-line. Jack began to move across, ready to cut the return off or, at the very least, limit Hunt's options. Hunt took the ball early, aggressively. It was time to take a few risks. With perfect balance, Hunt drove his return well away from Jack, who was hovering on the net. The quick return gave Tim little chance to prepare, but he managed a weak forehand that dropped just over the net. Illic charged to cover the shot, but in his haste didn't make good contact and the ball landed, heartbreakingly for him, on the tape at the top of the net before falling uselessly back on his own side. Thirty–fifteen.

Tim served again and nailed it. It was a great first serve, and Illic knew it. Instinctively he readied himself for the return. This time, he wanted to keep the ball in play, and he aimed straight for Jack, probably hoping Jack would not be able to move quickly enough to get a racquet to it. He was correct. As Jack twisted awkwardly to get to the ball, he mis-hit it, and it bounced erratically off his frame. Once again the crowd reacted as they watched the ball spin away, miraculously making contact with the inside edge of the sideline, wrong-footing both Hunt and Illic in the process and catching them out of position. Two bonus points, but how long could their luck hold? Forty–fifteen.

The crowd needed several admonishments from the umpire as he called for quiet. Even so, as Tim prepared to serve, there were a couple of voices who continued to shout encouragement. Tim stopped. With great composure he waited for silence, and then served. He sliced down hard on the ball, aiming for the centre-line but putting enough spin on it so that it bounced into the body of the waiting Hunt. Hunt, with great reflexes, sent it hard and fast back to Tim at the baseline. They rallied between each other for several shots, while Jack and Illic on the net worked hard to intercept and cut off any stray shots. Finally, Tim returned a shorter ball than he would have liked.

Hunt saw his chance and collected it in a low volley. He returned it with an uncanny touch and perfect accuracy into a beautifully timed lob. It should have sent Tim and Jack scrambling to the baseline, but Jack had anticipated the shot and was moving back before it had even been executed. He was already underneath the ball as it landed. He waited for what seemed an eternity as the ball reached the highest point of its bounce, then, as if it were a serve, he snapped it, low, fast, and straight down the centre of the court, confusing Hunt and Illic who had split to cover the net and were caught flat-footed. Five games to three.

The crowd erupted in a frenzy. They loved an underdog and the Anderson boys had been the undisputed underdogs in this match-up between a pair of wildcards and the highly experienced, top-seeded Hunt and Illic.

Illic won his next service game, but every point was a battle. Five games to four.

Jack was serving for the match. Amid spontaneous cheers and calls of encouragement, and while the umpire called on the crowd to cease, he stood up to finish the job. In workmanlike fashion, he demolished the opposition with two early aces. Even though Hunt and Illic rallied to equal at forty–all, they had lost their edge and, uncharacteristically, tightened up. Jack, with two powerful serves, almost single-handedly won the next two points, and held serve.

"Game, set, and match. 2/6, 7/5, 6/4, 3/6, 6/4. Mr Tim Anderson and Mr Jack Anderson."

The umpire's words were drowned out by the deafening appreciation of the hometown crowd, who had erupted once Illic had overshot the baseline with his last return.

Jack and Tim froze for a second in disbelief before gesturing to each other across the court in an exaggerated fist pump. The crowd went crazy. Conscious of the protocol expected, the boys turned their attention to their opponents, meeting them at the net to shake hands and acknowledge the umpire and the linesmen. Then, as one, they turned back and embraced each other, allowing themselves a brief moment to absorb the reality of their win.

"We did it, mate," Tim said into Jack's ear.

"We did!" breathed Jack, fighting to control his emotions.

Breaking apart they looked up at the players' box where everyone was kissing and hugging and crying. Karen waved to them and clapped exaggeratedly, as did Mr Mac.

"Such a shame Mum and Dad missed this," Jack shouted to Tim as they turned to face the crowd again, taking in their cheers and thundering applause.

What followed was a blur. A makeshift platform was wheeled out, the television cameramen set up, and a TV presenter took centre stage. Tim and Jack were shepherded beside him, along with Hunt and Illic. Larry Jones, a popular and heavily made-up Channel 7 sports journalist, was the interviewer.

Hunt and Illic faced the first questions.

"Well, Todd. You must be disappointed?"

"Very much so, Larry." At this the crowd, feeling generous now the game was over, gave a huge round of applause. Todd acknowledged the cheers before continuing. "We certainly gave it everything, and I believe we played some of our best tennis today. Tim and Jack certainly deserved their win. They were fantastic out there."

Again, the crowd went crazy. Larry addressed his next question to Anton. "Anton. You played an amazing game. What do you think the difference was today?"

"I thought we played some great tennis, but we missed the big points when we needed them," he replied, his Yugoslavian accent only slightly evident.

Shaking his head, Anton gestured to the crowd. "Tim and Jack played unbelievable tennis, but we were up against more than just two tennis players. I think we had to beat half of Melbourne," he said jokingly, referring to the crowd's parochial support.

This was met with a standing ovation as the losing team collected their trophies and moved to the side.

As the noise abated, Larry continued. "Well, folks," he said. "How good was that?" He stopped while the crowd did what was expected and cheered loudly once again. Tim and Jack grinned widely and waved to the crowd, and the cheering escalated even further.

As the noise died down, Larry carried on. "This must be something of a dream come true for you. Tim, did you ever think you and Jack would make it this far?"

More cheers ensued but they dropped to silence when Tim took the microphone. "No, Larry. This is definitely a dream come true for us. I still can't believe it. Todd and Anton made it very hard for us out here today and I think we are probably very lucky to be standing here now. But I have to give full credit to my brother, Jack, who played his heart out today." Again, there was huge applause.

Larry addressed his next question to Jack. "You had a bad fall in the second set, Jack. How are you feeling now?"

"I'm a bit numb, actually. I can't feel anything at the moment, but I think I might be a bit stiff tomorrow."

"No-one seriously gave you a chance of winning today, or even getting to the final. What do you say to everyone now, Jack?"

This time the crowd was silent. They hung on every word. Jack looked at Tim and took a deep breath.

"We may not have been playing the circuit for long," Jack acknowledged, with a shrug of his shoulders, "but we have worked hard on our game, and we've had a great coach in Paul Maclaren, who has taught us everything we know." He gestured up to where Paul sat, acknowledging Jack's compliment, while the crowd cheered.

"In fact, you've had quite a support crew haven't you, Tim, even your dad and grandfather are a part of your team. Is that correct?"

"Yes. Our dad was a big part of our training program, filling in whenever Mr Mac couldn't be there, and Pa was always ready to backup as well."

"And, of course, your dad has not been well. He wasn't able to be here today, we understand. And your mum was not able to be here, either?"

There was a sympathetic murmur from the crowd as both Jack and Tim prepared themselves for the inevitable questions about Mark. This was an emotional enough moment for them without Larry trawling through it. They both nodded.

"So, we thought we would bring your mum and dad to you."

While Tim and Jack looked puzzled, the big screen showing the Tennis Australia logo suddenly switched to a picture of Jenny and Mark, face masks on, surrounded by several nurses and doctors, waving at them from the hospital. A big thumbs up from Mark, while Jenny blew kisses. Another journalist at the hospital, also masked and gowned, moved into the camera view.

"Have you anything to say to your sons, Mark and Jenny?"

"We love you and we are so proud of you both. We knew you could do it! Can't wait to see you at home soon," said Mark, while Jenny, too overcome to speak, just cried and waved.

Tim and Jack were speechless but grinned and waved madly at their parents as the screen faded, and the logo appeared once more. They could not stop smiling as they were presented with their trophies and the winners' cheque for $15 000.

Later, at the press conference, when Tim was asked about what role his dad had played in their win, his voice broke and he nearly lost it. Drawing on the last of their emotional reserves, Tim and Jack spoke for the first time publicly about their dad's battle with cancer, his remission, and long recovery, which had left him immunosuppressed. Tim explained how this had caused his subsequent recent illness.

The journalists certainly knew how to extract the most from this human-interest story. Even as they told their story, Jack and Tim could hardly believe they had survived all this drama themselves, let alone played tennis. They made sure they gave Mr Mac full credit as their coach. This was another line for the papers to pursue, because Mr Mac's fade-out from the tennis world had been a mystery at the time, and now they sensed another feel-good story in the making. Pa was also not forgotten, because he had been the backup support when Mark got sick.

Finally they were finished, and Jack and Tim were free. Keen to escape the attention, they met with Nan and Pa, Mr Mac, and Karen in the players' lounge. It was short-lived though, and there was little time to really digest their win, because there were so many well-wishers coming up to congratulate them. There were also more interviews scheduled with various media and, as this was what they had agreed to when they entered the tournament, they had to go along with all requests.

Tim looked over at Karen a couple of times as if to say, "Get me out of here!" but for the moment they were public property, and Tennis Australia were not going to let this perfect moment of publicity go unheralded. Eventually, after an exhausting several hours of interviews and photo sessions, they were allowed to leave. They would return the next night to the tennis centre to attend an official function with the players and officials, sponsors, and others involved in the tournament.

In the meantime, they had one wish: to get to the hospital as soon as they could, to see Mark and Jenny. An official Australian Open driver was dispatched to get them there as swiftly as possible. As they walked through the hospital corridors on the way to the isolation ward there were lots of cheers and claps, and words of congratulation. Everyone knew where they were headed, so no-one stopped them for long. Finally, they reached Mark's private room. They donned masks and sanitised their hands before entering, and this time the tears did flow as they hugged, against doctor's orders, and proceeded to talk over the top of each other. The match was acknowledged only briefly. There would be plenty of time for that discussion later.

Instead of talking tennis, Jack and Tim were keen to check out their dad. Just seeing the continued improvement in him dissolved any last feeling of physical exhaustion after their hard match. Tim felt invincible and Jack was euphoric.

Finally, they stopped talking all at once and Mark had a chance to speak. "Enough of my health! I'm fine. But you two! I'm so proud of you, my boys! You are officially Australian Open champions. Who would have thought this could happen when we first went in to get those racquets?"

"Well, you did tell him we were almost semi-professional players," laughed Jack, reminding Mark of his boasting to the salesman in the sports store.

"I always thought I was a bit clairvoyant," chipped Mark. "And I bet that chap is bragging himself now about how he once sold you two racquets. The Australian Open Men's Doubles Champions, no less. Oh, it was such a great match," he enthused.

"You were always my champions," said Jenny, crying and hugging them both. "I wouldn't have cared if you lost but this is so wonderful. My boys! I'm so proud of you. And how are you, Jack? I thought you wouldn't be able to keep going. Where does it hurt?"

"I'm fine at the moment, but it did hurt when I first did it. But then the drugs kicked in and it helped. And the physio helped heaps. Then Tim stepped up, and here we are!"

"Oh, forget the tennis. I can't believe how great you look, Dad. That's the best present," said Tim, feeling his heart was about to explode with happiness. "Are the doctors still happy with your results?"

Mark nodded. "In all the tests they've taken over the last couple of weeks, when they tried to almost bleed me dry," he joked, "there's not been one cancer cell found. Dr Thompson said the results are excellent and that we should be very confident of remission continuing. The prognosis is very optimistic."

"What about your white blood cells? And the T-cells? What's happening there?" asked Jack, looking relieved but still feeling it hard to shake the familiar sense of concern over his dad.

"On their way up again today," said Jenny, squeezing Mark's hand.

"I'm still going to have to isolate here a bit longer. It killed me today. I wished I could have been there so much!" said Mark, shaking his head ruefully. "My immune system is getting there slowly, and those white blood cells are on their way up. I can almost feel them multiplying inside me. And you know, I keep thinking, if I hadn't got cancer, would we be here now? Would things have gone on as always if you hadn't gone to Winjarra when I got sick? Anyway ..." and he stopped, visibly upset for a moment. "You boys got me through all this. I can't tell you how in awe of you I am. How in awe we both are," he finished, with a sigh and a slow smile as Jenny took his hand.

"We missed having you there so much. I nearly blew it, too," said Tim, grimacing.

Jack nodded seriously. "You can say that again," he said as he punched Tim's arm lightly. "What the hell was that all about anyway?"

Mark sat back on the hospital bed next to Jenny, and the brothers settled themselves into the comfy chairs. Stretching out their tired limbs, they discussed the match until they could see Mark tiring and they left him to the nurse for his next round of observations.

Jenny came home with them to find Karen's family, Nan and Pa, and Paul Mac and his family were already in full party mode, celebrating. It would be a few more days before Mark would get home, but at least now the doctors were talking about a discharge date. For the moment, it was time for everyone who had helped the boys get to this point to enjoy the rewards.

Much later that night, when everyone else was asleep and the fanfare had briefly died down, long before the papers came out the next day, Tim and Jack, still feeling wide awake and unable to sleep despite their exhaustion, sat together on the back steps of the house. Both were companionably quiet, deep in their own satisfying thoughts.

Tim felt his world had been suddenly turned on its head. Mr Mac had already discussed with him the possibility of heading to the States and playing the circuit there. It was head-spinning stuff. There was also Karen, who had been a patient girlfriend, content to let their relationship drift along; Tim wanted her to be in his life, and if he committed to the pro circuit, that would mean more time apart.

Jack wondered about Year 12 and if he could get out of it somehow. He already knew his parents' answer, but it didn't stop him already starting to compose counterarguments in his head.

They looked up to the night sky as a shooting star flickered high above them. A perfect sign, just for them, to end this incredible day. They bumped fists and high-fived in a gesture of solidarity. It had all been said. Their matching glass trophies sat between them, in their velvet-lined boxes, on the step.

Karen was also feeling too wired to sleep, and she wandered out to sit with them. "Who would have thought, when you two dorks got on the bus that day, we'd be sitting here with these little trophies between us all? And at the time I thought I was the only tennis star at school!" she protested with a wry laugh.

They reminisced briefly about the early days at Winjarra High before Jack yawned.

He stood up tentatively, wincing in pain as he started to hobble across the patio. "I am not playing anything for a while: at least until I get this hip fixed, that's for sure. I think the anti-inflammatories are definitely starting to wear off. I'm getting an icepack, more drugs, and I'm off to bed. See you two lovebirds in the morning."

Tim watched guiltily as Jack limped off. Would he have injured himself so badly if he hadn't been trying to cover for Tim's average game?

"Don't even go there, Tim," said Karen, reading him like a book and putting her arm through his. "You recovered and played a magnificent game. In the end, when he needed you, you were there." Then she kissed him long and tenderly. "My very own champion," she murmured happily. "So, where to from here?"

"I don't know," Tim shrugged. "But I do know I loved it out there today. I know I took a while to get going, and I nearly stuffed it up … but the adrenaline and the rush I felt as we fought our way back into the match was so good. I loved that winning feeling. I loved it! I know I want to keep playing. And I want to prove that it's not just a one-off. I want to get good enough to be one of the best in the world." He stopped abruptly. "Do you think I'm a tosser for thinking like this?"

"No, you're not a tosser! In fact, if you stopped here and didn't follow this through, you would be insane. You and Jack have proven you can match it with the best in the world. It's time for you to put yourselves on the line. And I know you guys can get better and better. This is just the start!"

"It means Jack and I going overseas on the circuit. I'll be away for months at a time. And I'll miss you," Tim finished, kissing her gently on the lips.

Karen held his head in her hands and drew back so that she could look directly into his eyes. "We can survive this. We can do long-distance. I'll be busy at uni, and you won't be gone the whole year. You can fly back to Australia in between major events. And I can fly over to you. We're not kids anymore. We'll work it out. And besides, it's scary how much better I think you can play. I can't wait to see what you win next."

Then she kissed him, and for a while they forgot about everything, other than the feeling that they were exactly where they were always destined to be. Together.

The End

Acknowledgements

Winjarra is a fictional town in north central Victoria, but has its roots in the various country towns I was fortunate to live in over the years. I was always grateful for how quickly my family was made feel welcome, and the generosity of spirit within these communities to include newcomers into their fold. One of the first things we did when arriving into a new town was to join the local tennis club. We still have many lifelong friends from those Saturday afternoons spent playing competition and social tennis, in between chasing toddlers and changing nappies.

I have my mother, Shirley, to thank for introducing me to tennis at an early age. Along with my sisters, I played local competition tennis most weekends. Mum was an avid tennis fan and watching the Australian Open on television was a summer ritual. She always had a book in progress and the newspaper at hand, and so I also have her to thank for my lifelong love of reading.

Thanks to my son, Jacob, who read an early draft of this book and added some very useful suggestions, to my daughter, Luci, for her artwork on the cover and to Alix Kwan from Moxie Editing for her keen observant eye. My three sons, Carl,

David and Jacob, all played tennis and were lucky to be coached by some talented players. Their tennis journey gave me an insight into the regional competitions and satellite circuit, but any inaccuracies regarding these, the Australian Open and its rules of governance are mine alone.

Finally, thanks to my husband Greg, for his boundless enthusiasm and encouragement.

About the Author

Tricia Trevaskis was born into a family of six girls in Geelong, Victoria, Australia.

After gaining her teaching qualifications at Geelong Teacher's College, she worked as a primary school teacher while continuing to study for her Bachelor of Arts, majoring in Creative Writing.

Leaving Geelong, aged 25, she and her husband lived in various towns in regional Victoria and NSW, before heading with their family to Western Australia, in 2002.

Despite a brief foray into journalism, she always maintained her passion for teaching. With four children and five grandchildren, she lives with her husband, Greg in Bunbury, WA, close to the ocean and not too far from the golf course.

The Wildcards is her debut novel.

www.ingramcontent.com/pod-product-compliance
Lightning Source LLC
Chambersburg PA
CBHW010550170726
48285CB00011B/2842